MW01139336

In The Wrong Hands | Avi Domoshevizki

To my grandchildren –

for adding so much joy to my life.

In The Wrong Hands
Avi Domoshevizki

Editing: Julie MacKenzie
Translation from the Hebrew: Yaron Regev
Contact: avi253@gmail.com

ISBN 978-1987780628

Distribution rights in China arranged with
eBookPro Publishing

eBooκPro
www.ebook-pro.com

IN THE WRONG HANDS

AVI DOMOSHEVIZKI

If everyone is thinking alike, then somebody isn't thinking.

- George S. Patton

There is more to life than increasing its speed.

- Mahatma Gandhi

In order to seek truth, it is necessary once in the course of our life to doubt, as far as possible, of all things.

- René Descartes

PROLOGUE

The tears refused to stop flowing from her eyes, which were fixed on him in a silent plea. The pain spreading through her chest was unbearable. She prayed that the sight of the hotel room would not be the last thing etched in her mind before her soul returned to her maker.

When she'd begun fantasizing about an affair with him, she'd told herself she was probably delusional. But the realization that she would never forgive herself unless she dared and gave it a try had given her the courage to expose her emotions to him. When she had confessed her love, he'd just looked at her open-mouthed. He tried to dissuade her from thinking they could be together, but she persisted. Although she wasn't stunningly beautiful, she had a sort of magnetism about her. The kind that has blinded men ever since the invention of sex, and she knew it. Despite her youth, she had had quite a few relationships already. All her lovers had been young and good-looking, but also immature. Her attraction for them had never lasted more than a month. It was different with him. It was the first true love she had ever experienced.

Her mother, the only person with whom she dared to share her true feelings, simply scoffed. "You are too different," she'd said repeatedly. "In time your love will dissolve, and you'll understand that you've wasted your youth chasing after a hopeless dream." But time had passed, and her love had only grown stronger.

Sex with him was different. He'd proven to be a gentle, considerate lover. She had never imagined she would ever use the word "considerate" to describe such a pleasurable sexual experience. He was also the smartest man she had ever met. He was shrouded in a halo of silent mystery. Behind his back, people said he was brilliant, but an odd duck. If only those cruelhearted gossipmongers could know him like she did, they would surely change their minds.

A few months earlier, he had let her know that their affair was over. He had not bothered to provide any explanation and dismissed all her attempts to renew their relationship with aching frigidity. She kept hoping he would come around one day and understand that she was the only one for him. Just the day before, after another desperate attempt on her part, he had surprisingly agreed to meet. She suggested they meet in the same hotel room in which he had broken up with her, and he promised to be there. She had always believed in the power of fate. She had no doubt in her heart this was the right place for them to renew their love. She saw his willingness to meet as proof of the existence of justice in the universe.

He arrived, wearing his finest clothes and holding a bottle of fine cabernet. Soon enough, the clothes dropped from their bodies and they found themselves wallowing in the sumptuous sheets. The sex was just as exciting as she had dreamed it would be. Better than ever. He didn't even insist on protection.

"I'm not taking any pills," she whispered in his ear.

"That's all right. I love you." He surprised her with the words she had yearned to hear from the day they met. A delicious shiver passed through her. Never had she been so happy. When she climaxed and rested her head on his shoulder, thanking him for coming back, he gently embraced her and did not urge her to be quiet as he normally did. He poured her a glass of wine and gazed at her tenderly.

"Why aren't you drinking, my love?" she whispered. She closed her eyes as his hand stroked her cheek.

"It's a long story," he sighed. "My health is not what it used to be."

When the pain began throbbing behind her rib cage, she asked him to call for help. He smiled and told her not to worry. After all, she was too young to suffer a heart attack while having sex.

Black spots crashed inside her eyes. The pain became unbearable. She turned to look at him, her lips muttering urgent requests for help.

The last thing she saw was his cold smile as he removed the handheld vacuum from his bag.

CHAPTER 1

He was on his way to the meeting when his phone rang. "Young," he growled impatiently.

"Hello, Dr. Young. We do not know each other," a metallic voice informed him. "Allow me to get straight to the point. I believe I am in possession of a cure for your wife's cancer. A therapy, without which, as we both know, she will not survive. I will be happy to reveal this secret treatment, in return for your guaranteed commitment to providing me some future service in the field of genetics."

"Who is this? How do you know about my wife? Do I know you? Why are you distorting your voice?"

"My name is not important. But if you must have a name, you can call me Mr. Brown." The person at the other end ignored his questions. "What is important for you to know is that I am in possession of an innovative process for targeted drug delivery, the 'holy grail' of pharmacological science. I assume that you don't believe me. I know I wouldn't in your place. This is why, in order to build mutual trust between us, which I believe to be essential in any successful cooperation, I am willing to reveal to you the secrets of the technology in my possession and allow you to examine it before you are asked to agree to even the smallest obligation. Only when you are convinced that I have indeed provided you with the medical breakthrough you have been praying for, will you be asked to uphold your promise and commit to helping me when the time is ripe."

"If this is a joke or a prank, it's not very funny. Goodbye!" Young slammed down the phone, trembling with anger.

Dr. Sean Young was a physician by training and a known researcher in the field of genetics. From the very start of his career, he recognized that he did not have the necessary emotional skills required for treating others. The patients annoyed him with their ceaseless complaints and burdened him with the weight of their false hopes. Seven years ago, he had left his prestigious position at Massachusetts General Hospital and founded G-Pharma. It wasn't long after starting up the company that he realized his administrative skills were not much better than his interpersonal skills, and any insistence on remaining CEO would merely bring about the company's ruin. In an unusual move, he voluntarily chose to step down, assume the position of chief science officer, and recruit a professional CEO. After much deliberation, he chose Dr. Henrik Schmidt, whom he had met during his PhD studies.

Unlike Young, Schmidt had embarked on a management career and quickly gained a reputation as a pragmatic, goal-oriented leader. His business vision and his ability to pick winning companies soon made him sought after by the financial community. Despite committing to giving Schmidt a free hand in running the company, Young continued to dictate the company's technological and business goals. Over the years, he had proven himself to be a brilliant, headstrong man who would stop at nothing to achieve his objectives. His ultimate goal being the turning of G-Pharma into the world's leading genetics-based pharmaceutical company.

About a year ago, he had been told that his wife's cancer, which they'd believed to be cured, had returned and spread. As early as the first MRI scan, he realized her condition was hopeless. Due to his extensive connections at Massachusetts General, the attending physician agreed, in contravention to the professional opinion of all the experts, to operate on his wife. The surgery was brief and confirmed their worst fears. The cancer had spread and metastasized into many vital organs. The surgeon realized that any surgical intervention would simply result in death. He stopped the operation and gave them the bitter news.

G-Pharma dealt with developing targeted drugs aimed at curing cancer. Over the course of the past year, Sean Young had been using his wife as a guinea pig for the wildest ideas his mind could conceive of. He had frequently succeeded in stopping the cancer from spreading in one organ, only to have it metastasize in others with a cruel persistence. Young had no doubt that the mysterious caller's assessment of his wife's chances of survival had been cruelly accurate.

Young sighed loudly and buried his face in his hands. However slight the chances of the solution he had just been promised, he shouldn't have hung up. After all, the anonymous caller had strictly emphasized that he would need to carry out his end of the bargain only if the cure proved effective.

His desk phone rang again, and Young quickly snatched the receiver. It fell from his hand and knocked over a cup of hot tea, which spilled all over his trousers. He hissed a curse while picking up the receiver and placing it against his ear.

"I assume you have already reached the conclusion that hanging up was a mistake. Just so there are no more misunderstandings, this is your last chance to accept the deal I offered you." The cold indifference of the voice was almost frightening.

"If you really have a proven process that can help save my wife's life, I am willing to pay you any amount." Sean couldn't stop his voice from trembling.

"I don't need your money. I need you to develop a genetic mechanism for me, which I will define for you once you are convinced you are interested in the deal. Furthermore, the moment you deliver said product, two million dollars will be wired to your personal account."

"All I want is the technology." Young worked up his courage. "If you provide me with a solution that helps my wife, I'll do anything you ask."

A hollow, sickening laughter followed. "I won't force you to take the money, of course. But there is one crucial thing you must understand. The moment you agree to our deal, there can't be any turning back. Got it?"

"I understand. When can I see the material?"

"Soon. In the next few days, my assistant will bring you the promised information. Don't try to play any games with her. Those who have been deceived by her appearance and thought they could take advantage of her, were soon sorry they had done so. And I'm talking about the ones lucky enough to remain alive."

Young felt the blood drain out of his face.

"Once you realize I am giving you your wife's life as a present, I'll tell you what the price is. Have a good day."

Young stared at the silent apparatus. There was no way to avoid the painful truth — he had just made a deal with the devil.

CHAPTER 2

"I'm sorry," the prison guard at the reception desk grumbled, though his body language indicated that he couldn't have cared less, "all the visitation rooms are occupied. There is a long waiting list at the moment. I assume you've read the Metropolitan Correctional Center Attorney's Guide and are aware that rooms are available on a first come, first served basis, not on the basis of how—" the prison guard paused briefly, straining to erase the contempt from his face "—privileged the guest is."

Robert O'Shea maintained a poker face. He knew the quoted attorney's guide by heart and was aware that according to chapter two, section six, the law was on the side of the guard. "As you know, my client is to appear in court tomorrow morning, and I have not yet been given an opportunity to meet with him. I don't want to have to show up in court tomorrow and ask for another postponement, just because, once again, I wasn't allowed to meet my client due to your inflexible protocol. We both know that I could sit here for a whole day without one of your twelve visitation rooms becoming available. What do you say? Should I file another complaint with the court, or can we possibly reach some sort of compromise?"

"Sit down, please." The guard gave the crowded waiting room a quick glance. The luckless among those waiting were crouched or leaning against the walls with helpless resignation. "Let me check what I can do. I'll get back to you with an answer in about ten minutes."

The sour smell of perspiration filled the air. Both air-conditioning units hanging in the corners of the room clicked and clacked mechanically, failing miserably in their mission of cooling the place and settling for pushing the fetid air from one end of the room to the other. It seemed as though the prison architects had done their best to punish visitors, apparently believing the prisoners' crimes and transgressions were their fault.

The Metropolitan was considered the toughest facility in the state of New York and one of the worst in the country. Prisoners unlucky enough to have been "guests" in both notorious facilities said that conditions at the Metropolitan were even worse than those in Guantanamo Bay. It housed some of the worst and most notorious criminals, including drug lord "El Chapo," Bernie Madoff, the infamous white-collar criminal, and many others whom attorney Robert O'Shea knew intimately. People who weren't exactly saints. He regularly represented quite a few of the Metropolitan's residents, earning piles of laundered money for his troubles.

But just like the law enforcement authorities, Robert O'Shea had never believed the day would come when his best customer, Arthur "The Shark" Bale, would be charged with three counts of murder. Bale, an economist holding an MBA from the University of Chicago, had been arrested several times in the past on suspicion of laundering money for organized crime, but he was never brought to trial. Word on the street was that money laundering was only a sideline for him, just like the financial counseling firm he managed from a small office in the Trump Towers. Attorney O'Shea had always taken pride that these rumors remained unproven, and all the police and FBI efforts to obtain incriminating evidence had been futile. Until now.

O'Shea glanced at the Patek Philippe gold-plated watch he had spoiled himself with the day before in anticipation of the hefty fee this new case would bring and noticed that forty-five minutes had already passed. He rose, went to the guard, who completely ignored him, and fished out a sealed envelope from an inside pocket of his suit coat. "This is a court summons. Please see to it that the warden receives it immediately with my compliments. I hope he will be able to present Judge Morrison with a suitable explanation for this obstruction of justice."

Robert O'Shea smoothed the edges of his suit coat with clenched hands. Then, with practiced ease, he walked unhurriedly toward the long corridor leading to the exit. As he approached the door, he was stopped by a paunchy guard whose belt was heavily packed with a disproportionate number of deadly weapons. A serpentine wire twirled down an earpiece and into the guard's collar. "Mr. O'Shea, they are looking for you in the lobby regarding your visit. I'd appreciate it if you'd return there."

Robert O'Shea pretended to be weighing his options before he finally turned on his heel and walked back toward the reception desk. A side door opened at the far end of the entrance hall, and a burly prison guard with a military crew cut motioned for him to approach. "I was asked to escort you to your meeting with Arthur Bale. I'm sure you've been told all the private visiting rooms are occupied. However, the warden has agreed to make an exception and allow you to meet your client in his cell. The cell is constantly monitored, but the warden asked me to give you his word that all cameras and microphones will be switched off the moment you enter the room. If this arrangement is acceptable, please leave your briefcase and any electrical or blunt instruments and objects in your possession at the reception desk. Once you return, I will escort you to 10 south."

O'Shea went back to the reception desk. Without saying a word, he emptied his pockets and placed the contents, along with his watch, in his briefcase. He rotated the six dials of the combination lock and handed the briefcase to the guard on duty. Following a thorough frisk, O'Shea received authorization to continue. He placed the receipt ticket in his pocket and returned to the crew cut escort. O'Shea gathered all his mental strength to maintain an air of tranquility and not betray his true emotions. The 10 south wing was the maximum security section of the prison. The wing included six rooms, monitored twenty-four hours a day. The lights were on twenty-three hours a day, sometimes more, and the sealed windows prevented any sunlight from sneaking inside the small cells. The prisoners were not allowed to leave their cells, and most of them did not see or hear another living soul during their stay on the wing. Quite a few residents of that notorious wing had lost their sanity, and most of them complained about deteriorating eyesight. It was another ill omen added to the series of events slowly unfolding since his client had been arrested four days before.

"From this moment on, you are forbidden to make any sound until you enter your client's cell. Any violation of this instruction will result in the immediate invalidation of your visiting privileges, following which you will be accompanied outside the detention center."

The guard indicated with his hand that O'Shea should continue down the hallway.

Despite his seventeen years as a criminal lawyer, marching down that narrow concrete corridor sent needles of discomfort up and down O'Shea's spine. It seemed as if the hall, flooded with bright LED lights, would never end. The guard accompanying him walked disturbingly close behind him, occasionally bumping into him, taking enjoyment in his obvious discomfort.

O'Shea stopped in front of a grated door and turned his head, questioning.

The guard looked at the sweat pouring down the lawyer's plump face and soaking into the collar of his white shirt, clearly enjoying O'Shea's unease. Finally, he whispered something into a small transmitter that magically appeared in his hand.

The following silence was unnerving.

The faint sound of steel doors rattling shut was heard in the distance. O'Shea remained standing with his face to the locked door, ignoring the guard behind him. He was too experienced to fall into the obvious trap. One didn't need to be a genius to understand they were waiting for him to utter the smallest remark, so they could use it as an excuse for canceling his visit. At the end of the day, it would be his word against the guard's. Even the guard knew his behavior wasn't quite legal. Still, he could not resist the pleasure of seeing the distinguished attorney, who earned his fortune protecting murderous clients, suffer a little.

A sucking noise was heard, and the grated door slid open.

"Get moving. We haven't got all day," the guard grumbled.

O'Shea looked at the new corridor that opened before him and took a tentative step forward.

"To the elevator!" A large freight elevator waited to the right, its door wide open. "Inside!" The guard squeezed against the lawyer, even though there was room in there for a midsize SUV.

The elevator bounced a little then began to slowly crawl its way up. Neither of the two passengers budged. Finally, the large metal box staggered to a halt. The door creaked open. "Ninth Floor — Special Accommodation Unit," read the sign on the opposite wall.

"To your right." The guard pointed at a pair of closed gates at the end of the hallway. Cameras followed them, and the first gate opened with an electric whistle when they got within touching distance of it. The guard gave him a slight shove, and O'Shea heard the gate closing behind him. The guard took a key from his pocket and opened the second gate. He immediately directed the lawyer to a stairwell going up to the tenth floor. The heat was insufferable, and O'Shea estimated the humidity to be over eighty percent. At that moment, his tie seemed like the most unnecessary fashion accessory on the face of the earth, but he dared not touch it. He knew that even slightest sign of discomfort would be perceived as weakness. At the top of the stairs, he felt the guard clutching his arm with an iron grip and leading him toward the last of six sealed metal doors. The door opened, and the guard reluctantly let go of his arm. O'Shea stepped into the small cell without reacting to the blatantly illegal behavior he had just experienced.

He stopped in the middle of the tiny room, three feet from the steel toilet attached to the wall. In front of him, on a narrow metal bed, sat Arthur Bale, his head calmly resting against the gray concrete wall behind him. He wore a thick, spoiled-mustard-color prisoner jumpsuit. It seemed that since their last meeting, the hair at his temples had turned gray and wrinkles had etched themselves in the corners of his eyes.

"Before we begin, I was asked by an anonymous caller to tell you that—" The lawyer abruptly stopped talking as his client gave him a sharp look, while his left index finger pressed against his thumb moved across his lips, signaling O'Shea to be quiet. For the second time since he had entered the facility, O'Shea felt a cold wave crawling up his spine. Despite the many years in which he had served as Bale's personal attorney, he had never been able to get used to his client's soulless expression. It was not for nothing that his client had earned the nickname "The Shark."

"I don't care what you were asked to do," Arthur Bale shouted furiously, while moving to the center of the room.

"Lower your voice or this meeting is over." The words were muffled a bit coming through the door.

Arthur stopped next to his lawyer. "I think the cameras don't cover this spot," he whispered into O'Shea's ear, his heavy breath washing over the lawyer's face.

O'Shea didn't move an inch. One thing he'd learned during the years of his acquaintance with The Shark was to never, ever disrespect him.

"Talk! And don't leave a single word out," he hissed between clenched teeth.

"The idea devised by your man may be possible, but we cannot be certain about it. We would need unlimited financial and human resources," the lawyer whispered directly into Bale's ear.

The prisoner moved back and examined his lawyer through narrowed eyes. The room was completely silent. It was apparent that O'Shea did not understand his client's intentions.

The silence was finally disrupted by the prisoner, who said in an indifferent voice, "What are the geniuses from the FBI trying to pin on me this time?"

"Earlier today, I met with Julie Wilson, the prosecutor on your case. For the first time in our long history, it seemed as if she genuinely enjoyed hosting me in her office. Apparently, she is convinced that this time your case is hermetically sealed. She was so self-confident, that against protocol, she agreed to reveal the evidence in her possession. According to her, based on information obtained from a state witness, three graves were discovered by the FBI in upstate New York. The unearthed graves contained three murder victims. Two men, who were identified as members of 'Mad' Joe Murphy's 'Green Gang,' alongside a woman of about twenty-one, whose body was mutilated beyond recognition. The woman was identified with the aid of DNA tests as Patricia Roberts, a woman seen in your company on numerous FBI surveillance tapes. Wilson said that forensic experts had found your DNA at each of the three murder scenes and asked me to tell you, and I'm quoting: 'His arrogance has finally brought him down. He'd better prepare to spend the rest of his miserable life practicing a significantly more modest lifestyle.'

"I assume they are holding you in the most secure cell in the country because they know you wouldn't last more than a few hours in the same jail with any members of the Green Gang. I believe they intend to reexamine some additional evidence collected from older, unsolved murder scenes, tie you to those cases, and then try to close a deal with you in which you will incriminate other crime families in return for a witness protection plan."

Arthur Bale remained quiet, but O'Shea could have sworn he saw a hint of worry flashing on his face.

"I would like for us to begin and plan for…" The lawyer froze and stopped talking when he realized his client was staring at him and shaking his head, indicating the conversation was over.

"Tell the lady I am giving her a free hand to do whatever it takes. From this moment on, you will obey her instructions as if they came from my own mouth," he spat out in a whisper while his cold eyes searched for his lawyer's acknowledgment. "Don't ask questions. Just follow them down to the minutest detail. Also, postpone the date of the trial as long as possible. I need time, and I don't mind spending it in this cell. This is critical. Don't force me to switch lawyers due to unfortunate circumstances. Am I clear?"

O'Shea nodded. He was afraid to ask how his client knew the message had been relayed by a woman. He knew he had better follow his client's demands to the letter. Now that Bale's life was on the line, O'Shea's own situation had turned precarious and dangerous. He only hoped that the woman who had contacted him would be available to answer his call immediately.

CHAPTER 3

"I can't tell you how happy I am that we found each other again." Ronny Saar gave Sam a warm smile. "The offices you're renting us, at a loss, as we both know, are simply wonderful. My CFO was thrilled by my ability to close such an amazing deal."

Sam patted Ronnie's cheek fondly. "Trust me, I have enough real estate deals I earn a fortune from. Rest assured, I am not losing money on the deal, but at the same time, I can afford not to maximize my gains on the back of my little cousin."

Sam Storm had immigrated to America from Israel when Ronnie Saar was still in high school. Soon enough, word of Sam's meteoric business successes reached the kibbutz where Ronnie and his family lived. They said Sam had gambled on the booming real estate market and built a chain of successful malls on the West Coast. The kid who was never expected to amount to much, had turned into a multimillionaire overnight. The gifts he used to send his family, who had remained on the kibbutz, and the letters boasting about his accomplishments were received with mixed feelings. Ronnie remembered his parents explaining to him how bragging about his material success, as well as changing his name from Saar to the Americanized Storm meant that he had turned his back on his traditions and upbringing. Chasing material dreams, so they used to mutter, would never make up for the lack of genuine intellectual and moral values. One evening, Ronnie had overheard them speaking about the money the whole family had scraped together from their little savings in order to help Sam, or Shmuel, as he had been called then, to settle in America. Money the new millionaire had never bothered to pay back. Ronnie, who genuinely liked his brash, boisterous cousin, hoped that the numerous gifts he kept sending had covered the loan long ago.

The years had passed, and the constant flow of letters and gifts for the holidays continued. One day, a letter came, containing an invitation to Sam's wedding. Attached to the letter were five business-class airline tickets to New York as well as a reservation confirmation for a five-day stay at the Hilton, where the wedding would take place. The tickets alone cost far more than a kibbutz member earned in a year. Following a brief consultation, his parents, despite the vocal protests of their children, decided to refuse this expensive gift and not attend the wedding. Much to Ronnie's sorrow, Sam, insulted by this rejection, had severed all contact with his family in Israel.

Eighteen months ago, when Ronnie got married, he'd managed to track down Sam in New Jersey and invited him to the wedding. Much to his surprise, Sam and his wife had shown up for the wedding at the kibbutz. As a wedding gift, Sam suggested they switch houses, thus allowing Ronnie and Liah to spend their honeymoon in the States, while Sam and his wife would stay in Israel and catch up with the family. Ronnie and Liah gladly accepted the offer, and the two couples had kept in regular contact since.

So it was only natural that when Ronnie decided to relocate part of his business activities to New York, he had consulted Sam about leasing office space. Sam had just finished renovating some commercial complexes and offered to rent offices to Ronnie at bargain prices.

"Your little cousin can afford to pay." Ronnie returned to the subject he always raised in their conversations.

"How about this, Ronnie? I'll accept your offer and raise the rent to market price, but I won't charge you a penny for the next four years. In return, you will allot shares for me in Double N in the amount equal to the value of the rent you will be saving. This way, you will be able to invest the money in research and development, and I will be a shareholder in my little cousin's company and pester him to death by visiting him more often."

"Are you serious?"

"Very," Sam answered enthusiastically.

"I'll talk to the other shareholders, but I don't see any reason why we shouldn't do it. I'll have the paperwork drafted and sent for your signature next week."

"Excellent. I —"

Loud voices from outside the room interrupted their conversation. "Maybe you don't have any work to do, but I can't concentrate with all this noise outside," called an impatient voice. "I'm taking all the material with me and working from home."

"Excuse me for a moment," Ronnie apologized and stepped out of his office.

Sam hurried after him and leaned against the doorjamb, following Ronnie's conversation with interest.

"Guys," Ronnie addressed the employees who had wandered out of their offices to see what the fuss was, "please go back to work." Everybody hesitantly left the scene, and only then did Ronnie turn his attention to the agitated scientist standing by the reception desk. "What's the matter, Simon?"

"I can't focus on preparing my presentation. I need peace and quiet. I'm taking all the technical material and I'm going to work from home. I'll call if I need any help. I —"

"That's all right, Simon," Ronnie interrupted and placed a reassuring hand on his arm. "If you feel more comfortable working from home, just do it. Don't let the pressure get to you. Come into my office for a moment, and we'll go over everything we need to prepare for Monday. Then you can go home and work quietly."

Simon gave him a grateful smile.

Ronnie threw his arm over Sam's shoulder. "I apologize, but as you can see, I have some urgent business to attend to. I don't think this will take more than half an hour. If you feel like waiting for me, we can go for dinner together."

Sam looked at his watch. "Nah, actually, with the traffic at this hour, I am already running late for a meeting in Jersey. Business before pleasure." He threw his hands up in false exasperation. "I believe we'll see each other next week, though." He turned to leave, then stopped, winked at Ronnie, muttered, "Good luck with your kindergarten," and left the office humming an unfamiliar song.

CHAPTER 4

A flickering blue light rippled from the roofs of the chaotically parked patrol cars, intermittently illuminating the dark alley. A brawny man in his fifties with a budding paunch approached the crime scene.

"You can't go in there, sir," a young, confident-looking police officer called out to him. He looked like the sort of cop who takes his job too seriously.

The older man unconsciously hiked his pants up then opened his jacket a little, exposing a gold shield with the words "Federal Bureau of Investigation," embossed on it. "FBI," he muttered off-handedly. "Please direct me to the officer in charge," he added as his eyes reflexively scanned the crowded crime scene.

"That would be Detective McCarthy. Over there." The uniformed officer pointed at a man in his fifties wearing a pair of jeans and a pale green polo shirt.

"Thanks." The agent stepped over and around the forensic team members as he made his way to the detective. McCarthy was speaking with two police officers who were leaning against a patrol car.

"Detective McCarthy? Special Agent Miller." The burly man extended his hand, which was met with a formal handshake.

"Thanks for coming. I called you because our district got a memo requiring us to alert the FBI in cases of armed robbery resulting in homicide. This incident didn't end with the victim's death, but the rest of the characteristics seemed similar to me. I understood from the memo this is the fourth such case in the past two months."

Miller nodded distractedly.

"I'm in the middle of questioning the officers who found the victim." The detective nodded in the direction of the patrol car.

"Why don't you start over and save us all some precious time?"

One of the officers, a sergeant, stretched up to his full height in an attempt to impress the detective. It did not go unnoticed. "At 5:24 pm, a call came into the station about suspected violence in the area of this alley. My partner and I were about four blocks away, so we responded to the call. We got to the crime scene seven minutes later, at 5:31. I went to check on the victim while my partner looked around to see if he could find the perp. Unfortunately, except for a few young passersby, there was no one around, and he didn't notice any suspicious activity or identify any potential suspects."

The sergeant looked at his partner, who nodded his agreement.

"When I got closer and could see the victim's condition, I would've sworn he was dead. The number of blows he'd taken to the head with a wooden plank didn't leave him a chance. Just to make sure, I decided to check his vitals and was surprised to find a faint pulse. I immediately called in an ambulance, sealed off the area and called you, Detective. That's all I know."

"How do you know he was attacked with a plank?"

"We found one next to the victim, all bloody."

"May I see the crime scene?" asked Miller.

McCarthy took him deeper into the alley. A forensic investigator was kneeling there on the asphalt, clad from head to toe in white coveralls.

"Any initial conclusions, Clive?" The detective approached him.

The investigator raised his eyes and stood up as soon as he recognized McCarthy. "Hey, Mac, we have to stop meeting like this," Clive repeated the lame joke he used every time they were unlucky enough to share a crime scene.

"I'll do my best." McCarthy cracked a weak smile and pointed at the man standing beside him. "This is Special Agent Miller of the FBI. We'd both love to hear your first impression."

"It's still too early for any conclusions, but if I had to guess, I'd say this is a classic case of a robbery gone wrong. I found a piece of wood that had been taken off a crate." He pointed at the evidence markers a few feet away. "I found traces of black wool on the bloodied plank, probably from a glove the killer wore. You can immediately notice the wool is old and tattered, the sort homeless people and junkies wear even during summer. Based on the condition of the victim's head, there was a lot of rage involved with the assault. The victim must have refused to hand over his wallet or his bag."

"Why do you think he had a bag?" Miller asked.

"No money or wallet has been found. But in the inside pocket of his jacket, there were a few business cards with the name Dr. Simon Fine and a company by the name of Double N, whose offices are in this neighborhood. The vic was Head of Development—Genetics. My guess is that Fine left his office on the way to a meeting or stopped to have a drink in one of the bars in the area. Most of the high tech people around here carry a bag with them for their laptops, among other things. This is only a guess, of course." The forensics investigator shrugged.

"Hmm…hmm, hmm…hmm." Miller was humming to himself and stopped when he noticed the two staring at him.

"This is the first time the victim wasn't killed. Perhaps the assailant assumed Fine was dead and that was why he didn't finish the job. Still, the extreme violence is similar to the level demonstrated in the previous cases. Until we can question the victim, I think it's best if we work on this case together." He turned toward Clive. "I suggest you continue to investigate this case as if the FBI weren't involved. I will update you with any findings, and I expect you to do the same."

Miller looked at the detective wearily. "If I were you, I'd start with the questions of why a respectable scientist was in the alley and why he didn't just give up the bag. Until you have some answers, good night to us all."

CHAPTER 5

A light knock at the door of Dr. Young's office was followed by his secretary's head popping around the corner. "Your appointment is here."

"Show her in, please."

The door opened wide, and in stepped a gorgeous woman in her early thirties, wearing a yellow summer dress showing off a lithe, athletic body. She wore high-heel sandals and held a walking stick in one hand. Undoubtedly, she was an attractive woman, and her unusual appearance merely served to emphasize her sensuality. But Young didn't care about that. He was interested in only one thing — the MacBook Pro she was carrying.

Young politely stood up and motioned at the two sage green armchairs in the corner of his spacious office. "Please, sit down."

The woman completely ignored his two gestures and placed the laptop on his desk. There was a sticker on the computer, just above the famous Apple logo: "*Mathematics is no more computation than typing is literature.*"

Young looked at the sticker with contempt. He had always despised those who tried to prove their intelligence by using so-called sophisticated quotes. As far as he was concerned, independent thought was the only attribute differentiating those who deserve the title "human being" from the rest of the animals.

"Allow me to reiterate our agreement." Her calm voice completely belied the hidden aggressiveness accentuating her words. "As promised to you on the phone two days ago, this computer contains all the technical information we discussed. I believe the unique nature of the solution will convince you to accept our deal. Just to remind you" — she glared into his eyes — "we are giving you this information for one very explicit reason — your commitment to develop, based on the technology you will find on this computer, an innovative product that will meet the specifications you'll soon receive from us. I will be providing you with the specific demands once you confirm that the material on this computer is indeed valuable and relevant to finding a cure for your wife. You may be happy to hear that we have no objections to G-Pharma taking full commercial advantage of this information."

"That's what we agreed." Young extended his hand toward the computer, but the woman pulled back the Mac before he was able to touch it.

"I'm not finished," she continued in the same tranquil voice. The icy look in her eyes left no doubts regarding her seriousness. "In four hours, I will be back for the computer. You are not permitted to delete, copy, or change any of the information it contains. I expect your answer upon my return. Should you decide not to cooperate, we will part as friends. I ask that you look me in the eye and confirm that you agree to accept this computer from me and in return, you will allocate resources for the developments we will request, whatever these may be."

Young was tongue-tied, trying to consider his options.

"It was nice doing business with you." The woman turned to leave the room.

"Hold on. How did you obtain this information, and is it legally yours?"

"It's a little late to be asking those questions now. When we introduced the deal, you agreed to it unconditionally. The way I understand the situation, you have two options. Option one, do whatever I ask and decide down the road if you want first right of refusal and exclusivity for the discovery. Should you decide the technology does not interest you, the information will be returned to me and I will offer it to one of your competitors. I am convinced that the scientific innovation described in the computer files is crucial for a large number of genetics companies and that I will easily find another firm that will grab the opportunity to have these game-changing methods no questions asked. Option two, you can refuse the offer right now, and know this will be the last time you see me or have access to the information contained on this computer. All I ask is that you make up your mind. Quickly." The knuckles of her hand holding the door handle whitened.

"Why is this whole charade important to you, having me look you in the eyes and promise something I don't even know if I am able to perform? You've seen too many B-movies…"

"I believe a handshake deal is worth more than any written agreement. But only when both parties are fair-minded. I've done my part. Based on your reaction, I guess I was wrong for taking you to be a man of his word. Goodbye. Next time you see your wife suffering, remember that you could have saved her."

The woman left the room with a slight, almost unnoticeable limp and closed the door behind her.

Young remained seated, deliberating. Finally, he got up and hurried after her. He found her lingering outside his office, examining the paintings on the walls. The weak smile that flashed across her lips made him realize she had expected him to rush after her.

"I believe we have a few more points to finalize. If you could please come back to my office for a moment." He tried very hard to conceal his sense of defeat as the woman passed him on the way into his office. He followed her, wearing a conciliatory smile on his face. "I'm sorry for my reaction. I really appreciate that you've brought this information to me and were kind enough to offer my company first right of refusal. Should the material on the computer be as groundbreaking as you claim, I give you my word that I will do anything in my power to develop whatever you ask me to." And with the smile still on his lips, he added, "Even if this is only a cure for the chronic inflammation of the hip joint you are suffering from."

The woman gave him an icy look.

Young lowered his head and extended his hand. She shook it lightly. "Thank you. I will see you in four hours. Should you want me to return sooner, just call the number I dialed from earlier this morning. Remember, any attempt to alter the material on the computer will be considered a major breach of the agreement. And one more thing, the computer and its keyboard are coated with a thin layer of plastic. I suggest that you do not remove it; it is for your own safety to not leave any fingerprints."

This time Young escorted her to the elevator. As soon as the doors closed on her, he rushed back to his desk and turned on the laptop.

"*Password required*," a message flashed on the screen. He hurried outside and snapped at his secretary, "Tell our Information Systems Manager that I want the best computer guy in our company to come to my office immediately. I'm waiting." Then he slammed his office door behind him.

Three flights down, the woman exited the elevator. "The computer has been delivered," she whispered into her phone, "and the microphone has been attached to the door handle."

"Let's hope it works. Update me with any developments," said the man's cold voice before the call was disconnected.

CHAPTER 6

Young was still staring at the blank screen on the Mac in front of him when the sounds of an argument disturbed him from his thoughts. The door opened, and into the room strode a young man wearing a light-blue T-shirt that'd been washed one time too many, a pair of busted-knee jeans, and mint-colored Havaianas flip-flops.

"It's all right, Suzie," Young reassured his agitated secretary, who'd rushed in after the intruder.

"They told me you were looking for me." The man flopped down in the guest chair and stretched out his long legs.

Young ignored his impudent behavior. "This computer contains important information. Unfortunately, it is password protected. Do you think you can crack the password without causing the information to be automatically erased after too many failed attempts?"

"Let me think for a minute." The young man scratched his head, while his narrowed eyes examined the computer. "The information won't be erased, but, and it's a big but, it might lock itself after a few incorrect attempts. If I get the password right in the first few shots, we'll be able to do it quickly. If not, I'm sure I'll be able to hack into the computer, but it might take a while." The computer guy leaned back in his chair with a smug expression on his face. "Before we continue, let me just try something simple. Most of the people I know, no matter how smart they think they are, are complete idiots when it comes to storing information. This is how hackers can earn a living. It would be helpful to have more information about the owner of this computer: name, Facebook or LinkedIn account, and so on. This could help me get the answer you want much faster."

"What do you mean?" Young's voice betrayed his anxiety.

"If you know who the computer belongs to, perhaps you could simply ask him." The young man suggested with mock innocence.

Young quickly dialed the number of his earlier visitor. "I need a password or some information about the laptop's owner."

"I'll get right back to you." The call was disconnected.

The programmer took a smartphone from his pocket and tapped the screen with lightning speed. Based on the chiptune music coming from the phone, he was playing some sort of game.

"Why don't you stop —" Young started angrily.

The telephone on his desk rang before he could finish. "I'm happy to hear you've decided to explore the contents. Unfortunately, I don't know anything about a password or any details about the computer's owner. Try to get an expert hacker to break into it. Our time limit still stands." She hung up without waiting for his reply.

"I don't know what the password is. I need a brilliant hacker. Do you happen to know one?"

"Well…actually, I do. You're looking at him." The programmer snorted another nervous laugh.

"I've had enough of your childish behavior!" Young slammed the desk with his open palm. "Put down the phone and cut the crap, or I'll have you fired. I'm sure I can find an expert who takes his job more seriously."

The programmer wasn't intimidated. He knew that people with his skills were in high demand. His flickering eyes revealed his enjoyment of being in a situation where this tailored vice president needed his help so desperately. He squinted and looked up at the ceiling, pretending to consider the two options presented to him. Then he turned on the laptop he'd brought with him. Young stared with growing frustration as the programmer's fingers flashed over the keyboard in a mad dance. Following about ten minutes that seemed to last forever, the hacker eased back in his chair. "I'm asking your permission to make one attempt. If I'm wrong, nothing will happen. But if I'm right, we could buy ourselves a whole lot of time." He gave Young the determined look of a poker player who had just gone all in.

"Please," Young said through gritted teeth, spreading his hands in invitation.

The computer guy typed six letters into the password field, paused a moment, then hit "Enter." Nothing happened. He rubbed his eyes with the back of his right hand then quickly typed something on his own computer. "All right." A smile curled his lips. "I was hoping for a simple solution, but I have to give credit to the guy who owns this laptop. The password is more complicated than I thought it would be." Before Young was able to reply, the young man typed twenty-two letters and pressed "Enter" again. The password box disappeared, and the desktop immediately came to life.

He turned the computer to Young, and the latter's eyes widened with appreciation. "Like I told you, even the greatest geniuses make stupid mistakes. In this case, the sticker on the laptop cover: 'Mathematics is no more computation than typing is literature.' I googled it and found out it's a quote attributed to John Allen Paulos. So I figured if the computer owner likes him so much, he'd use his name for the password. I was wrong. He's more sophisticated than that. But I'm experienced enough to know I was going the right direction. Then I got it. Paulos is a man who sees math in everything. He even has a YouTube explaining it. So I gambled that the password would be the name of that video, 'Seeingmathineverything,' and bingo! I was right."

"And what if you'd been wrong?" Young didn't know whether to be happy or angry at the irresponsible, yet successful, second attempt.

The hacker pressed his right hand against his heart. "Actually, there was a good chance I'd be wrong. The password can be written in quite a few ways. But even if I'd been wrong, I probably would have had several more attempts before a system lockdown. But I'm usually right when I'm making an educated guess. All you need to do is get into the encrypter's head and voilà — it's as clear as day."

"And now the documents can be copied?"

"You can copy, read, or do whatever you want with them. If the computer is turned off, you still have the password." The programmer pulled the Mac over, performed a few more actions, then returned it to Young. "I switched off network and web connectivity. I assume this computer wasn't obtained in an entirely legal way. If it's connected to the network, it can easily be traced. If you want to examine additional files stored on the server the computer was originally connected to, you'll have no choice but to reconnect it to the network. If it comes to that, I strongly recommend that you call me. I know a trick or two that could mislead those trying to locate the computer or its IP address."

Young did not reply.

"So, are we done here?" the young man asked with ill-concealed arrogance while brushing imaginary dust from Young's desk.

"You're dismissed. I appreciate your assistance in this matter." Young's excitement made him forgive the hacker's irritating behavior.

"The pleasure was all mine. By the way, in case you need me again, my name is Pete. My mother had a thing for Pete Townshend from The Who. Pete Rogers. Rogers because that was my mom's last name. Don't know Dad's," he said and bounced out of the room.

CHAPTER 7

Ronnie sat in the visitor chair at the foot of the hospital bed and looked at Simon Fine's swollen face with a mixture of pity and shock. On the table at the other end of the bed lay an impressive bunch of flowers with a get well card from the Double N staff. Earlier that morning, Michelle, his new secretary, had come into his office and tearfully announced, "I'm going to visit poor Simon and bring him a huge bouquet of flowers."

All of Ronnie's attempts to explain that he could deliver the bouquet himself in a few hours were firmly rejected.

"It's important that Simon sees the flowers the moment he wakes. You should trust my female instincts on this," she urged while crushing a tear-drenched handkerchief in her fist.

Now that he saw the color the bouquet added to the room, whose walls were nearly blinding in their whiteness, he thanked her in his heart for having been so stubborn.

The scientist had regained consciousness a few hours before, but he was heavily sedated and extremely hazy. "Water," Ronnie heard him whisper.

Ronnie searched the room with his eyes. "Hold on, I'll go out and get you some water."

"Water," Simon continued to mutter.

"There's no water here, Simon, I'll get you some in a minute."

Ronnie gently patted the back of his hand.

"Michelle…" Simon grabbed Ronnie's arm then mumbled something incomprehensible. His hand slid from Ronnie's arm, and his eyelids began to fall. Ronnie's attempts to spur him on were met with a blurry look.

The sudden noise of the door opening behind him startled Ronnie. Three men entered the room. The first was wearing a doctor's green scrubs, and the two men accompanying him wore dark suits and looked like FBI agents.

"And who might you be?" one of the suits addressed Ronnie.

"My name is Ronnie Saar. I am the CEO of the company where Dr. Fine is employed. And you are?"

"I'm Special Agent Miller, and this is Detective McCarthy." With the official tone of a man used to being obeyed, he added, "I'd like you to leave the room, please."

Ronnie stood his ground. "With your permission, I'd rather stay. Simon is a top genetics expert on my team. If he starts talking genetic science, you won't be able to understand a single word he says. I'm sure I can help, and I promise not to take an active part in the conversation unless you ask me to."

"All right," Miller grunted and turned to the doctor. "Please lower the sedative dosage and bring him around so he can communicate with us."

The physician examined Special Agent Miller with narrowed eyes, carefully considering his options.

"This investigation involves a serial killer. While you're wasting time making up your mind, he's already planning his next murder," Miller barked.

A hint of hesitation crossed the doctor's face. Finally, he used the roller clamp to stop the flow of sedatives dripping into the patient's arm. He took a thin syringe from his pocket and emptied its contents into a short extension of the IV tube.

"Dr. Fine, this is Detective McCarthy of the NYPD. Can you hear me?"

Simon's face twitched with pain. "Yes," he whispered.

"We'll try to be as brief as possible, so this nice doctor here can soon restore the flow of pain medication."

A stifled groan erupted from between Simon's lips.

"What were you doing in the alley, and were you able to see your attacker?"

Simon gave a slight nod. "It all happened so fast," he whispered.

"Tell us what happened," the detective encouraged him to continue.

"I was walking by the alley... I thought I heard a woman calling out for help. I stopped for a moment to see what was happening, and then someone grabbed me and dragged me into the alley. I tried to run, but he chased me." Simon shuddered.

"Did you see him?"

"He was faster than me... he had some kind of... rod in his hands, and he hit my legs with it. I fell... Please, I can't stand the pain." He looked at the doctor with pleading eyes.

"In a minute. Did you see the attacker?"

"I remember he was wearing a coat in spite of the heat, a stocking hat, and black gloves. I didn't see his face." His voice weakened and sweat began to collect on his forehead.

"Height? Physique?" the detective hurried to ask, realizing time was getting short.

"Similar to mine. Skinnier. Emaciated... You've got to give me something for the pain, or I'll pass out," Simon's voice had lowered to an almost inaudible whisper.

Miller nodded, and the doctor attached the IV line back to the main bag and used the roller clamp to restore the regular flow of liquids that dripped into Fine's arm.

"Simon," Ronnie spoke up, despite the lawmen's visible displeasure, "did you have the bag with the technical materials when you were attacked?"

Simon turned his head curiously, as if surprised to see Ronnie beside his bed. His eyes began to close.

"Simon, please," Ronnie raised his voice in the hope that his friend wouldn't fall asleep.

"Bag… laptop … documents," Simon mumbled before falling asleep.

"Did you find a backpack at the crime scene?"

"No. Why is it important to you?"

"Maybe the attacker wasn't your serial killer, but someone dealing with industrial espionage."

"And how would the attacker know your employee was carrying trade secrets when even you, the company CEO, aren't sure of it?" Miller gave him a condescending look. "And why would he beat him up so badly? The assailant could have simply taken the bag and run away. When you come up with some reasonable explanations, I'll be happy to listen to them. Until then, please allow us, the professionals, to conduct the investigation our way." The agent turned to Detective McCarthy. "I think we're done here."

Ronnie watched the two men leave the room. When he turned back to Fine, he found the doctor shaking his head with raised eyebrows. "I suggest you go about your business. Your friend won't wake up before tomorrow morning."

CHAPTER 8

Every item in the mahogany-paneled conference room screamed money and prestige. The massive conference table was surrounded by twenty Vitra Skape high back chairs. The snow white of the chairs stood in stark contrast to the otherwise dark furniture in the room. Dr. Young sat by himself at the head of the table, coolly examining the luxurious furniture. The corners of his mouth turned down sourly as he remembered when he had learned the twenty chairs cost over seven thousand dollars apiece. Despite the explanations of the CEO he'd hired about the importance of a prosperous appearance in creating a company's image, he was still unable to help feeling the money spent on those stupid chairs could have been used in a number of wiser ways.

The cell phone in his pocket rang and brought him back to reality. It was his wife's caregiver.

"Yes, Roberta," he answered with concern.

"The missus feels very bad. She is in great pain. The missus wants a sticker on her back, but she already has one. That's dangerous. What to do?"

"In the medicine cabinet, you will find a blue vial. Inside, there are twenty-seven cannabis oil pills. Give her one pill and update me on her condition in thirty minutes."

"The missus wants sticker," the caregiver repeated.

"Tell her that if the cannabis doesn't help, we'll let her have another patch," he said with pain in his voice. "And tell her I love her."

The door opened, and Young's deputy, Fred Nilsen, stepped into the conference room. The look on his face hinted at his annoyance at the urgent summons to the company offices on a Saturday evening.

"I'm in the middle of a family crisis. My wife's parents are supposed to come for a visit in an hour and with them, unfortunately, her two brothers and their parasitic wives. My wife is convinced I invented a phone call from my boss just to get away from her family. I wish I had the guts to do something like that." He gave a little chuckle but quickly went quiet when confronted with his colleague's frosty stare.

Dr. Sean Young was known in the company as a genius with very little in the way of social skills. He held thirteen patents in the field of genetics and a similar number in microbiology. Even today, seven years after he had established the company that currently employed over a hundred and fifty workers, most of them scientists, he was still considered the organization's most valuable asset. In all that time, he had never associated socially with any of his colleagues. He was zealously protective of his privacy, a tendency that had become even more extreme once he'd learned of his wife's cancer.

Three senior members of the company's research team entered through the open conference room door and took their places around the table. The five men in the room were the development department's "commando team." The spearhead of innovation. Every single one of the company's products had begun as an idea in their minds then developed as a prototype in their secret laboratory, a laboratory none but the five of them were permitted to set foot in.

"I wanted to update you on two topics," he began without apologizing for having called them to the office on the weekend. "Dr. Schmidt has managed to obtain an additional funding of fifty million dollars for further development. The initial results we demonstrated so far have convinced our investors that we are on track and that it will be worth their while to finance the next stage of developments, dealing with the genetics of cancerous cells. They have agreed with the thesis we presented that at this current rate and based on patents we have already registered, we will soon be ready to start FDA testing."

A wave of eager whispers swept around the table. Clearly, this was the news the team had long hoped to hear. Now they would be able to continue to develop all their technological whims undisturbed.

"Enough!" Young's voice rumbled, and his lips whitened with rage. Silence settled in the conference room. Their manager's furious outburst was not in keeping with the good news he had just announced. On the contrary, it was apparent that he was in distress. None of those present dared ask him about the nature of his behavior.

"Now to the second subject. But before I begin, I ask that you carefully read the confidentiality agreement you will soon be given and are requested to sign." Young took eight copies of a document out of his briefcase and handed them out. "Please sign two copies. After you sign, I will sign as well and return a copy for each of you to keep."

The four men exchanged glances, after which Fred, the most

senior among them, spoke up, "We've already signed an NDA. Why should we sign another one?"

The three others nodded in agreement.

"I am going to present you with a technological breakthrough the likes of which you have never been exposed to. Also, I must share additional information with you that is not related to the company. I will understand if you refuse to sign, but I cannot reveal anything to you before you do. This is the moment of truth. Each of you needs to ask yourself whether or not you trust me."

The murmuring stopped as the scientists immersed themselves in reading the document. Occasionally, they rubbed their faces with growing incomprehension and concern. Finally, they all finished reading and placed the document in front of them. None of them signed it.

"I understand that you all refuse to sign. Thank you. This meeting is over." Sean Young collected the documents without another word and marched to the door.

"Dr. Young," the youngest of the four called to him, "I've signed my fair share of confidentiality agreements. This is without a doubt the most draconian agreement I've encountered. If it weren't for my respect for you, I'd have left the room long ago. I think the mere fact that we have all chosen to remain speaks for itself. I believe we deserve some explanation about the nature of the secret you plan to share with us, before we agree to sign."

Young returned to his chair and sat down heavily. "All right." He sighed, an expression of genuine distress on his face. "About a month ago, Fred and I discussed the most challenging topic facing all genetic researchers, one I know you're all familiar with. Indulge me in a brief update on the subject of our conversation.

"As you know, every cell in our body carries the same DNA, but different cells have different gene activity. In order for a particular gene to be muted, the cell activates an epigenetic mechanism that controls gene expression. The collection of these changes, or humps, as some of us call them, formed atop the DNA are called methylation."

Everyone nodded; they were all well versed in the subject.

"The question we asked ourselves was whether there is a way to calculate the methylation of each and every tissue in advance, so that we could develop a targeted drug delivery system that would influence only the damaged tissue without affecting the other tissues in the body and without causing any side effects. It was clear to us that the first to solve this problem would own the holy grail of modern medicine. Now, I think I have the solution. If you would like to be part of the team working on it, you must sign the confidentiality agreement before you, with all the draconian fines included in it." Young piled the documents in the center of the table.

This time, all four scientists hurried to sign then pushed the papers toward their manager. The looks on their faces said it all. It was rare for any scientist to come across a breakthrough of such magnitude. The Nobel Prize was suddenly on the horizon.

Dr. Young collected the documents, signed them, and returned a copy to each of the participants. Then he slowly gathered the four remaining documents and placed them back in his briefcase. It was apparent that he was considering how to proceed. Finally, he connected his laptop to the giant screen covering the wall behind him. A series of complex equations appeared on the screen, surrounded by densely written explanations in his handwriting.

Once again, the scientists became immersed in reading. The air seemed to have been sucked out of the room. The silence was disturbed only by the sounds of markers squeaking, as one by one the men stood up from the table and approached the whiteboards normally hidden behind the mahogany paneling. The intensity of the discovery had made them completely forget their weekend familial duties. The mathematical challenge they'd been presented was intellectually dazzling. They had never encountered such ingenious work.

"Astounding," Fred muttered and gave Young an appreciative look. Various cries of admiration were heard from around the table. They all realized they had been offered the chance to write their names in the annals of medical history. If only their manager would agree to share the glory with them.

Young seemed to have read their thoughts. He raised his hand and asked them to settle down. "I think we all agree that what I've just shared with you represents an impressive breakthrough." He chuckled uneasily. "There is no doubt in my mind that the described mechanism can become the basis of an ultimate solution leading to the eradication of cancer from the world. You will be the team that will do it, and I promise you, here and now, you will equally share the credit for this discovery, should you meet the schedule I have in mind."

The scientists exchanged bewildered looks. "Why are we pressured for time? Do you think someone else has the same technology?"

"No," Young said firmly, "but my wife has cancer that has metastasized throughout her body. I believe she has no more than a few months remaining. Together, you and I will help her get well again."

"Are you saying," Fred interrupted, "that you intend to try the mechanisms we will invent on your wife without testing them on animals first?"

"Yes. Without her knowledge, I've been experimenting and trying various solutions for the past few months. Some proved effective, others didn't. Unfortunately, even the more effectual solutions aren't focused enough, and the disease continues to spread. I've no other choice."

"Without her knowledge?"

"Indeed. And that is why you have all signed a confidentiality agreement. Tomorrow, I will be in the laboratory to begin work. I hope to see you all with me." Young began to gather his belongings. He could not shake off the disquieting feeling that had settled deep in his chest following the phone call from his wife's caregiver. He wasn't at all convinced that he had several months to save her.

CHAPTER 9

The telephone on Ronnie's desk buzzed. He picked up the receiver sluggishly.

"Someone from the FBI," said Michelle, sounding a little concerned.

"Transfer the call, please."

"Hello. This is Special Agent Miller. Am I speaking with Dr. Ronnie Saar?"

"Yes." Ronnie held his breath.

Miller got straight to the point. "I need you to tell me if Double N is involved in anything the authorities should know about."

"I can't think of anything that would justify a violent attack on one of my employees. We're a small startup company, and most of our activities are conducted in Israel."

"Do you have any competitors that might be interested in information held by your company?"

Ronnie was surprised. "Yes, practically everybody active in the field. Why do you ask?"

"Anyone in particular come to mind that would be willing to resort to violence?"

"I assume all the major players in the industry would give practically anything to get their hands on what we've developed. The fact that I cannot imagine a business organization taking such a drastic step, doesn't mean it couldn't happen."

"That's true." Ronnie could actually sense the smile on the other end of the line. "But perhaps the following information will put your mind at ease, at least concerning your company's proprietary technology. Fine's backpack was found yesterday. It was tossed into a trash can in a nearby alley. The backpack contained paperwork belonging to your company and a laptop. Fine's wallet wasn't found, which supports the police suspicion this was a run-of-the-mill mugging. Probably committed by a homeless person or a junkie.

"I, on the other hand, have not yet discarded the idea that this attack was part of a series of violent acts committed by a killer I am after. Only wool remains from a glove, which matched those found on the weapon, and the victim's fingerprints and genetic traces were found on the bag. Furthermore, the computer appeared to have only Dr. Fine's fingerprints on it. I expedited all the forensics, and at this stage, the police have agreed to return the contents of the backpack to your company."

"And how do you explain why a homeless person didn't try to sell the computer? Even for a pint of whiskey?"

The agent didn't hesitate. "According to the testimony of the police officers, they arrived on the scene very quickly and were followed by additional officers, who deployed in the area and searched for the assailant. Our working theory is that the perp got scared and tossed the incriminating backpack."

Ronnie's mind was working feverishly. "How come you didn't find the bag the day before? And how do you explain why the trash cans hadn't been emptied since the day of the assault?"

"Apparently, waste disposal services in New York tend to leave half-empty trash cans for the next round. As for why it wasn't found before — I've no idea. Maybe it was negligence, maybe it was just bad luck. Anyway, I gave your assistant the name and address of the police officer holding Dr. Fine's backpack. Have a good day." The call was disconnected before Ronnie had a chance to reply.

Three hours later, three men and a woman sat around the conference table in Ronnie's office. The large window overlooked 30th Street in the Chelsea neighborhood. A tense silence filled the room. They were all waiting for Michelle to return. She had gone to pick up Simon's backpack over two hours before and was expected back any minute.

Ronnie scanned the faces around the table. The four of them, two Israelis and two Americans, were scientists who had worked with Simon on the company's most innovative developments. Ronnie had separated them from the team in Israel and moved them to New York so they would be able to continue their unique research without being interrupted by routine assignments. In the days following the mugging, there was no question that that the joy of creation characterizing that special group of people was gone.

Ronnie saw Michelle hesitantly approaching from beyond the glass door and beckoned her inside.

"Sorry for the delay, but the number of documents I had to sign could fill up an encyclopedia." She sighed, then placed a plastic bag in front of Ronnie. With tears filling her eyes, she muttered in a strained voice, "I'm so sorry for what happened to Simon" and rushed out of the room.

The four exchanged confused glances, but their eyes quickly returned to Ronnie as he spread the contents of the backpack on the desk. There were neat packages containing a detailed printed presentation of the design review, a book called *Statistical Genomics: Advanced Methods and Protocols*, and Simon's laptop. Simon's wallet and a Montblanc fountain pen he always carried were conspicuously absent.

"It seems like the thief wasn't after the company information after all," one of those sitting around the table said with a sigh of relief.

Ronnie bit his lower lip. "Let's adopt for a moment the viewpoint that only paranoids survive and presume that the opposite is true. It might be that the backpack contained some other documents that were taken. Also, information from the computer could have been copied. I suggest that we find out whether the computer contains information that, if leaked, could irreparably harm our company. If that turns out to be the case, I believe we will have to assume the information is now in the hands of elements hostile to our company and determine the implications of such a breach."

Eugene, the company's senior mathematician, shook his head in disagreement. "Ronnie, as you know, according to your strict instructions, all company computers are encrypted and protected by an access passcode. Even if they removed the hard drive from the computer and tried to copy it, such copying would be useless. Also, if someone tried to guess the password more than three times, the computer would have been locked. It can be unlocked only when two conditions are met — it is connected and synced to the company's server and is fed by a dynamically changing password that only I and our security manager in Israel are in possession of. From the moment I learned about the theft of the computer, I've been checking regularly for any attempts to connect it to the network. No such attempts were made. So, unless Simon gave the thief the password or his fingerprints, the computer could not have been accessed."

Ronnie turned on Simon's computer. A password request box appeared on the screen. He looked at Eugene, who began to search for the information in his own computer's database. "Seeing math in everything. All lowercase and no spaces," Eugene dictated slowly. The password was entered, and the desktop screen came up. Everyone's eyes were immediately drawn to a folder titled "The Breakthrough."

"Hold on, Ronnie," Eugene called, stopping Ronnie from opening the folder. "Not that I believe breaking into the computer is possible, but let me check something before we open any of the documents. On each computer, I installed a logger that records every keystroke. If anyone fooled around with the files we'll know soon enough."

Ronnie pushed the computer toward him. The tension was visible on the faces of everyone in the room as they followed Eugene's changing expressions with interest and growing apprehension.

"I don't understand how it could have happened" — the mathematician's face crumpled — "but there's one thing I'm sure of. All the documents in this file were opened the day after the attack on Simon. We must assume they were copied as well."

A heavy silence settled in the room as the implications of Eugene's findings began to register in everyone's minds.

"We all remember Simon's shouting." Ronnie's expression became troubled as he recalled the incident. "He sat with me and explained that he needed complete silence in order to prepare the design review presentation. I made an exception and allowed him to take home all the materials relevant to our recent breakthrough.

My working assumption was that our computers cannot be hacked. I guess I was wrong. Big time."

"So you're saying we're screwed?" Eugene looked terrified.

The silence that followed was more telling than any answer.

CHAPTER 10

Sean Young's head trapped the telephone receiver against his shoulder. "You think I don't understand what's going on? A scientist from a competing genetics company was violently attacked in New York, an assault that fell short of murder only by sheer miracle, and the next day you bring me information only a handful of people in the world could have developed? I don't care if you're behind the attack or if you just got lucky and found the computer," he spat, "I never agreed to be a part of any act of violence. But now, because of you, I'm up to my neck in this mess. As of now, our agreement is canceled. You can come and retrieve the material you gave us." Young took a letter opener from his desk and began to obsessively clean his manicured nails.

"I don't think you're in a position to change your mind. I suggest you take a moment to reconsider your last statement. Allow me to remind you what was explicitly agreed between us. It was made perfectly clear that once you agreed to the deal, there would be no turning back. Furthermore, did you really think I didn't know you copied the material?" she asked, sounding almost amused.

"I didn't co—"

"You need this scientific breakthrough to save your wife, and that is why you will perform the assignment you've been given." The call was disconnected.

A chime indicating incoming mail sounded from his computer. His eyes involuntarily drifted to the screen. Two messages from an unknown email address appeared in his inbox. He read the subject of the first email. *The assignment you have committed to perform.* He curiously opened the mail and began to read. His eyes widened with horror. The full extent of his entanglement began to dawn on him. Young closed the computer and looked at the telephone on his desk. He knew what the right thing to do was. But he also knew the terrible price he'd have to pay for doing it. His wife, the love of his life, would die. Beads of cold sweat formed on his forehead. He was reaching for the phone when the subject of the second email caught his eye. *Recordings to be released to the press in one hour.* The words sent a twist of pain straight to his stomach.

Young extended a shivering hand to the keyboard and opened the email, to which two files were attached. He clicked on the first file. It was a recording, made without his knowledge, of the conversation they'd had when she had given him the MacBook. He cursed his carelessness, hurried to close the file, and clicked on the other one. He heard his conversation with the development team. When he reached the end of the recording, a slide popped up on the screen, quoting the sentence with which he had summed up the meeting.

"*Yes. Without her knowledge, I've been experimenting and trying various solutions for the past few months. Some proved effective, others didn't. Unfortunately, even the more effectual solutions aren't focused enough, and the disease continues to spread. I've no other choice.*"

Young removed his hand from the receiver. Should the contents of the recording be published, he would never again be able to work as a researcher or a physician. He would end his life in shame. Perhaps even behind bars.

"How the hell did she make those recordings?" He felt the blood draining from his face. "That conniving bitch," he whispered in frustration, recalling his decision to meet her in the conference room when she had come to pick up the computer, and the interest she had shown in the fancy furniture.

"Get me Pete Rogers," he screamed at his secretary.

Minutes later, the door opened and Rogers stepped inside with a newspaper folded under his arm.

"Great. Please go to the conference room. I —" Young stopped when he saw Pete still standing in front of his desk, ignoring his instruction.

Pete tossed the newspaper on the desk.

Young stood up and leaned forward, resting his fists on the table. "Wasn't I clear enough? Go to the conference room. I need you to make sure it hasn't been bugged!"

"I'm willing to bet this man would really like to know where his laptop is." The programmer didn't budge, keeping his eyes on his manager with a challenging look.

"I have no idea what you're talking about, but I'm not going to ask twice. Please get out of my office and come back when you have some answers."

Rogers placed his hand inside the folded newspaper and in one sharp motion spread it open on the table. He motioned with his eyebrows at the newspaper. *Did the Serial Killer Fail?* the headline shouted.

"This is what I want to talk about, and I believe everything else can wait."

"I don't understand what you or I have to do with this article," Young said, but with very little conviction.

Pete Rogers sat down and crossed his legs, exposing a sockless moccasin from which sprouted an exceptionally hairy leg. He picked up the newspaper and began to read out loud:

"*The Serial Killer Strikes Again! A man was brutally attacked in a Chelsea alley and survived only thanks to the quick response of the NYPD*, et cetera, et cetera." His eyes flitted over the article. "*The victim is an Israeli citizen by the name of Simon Fine. Fine, forty years old, has a PHD in genetics from Harvard. Dr. Fine works at Double N, with offices in Israel and Chelsea*." He refolded the paper and placed it back on the desk. "I don't believe in coincidences. A brutal attack on a scientist, a genetics expert, an Israeli… should I go on?" He stared at Young impassively.

Young maintained his silence.

"And then, one day after the robbery, you ask me to break into a computer containing documents, some of which were written in a strange language. Something in the article makes me think it was Hebrew. I think I deserve an explanation."

"I have none to offer. But it is a strange coincidence, indeed." Young forced a smile.

"I checked the victim's LinkedIn page, which mentions, just like the newspaper does, that he works for a company by the name of Double N." The programmer's monotonous tone sent shivers down Young's back. "A company whose logo appeared on quite a few of the documents I went through after cracking the password."

"So what are you asking?"

"Why shouldn't I go to the police with this story?"

"Because I have nothing to do with the robbery." Young gave

him a cold look.

"Then you shouldn't have any problem with me going to the police." Pete sat up in his seat and slowly started to rise.

Young closed his eyes and took a deep breath. Finally, he leaned back in his chair and crossed his arms over his broad chest. "Sit down, please. As I said, I have nothing to do with the robbery. If I did, your decision to come into my office and threaten me would probably have ended badly for you. The reason I don't want you to go to the police is simple. Every bit of dirt or juicy story that comes out in the press immediately influences the price of our stock and starts a whirlwind that costs us valuable resources, resources that we do not have the luxury of wasting. Dealing with something like that might harm every aspect of the company's activity. So, let's finish this conversation quickly. What do you want in order to forget about all this?"

"You mentioned stock. I have a small number of company options at the moment. I'm willing to bet even your secretary has more shares than I do. In fact, I know she does, because I broke into the company's human resources files and saw the actual allocations. By the way, you have lots and lots of shares. If my assumption is correct, and the information I managed to retrieve from that laptop will significantly increase the company's market value, then I do believe the right number of shares will help me forget this whole story. And you, as the company founder, can make this happen."

Young was surprised to see how quickly the young programmer had moved from indignation to greed. They stared at each other across the desk.

"How many options do you currently have?"

"Five hundred."

"I'll see to it that you're given five thousand additional options."

"I was thinking fifty thousand." Not a muscle on Pete's face moved.

"Ten thousand is the most I can offer. Anything over that requires the board's approval. So as I see it, you have two options: walk out of this room and go to the police, or get ten thousand options, which I estimate will be worth over a million dollars a year from now."

The two men still did not take their eyes off each other. Finally, Pete Rogers picked up the newspaper and tossed it in the wastebasket.

"I'll be sure to check the conference room right away, sir," he said in a clear voice, and without looking back, he left the room.

CHAPTER 11

"What did you do with the laptop? Why didn't you return it to me?" he whispered viciously the moment she answered the phone.

"I assumed that if the police found the computer, they would have no reason to believe the attack was related to any information that might have been on it. Therefore, I made sure that no additional fingerprints were left on it and threw it in a trash can in a nearby alley. I even left a guard on the scene to make sure nothing happened to the laptop until the police found it."

"The police have the computer? Are you insane?" His voice was trembling with rage. "I told you I needed the computer after you got it back from Young."

"I thought any additional meetings between us might expose you, and I promise, they found no traces that anyone tampered with the computer. Besides, I don't understand what you need it for. After all, you had it even before we gave it to Young." Curiosity mixed with worry colored her voice.

"I knew you couldn't be trusted. I should have destroyed the computer myself. There's a good chance you've ruined everything," the man erupted. "If Young's people did not manually change the 'last update' information on the files, or if the computer contains a key-logger and Young's hacker didn't worry about it because he didn't know the computer would be returned to its owner, then your clever intentions have just gotten us into BIG trouble."

The silence on the other end of the line said it all. The man hung up and furiously punched the wall in front of him. If that woman weren't protected by her lover, he knew nothing could have stopped him from strangling her with his bare hands.

CHAPTER 12

"I went over the recordings as you asked me to do. As expected, after I sent Young the recording from his meeting with the team of researchers, he found and destroyed the transmitter I hid in the conference room."

"What about the one attached to the door handle?"

"It works wonderfully. Better than expected. You should listen to the audio file I emailed you a few minutes ago. I'll wait on the line."

From the open file played an emotional conversation between Young and an unknown person. The man listened to the entire exchange with interest.

"Sometimes all you need is a little luck. I think we've just found the hacker we need. I suggest you send over one of your goons. Have him explain to the hacker that he is in over his head, hiding information that could have helped in capturing a criminal. At the same time, offer him a hundred thousand dollars for cooperating with us. I want him to break into the DHS database and replace a retinal scan file. Once he agrees, I will give you the exact details."

"And if he doesn't agree?"

"That is not an option. If the money we offer him, along with the money he will earn from the rising value of the options he is about to receive, doesn't convince him and for some obscure reason he decides to play the hero, I give you a free hand to convince him your way."

"Done."

In his mind's eye, he saw the sadistic, satisfied smile spreading on her face. He hoped her mistake in returning the computer to its owners wouldn't ruin the perfect plan he'd spun. At the same time, he was bothered by the realization that one day, her addiction to violence and her insistence on taking care of things in her independent, unique way would bring about a mistake he might have to pay for as well.

CHAPTER 13

"Not now!" Young shouted when he heard the knocking on his laboratory door.

The door opened, and his deputy entered the room.

"I said not now!"

Fred sat down in front of his manager. "We need to talk. Now. Otherwise, you might lose your entire team of scientists. I was barely able to convince them not to just walk out without notice."

Young's red eyes spoke to the fact that he hadn't slept properly for days. "Talk. Quickly."

"The tension between you and the staff has become insufferable. Over the course of this past month, we've all willingly shut ourselves in the laboratory in a desperate attempt to meet your unreasonable demands. We all realize your wife's situation is getting worse, which explains your irrational behavior. But we don't understand why you stay cooped up in your private laboratory instead of joining us and helping. The few times you've come out, you ranted at us for being dilatory and for what you consider to be our unwillingness to make an effort. But you blatantly keep ignoring the reality that all of us, without exception, are working around the clock, eating in the laboratory, and only rarely leaving to take a short nap, shower and keep in minimal contact with our families, who can't understand our behavior. Things have to change right now. And if that's not enough, Schmidt is constantly pestering us. He wants to know what we're working on. The employees who signed the confidentiality agreement feel trapped between the devil and the deep blue sea. They are afraid of losing their jobs."

Young collapsed in his chair and buried his face in his hands. The silence in the room was disturbed only by the buzzing of the centrifuges. After what seemed to Fred like an eternity, Young rose from his seat and went out to the scientists waiting outside.

"I'm sorry about my behavior," he began, while signaling with his open hand for them to sit down. "I'd like to thank each and every one of you for his sacrifice. It's important for me to person-ally tell you that your investment and involvement have not gone unnoticed and aren't taken for granted. In addition to the work you're doing, which, as you all know, is extremely important to me on a personal level, as the company's chief scientist, I have quite a few other tasks to perform. I am under immense stress. This is not an excuse. It is a fact. From now on, if you have any concerns, don't hesitate to come and talk to me personally. In any event, from now on, I will try to spend significantly more time with you guys."

"And how is your wife?" asked one of the scientists.

Young's eyes moistened. "I can't tell. Over the past week, I've been injecting her with a preparation that includes the mechanism designed to carry the drug directly to her liver. Tomorrow, I will take a blood sample from her and we'll see. She is extremely weak and in terrible pain." He distractedly brushed away a rebellious tear. "Please, take the rest of the day off. We all need that. I insist that you leave right now. I will take care of closing the laboratory." His voice had grown stronger and louder by the end.

The researchers looked away, embarrassed for him. Except for his angry outbursts, they had never been exposed to their manager's emotions in such a visceral and direct way.

"Go home," he urged them.

The four of them retreated to their workstations hesitantly and collected their things. Young sighed with relief. He had sought an excuse to send them home all along. When he was all alone, he locked the laboratory door. The spinning of the centrifuges subsided, and the only sound was the background hum of the refrigeration equipment. Young took three empty water bottles from his bag and poured the contents of the centrifuges into them. Then he returned the bottles, now full of the liquid he'd been asked to prepare by the woman who had visited his office, to his bag. He slung the bag on his back and left the laboratory.

"The compound is ready," he blurted when his call was answered.

"Excellent. One of my men will wait for you in the lobby of the Iroquois in half an hour."

"I'll be there."

He had long ceased to delude himself regarding the consequences of his actions. He no longer cared. So long as there was a chance of saving his wife's life, the price, no matter how high, was of no importance. True, the bottles he carried contained a destructive mechanism, but he simply thought of it as a weapon. Just like weapon manufacturers, he wasn't responsible for the possible consequences of using the products he and his staff had developed. At the end of the day, it would be Brown and the woman working with him who would decide whether or not to pull the genetic trigger.

His step became more confident and a light smile touched his lips. He knew he was a brilliant scientist. Now, more than ever, and against all odds, he believed he would be able to save his beloved wife's life. Then he would find a way to take care of those who had mistakenly thought they could blackmail him.

CHAPTER 14

"Cheers!" Ronnie and Gadi raised the pint glasses that had just been served to them.

The two friends sat at a corner table in Murphy's Bar in Tel Aviv. Since Ronnie had opened the offices in America, he divided his time between the two countries. When Ronnie was in Israel, the two met often, but this was the first time they had done so without their wives.

Ronnie eased back in his chair. "How's Juanita?"

"Since becoming Liah's best friend, she's learned how to bitch and moan and make demands. I think she somehow got infected by Liah's Jewish mother genes." Gadi pursed his lips in mock irritation.

Gadi Abutbul had met Juanita, a young American woman, when he'd traveled to New York to help Ronnie solve a mystery involving the murder of three men associated with the company he used to chair.[1] She followed him back to Israel and the two were soon wed in a civil ceremony. Liah, Ronnie's wife, took Juanita under her wing and right away they became inseparable.

"I should probably warn you that now that she's pregnant, Liah

---

1   Read about it in *Green Kills*, the first in the Ronnie and Gadi series.

has honed her bitching and moaning to perfection," said Ronnie with a smile, and the look in his eyes spoke of his love for Liah. "Please thank Juanita for me for all the help she's been giving Liah. When I spend so much of my time in New York, Juanita is a perfect replacement for me."

"I'm sure if you asked Liah, she'd tell you I could serve as a much better replacement. Actually, you're such a shitty husband that anyone could be a better replacement."

Ronnie gloomily lowered his eyes. "I guess you're right."

"All right, no more whining. When are you going to get to the reason you wanted to see me this evening?" Gadi pushed his empty beer glass to the center of the table while giving his best friend a piercing look.

Ronnie Saar puffed his cheeks and emitted a series of short sighs. Then he pushed back his chair, scratching one more scar into the surface of the tired parquet floor. "About a month ago, one of my employees, Dr. Simon Fine, was brutally attacked. His backpack, and everything it contained, was stolen from him. The police believe some homeless beat him because Simon refused to give him his wallet."

"But you think there's more to it than someone unlucky enough to be in the wrong place at the wrong time." Gadi gave his friend an inquiring look.

"I don't know. Simon's backpack was found two days later in a nearby garbage can. Police suspect that the attacker got scared of the cops, who arrived pretty quickly, and got rid of the backpack before he got caught with evidence on him. Other than the wallet and a fancy fountain pen, nothing was missing." Ronnie tried to arrange the thoughts racing through his mind.

"Two days later? Don't they clear the garbage every day in New York?"

"That's a question that has been on my mind too. According to the police, and I double-checked their claim with city hall, the garbage is supposed to be removed every day, but sometimes, if the trash cans aren't full, the garbage collectors leave them for the next day. But that's not the strangest point. Simon's computer was encrypted and password protected. Eugene, a genius mathematician who works for me, is responsible for, among other things, the Chelsea office information security and data protection. He knows everyone's passwords. In an analysis he conducted, he discovered that the security on Simon's laptop was compromised and all the files had been opened some time after the attack, and therefore we must assume they were copied as well."

"So what are you saying? That Simon had a partner and they stole information from the company together? That his partner betrayed him and tried to murder him? And why did they return the computer, anyway? Come to think of it, I'd like you to explain how come this is your second company and the second time in two years that your employees have been either attacked or murdered."

"I don't have an answer to either of your questions. The police have also raised some questions I was unable to answer. It's all so surreal, and I can't explain anything."

"What questions did the police have for you?"

"More or less the same questions you just asked: How could the robber have known Simon was carrying classified information in his bag? If Simon was his accomplice, why was he beaten so severely? Why didn't they stop at threatening him when his backpack was taken?"

Gadi rolled his eyes in mock despair. "You've already told me what you guys are working on in a general way. If I'm not mistaken, it's something to do with genetics. I studied genetics for my criminology degree, but I understand that the field is developing faster than the speed of light. Things that sounded like pure science fiction five years ago are now a reality. If you explain to me what you guys are doing, I might have an idea about where to start looking."

Ronnie pinched the bridge of his nose then laced his fingers under his chin and started to talk. "The world of medicine is about to drastically change. Until recently, drugs were distributed through the bloodstream and thus spread in the entire body. The next generation of drugs will be targeted and will reach only the sick tissue, leaving the rest of the body unharmed. Think of the way chemotherapy is used to treat cancer. While it is true that the cancer cells are often destroyed, the drug's toxic materials are spread through the entire body, also affecting healthy organs and causing severe side effects. I'm sure you've seen the hair loss. Trust me, the damage that isn't visible is far more hideous. My scientists developed a 'guided missile' that can deliver drugs to specific tissue. The same mechanism can be used to replace a damaged gene with a healthy one."

"From what little I've read about the subject, I know there are many companies working on this. What makes yours so special? Why would anyone go so far as to attack one of your employees, beating him nearly to death, just to steal information from you?"

"Good question. Today, the 'guided missile' I talked about knows how to target particular types of damaged cells, mainly cancerous ones. We've added a homing mechanism, something like Waze, that knows how to reach any particular tissue in the body, cancerous or healthy, as if it had received the tissue's exact address."

"Why healthy tissue?"

"When I say 'healthy' I only mean not cancerous. Inflammation is a good and simple example," Ronnie explained. "Imagine how the medical world will look if when we know about an infection that has caused inflammation in the urinary tract, we will be able to deliver the proper drug only to that location."

"Ouch. Thanks for using such a painful and familiar example." Gadi winced. "And where does this system get the delivery address from?"

Ronnie took a sip from his beer. "This lies at the very heart of the algorithm we've developed. The system knows how to calculate the exact delivery address of each tissue in the human body, based on the particular main functions it performs."

"You're starting to lose me. Correct me if I'm wrong. Your solution works like a courier service. Let's suppose a customer comes along and asks to send flowers to a girl he loves. What you're saying is that, based on a description of the girl's most prominent characteristics, the company will find her exact address and deliver the flowers there?"

"In principle, yes, but we've additionally developed methods that allow us to haul any necessary load on the courier company's vehicle. To use your example, not just flowers, but candy and teddy bears. In our case, genetic correction mechanisms, chemo, or anything else that is necessary to cure or modify a tissue."

"All right. I'll stop asking questions now, because I'm afraid you might overwhelm me with information that would make me go and slit my wrists. But if I understand correctly, you are implying that another pharmaceutical company is behind this assault, right?"

Ronnie raised his hand and flagged the waitress. "Two more pints of Carlsberg, please." He followed her with his eyes as she left, and when she was far enough away, he said, "Not necessarily. It could also be a cosmetics company hoping to develop the next must-have glamour breakthrough, or some country with malicious intent. We developed the technology for beneficial purposes, but in the wrong hands it could be used for developing biological weapons."

"Give me an example."

"Research has been recently published on anopheles mosquitos that were genetically programmed to become resistant to malaria, so they wouldn't carry the disease. It was also proven that future generations of the mosquitos possess the same 'good' gene preventing them from carrying the disease, building hope that humanity will be able to finally eradicate malaria."

"So what's the problem with that?" Gadi asked.

"The problem is that the same exact technology can be used to program mosquitos that would carry much worse diseases, or alternatively, have every mosquito in the world become a malaria carrier. In short, it all depends in whose hands the technology lies."

Ronnie paused. The waitress returned to their table and set two beer glasses on a pair of coasters. "Anything else?" she asked, shamelessly checking out the two handsome men.

"No thanks." Gadi favored her with a casual smile then returned his eyes to Ronnie. "So everyone and his sister needs what you've developed?" He gave his friend a questioning frown.

"Now you understand why I feel so helpless when I'm trying to understand who was behind this attack on Simon."

"What do you want me to do? You want me to fly to New York with you and help you find the fucking bastard behind the attack?"

"Not at this stage. Right now, in my absence, I want you to keep

Liah safe. But, and I can't stress this enough, she can't know someone is guarding her. I don't want her to be under any stress while she's pregnant. If I need you down the road in New York, I'll let you know."

"What makes you think she's in danger?"

"Nothing in particular. But I'm not about to let go. I need to get to the bottom of this before it's too late. Since I have no clue who's behind all of this, I risk stepping on the wrong toes. Who knows how these people will react?"

"What are the chances they'd come all the way to Israel just to intimidate you? They could do that much more effectively in New York."

"Gadi, you're being logical, and you're probably right. Chances are close to zero. But I can't help being emotional and possibly irrational when it comes to the woman I love more than anything else. Last time, when we investigated the deaths of two patients in two different hospitals, we never imagined someone might come after us personally. I'm sure you remember the killer who went after Liah." His voice had inadvertently gotten louder.

Gadi's expression turned serious. He recalled the event very clearly. Liah and Ronnie were still living in New York. She was a senior-year medical student and he was a partner in an American venture capital fund and the chairman of a successful pharmaceutical company. Just as it seemed life couldn't get any better, the company's CEO was found dead in his hotel room. Then Ronnie, along with Gadi and Liah, found themselves swept into a whirlwind of events that had put their lives in danger and nearly left them dead.

"I'm aware that I'm probably wasting your time," Ronnie summed up, "but I have to be sure nothing happens to her."

"You take care of yourself," Gadi said earnestly. "I'll make sure nobody gets close to Liah."

CHAPTER 15

Ronnie leaned against the headboard and closed his eyes. Liah's head rested on his chest, while his arm was wrapped around her protectively. The scent of her shampooed hair clouded his senses. A cry of protest rose from her lips as his embrace intensified and crushed her exposed ribs.

She looked up at him, leaving her cheek on his chest, and whispered, "What's bothering you, Ronnie?"

Ronnie remained motionless.

"Please look at me." She tried to prop herself up, but the weight of his embrace did not allow her to move.

His eyes slowly opened, he leaned over, and kissed her lightly on the cheek. She pressed her hand against his chest and pushed herself into a sitting position, keeping her worried eyes on his face. Ronnie's hand drifted across her breasts and slid toward her belly, which rounded gracefully with the contours of a perfect pregnancy.

"I love you more than I can bear," he whispered huskily.

"You're scaring me. I know you better than you're willing to admit. I know something is bothering you."

Ronnie continued to stroke her belly, avoiding her eyes. "I want you to come live in New York with me. I'm sure we could get you an internship at Mount Sinai. You know I have good connections there."

"I thought we'd already been through this." Liah shook his hand off her body and began to get dressed. "I'm lucky enough to have one of the top head and neck surgeons in the country as my mentor at the Kaplan Hospital. He is a brilliant surgeon and a nice person. I'd even say he is cute. A wonderful teacher. Most importantly, he believes in me and allows me to participate in the most complex surgeries. While you're in America, I'm working around the clock with him. The other interns can't wait to get home, not me. I'm willing to participate in any surgery at any time. By now, thanks to him, I've performed more operations than all the other interns combined. I'm not about to abandon this opportunity just to get to a hospital that may be more famous but doesn't have Dr. Schindel."

"Are you in love with him?" Ronnie wore a theatrical, worried expression on his face.

"You're not funny. And yes, Doron is the kind of man you can't help but fall in love with. If I remember correctly, you fell in love with him too after only one brief meeting. Now, are you done evading giving me a straight answer? Why are you bringing this up again? I thought we agreed that with all the difficulties involved with us being apart, this is still the right choice for me. So what happened?"

"Missing you while in New York is killing me."

"Bullshit," she angrily snapped at him.

A cloud of sadness passed over his face. Ronnie lowered his head in defeat. "I can't convince myself Simon's attack was random. And if I'm right then this whole business isn't over yet. I can't be sure that the attacker found all the information he needed. It's better for me that you stay out of the line of fire, but the thought that you're not with me in these difficult times is tearing me apart."

"So what are you saying, Ronnie? That against all reason, you want to draw me into the danger zone just because…" Liah paused, searching for the right words, "it's hard for you without me?"

Ronnie gently reached out and pulled her to him. Liah placed her head in the hollow of his shoulder and said nothing.

"You're right. Forgive me, I shouldn't have brought this up. Promise me you'll take care of yourself." He pressed himself against her warm body and looked into her eyes. "I don't want us to say goodbye while we're angry at each other."

His kiss gently touched her lips was answered hungrily, and they quickly found themselves rolling between the sheets with a passion accompanied by tiny rebellious kicks coming from Liah's belly.

"He's angry," she said. "You're pissing him off too." She emitted a cry of protest as the alarm clock went off. "I have to go to my shift. When is the taxi coming to pick you up for the airport?"

Ronnie glanced at his watch. "In twenty minutes." He tried to take her in his arms, but she slipped away from him.

"I really don't care if you miss your flight, but I'm definitely not going to be late for my shift at the hospital."

The two showered quickly and dressed quietly.

"Take good care of yourself." Liah was unable to hide her concern.

"I promise."

She gave him an appeasing look. "I'll talk to Doron and check with the hospital about a one-year leave of absence. You never know, I might be joining you before long. After all, I'm due pretty soon, and I was planning on taking a long vacation anyhow."

"I love you." Ronnie looked at her gratefully as she picked up her car keys and left the house. He double-checked that both his passports, Israeli and American, were in his travel bag, stepped outside, and locked the door. The taxi was already waiting and left for the airport as soon as he dropped into the back seat. On the way, he went over his plans, but nothing could have prepared him for what would happen in the next twenty-four hours.

CHAPTER 16

The pulled-back hair of the woman sitting in the lobby of the Department of Homeland Security radiated a sixties-style elegance. She studied the documents piled in her lap with great concentration. Occasionally, she raised her eyes to look at the employee entrance gate. She sported a striped two-piece suit and heavy brown horn-rimmed glasses. To the onlooker it would seem as if she were waiting for her host to come and pick her up. The message she'd just received through the tiny earpiece made her lift her eyes and examine the lobby with deliberate indifference. Through the entrance door stepped a young man clearly of Indian descent. Wiping his forehead with the back of his hand, he marched toward a guarded door set in the middle of a reinforced glass wall.

Behind the wall were the elevators that every morning delivered the thousands of DHS employees to their work areas, each according to their security clearance. The man swiped his employee ID card in the magnetic reader and pressed his eye against the retinal scanner. A jangly sound filled the air, and the door remained closed. The man nervously blinked and wiped imaginary beads of sweat from his eyes and repeated the procedure. The same buzz of denial sounded again. He swiped his magnetic ID card once more and hurried to press his forehead to the scanner again. To no avail. The door remained closed.

People behind him began to sway uncomfortably.

"Sir, please step aside," the guard commanded.

The dark-skinned man seemed to be straining his memory to try to recall the guard's name. "Eh… you know this is a mistake. You know me. My name is Sunil Gupta, and you've seen me come in here every morning for the past five years. Something in the machine is off."

"I won't ask you again. Please step aside," the guard repeated in a threatening tone, advancing a little toward the man with his hand moving toward his gun.

The woman in the suit, like the rest of the people in the lobby, closely followed the unfolding events. It was apparent that Sunil was frightened. Following the previous month's attempted terrorist attack on the Pentagon, the guards had been instructed to show zero tolerance for any potential threat. Sunil raised his hands in surrender. He left the entrance gate station and went to the waiting area, where he sat with a sigh in one of the armchairs but immediately rose with impatience. The swarm of employees successfully undergoing the scanning, then being swallowed into the heart of the building merely fueled his frustration. His eyes examined the lobby, expecting someone to come and explain the reason for his irritating rejection. His eyes lingered for a moment on the beautiful woman who was sitting in the armchair next to his, studiously reading one of the documents before her. She demonstrated no interest in what Sunil was going through.

He pulled his cell phone from his pocket and dialed. "Liz, this is Sunil Gupta. I'm in the lobby. For some reason, the retinal scanner in the lobby rejected me. Could you please send someone to help me sort things out?" Puzzlement spread on his face. He returned the phone to his pocket, his eyes nervously scanning the lobby. Finally, he noticed two security guards emerging from a side door and advancing toward him. Relieved, he rose and began to walk toward them, but he froze as one of the guards drew his gun and cried out, "Stay exactly where you are!"

Sunil obeyed.

"Sir, you need to come with us, please," the other guard gave him a cold look, and when he noticed Sunil's hesitation, he wagged a threatening finger at him. "Sir, I won't ask you again."

The search of his body was quick, and when they were satisfied Sunil was not in possession of any weapons, the guards grabbed his arms and led him to the door from which they'd emerged.

"My name is Sunil Gupta. I work here," he shouted with a hoarse voice while struggling to break free.

"Not according to our security system," the guests in the waiting area could hear one guard grumbling as they continued to drag him behind the steel door. "You may have his ID card with your picture on it, but your retinal scan proves you're not who you claim to be. Rest assured that we're going to get to the bottom of this very soon."

The elegant woman rose from her seat in the lobby and walked toward the exit door, typing a message on her cell phone: "All right, Pete Rogers has done his part. The ball is rolling." She pushed the revolving door with her free hand and exited the building with a slight limp.

CHAPTER 17

"Pete Rogers speaking."

"I have to admit you performed well. I need you to retrieve one last piece of information, and then you won't hear from me again. Ever."

"Who is this?" Pete was unable to hide his growing concern.

"That's none of your business. All you need to know is that the man who paid you a visit works for me. I hope we can come to an understanding without me having to send him for another round of persuasion." A mock weariness snuck into the speaker's voice.

"This wasn't our deal," Pete erupted. "I took enough risks when I broke into the Department of Homeland Security computers and planted fake retinal prints in Gupta's personal data file. I'm not going to do anything else," he stammered nervously.

"I really don't have time for your nonsense. Now listen and listen well." The speaker's voice turned ice-cold. "Up to this point, you've been lucky that our relationship has developed in peaceful and rewarding ways. But... there are other ways. Significantly cheaper for us. If you want to play tough, that's your choice. Trust me, at the end of the day, you'll do exactly as I say."

Pete shivered when he recalled the man who had waited for him one morning outside his door. At first glance, the man had looked like any other passerby, but a brief look at his steely eyes and something inconceivably intimidating about his catlike stance made it clear that his profession had something to do with deciding human fates — and grim ones at that.

"What do you need now?" Pete tried to keep his voice steady but failed miserably.

"I need you to break into the servers of DHS again and perform the following two tasks: One, find out if they are onto your previous break-in. Two, I need you to get Sunil Gupta's DNA test results. I believe they will be ready in five hours. When the time comes, I will provide you with a temporary email address to which you will send the information."

"I might need some more time. Correct me if I'm wrong, but I don't think you want me to rush it and get caught." The confidence had returned to Pete's voice.

"All I care about are the results. If I don't get them in time, you'll wish DHS *had* taken you in. Once I have Gupta's DNA report in my hands, the second part of the payment will be wired to your numbered account." Without any warning, the man disconnected the call and left Pete breathless. For the first time in his life, he felt the bitter taste of horror.

CHAPTER 18

"Hello, Kate. I assume you know who you're speaking with," the familiar, flat voice spoke from the phone.

"Hold on a moment," she answered. "I'll be right back," she mouthed at the waiter, whose eyes followed her as she left the restaurant leaving her main course on the table. She stood on the sidewalk, resting on her walking stick. "I'm very busy," she blurted angrily.

"I couldn't care less," the speaker maintained a tranquil tone, which suddenly sounded intimidating.

"Speak!"

"The good news is that Pete Rogers has done a good job again. Our scientist inspected the DNA test results Pete sent me. You can tell the boss we are ok to move on to the next stage."

"Thanks. I'll tell him. That's all?"

`"I am in possession of a package that is supposed to reach Bale. I will send it to your office. See to it that the contents of the package are consumed by him at least a week before he intends to set the plan in motion. I will deliver another package to you personally in three days. I will let you know the rendezvous point a day in advance. I suppose we will need to meet at least a few more times before we can be sure the program is successful."

"All right. Goodbye." She began to march back toward the

restaurant door.

"Wait. I'll be the one to decide when this conversation is over."

"Yes?" Kate stopped in her tracks, giving a reassuring smile to the worried waiter, who kept eyeing her, ready to give chase if she chose to leave without paying.

"I suggest that you follow Gupta. What will happen to him isn't a coincidence. In addition to our joint project, I've come up with another initiative. You know how much I like thinking outside the box. Believe it or not, the information we obtained from Double N has helped me come up with the ultimate weapon in no time at all. I believe that in the coming years, we will be able to make a hefty sum of money thanks to this invention."

"What are you talking about?" she whispered, feeling her confidence melting.

"Do as I ask, and you'll soon understand. By the way, I believe — no, I'm actually totally convinced — that Pete Rogers has outlived his usefulness. I suggest that you make him disappear. Unlike you, I've listened carefully to the tapes. Pete is blackmailing Dr. Young. Right now, the good doctor is the most important link in the chain. Conclusion? Rogers need to go away."

"You—"

"Shh… relax. I don't understand what the excitement is all about. After all, you're always so proud of your unique ability to make problems go away. Right now, Rogers is a problem. He knows about Young, about you, and about Gupta. In order for him not to be a problem anymore, either he, or the people he's been in contact with, need to disappear. I assume this is an easy choice to make."

The woman stared at her silent phone. A crooked smile curled on the corners of her lips. She loved these missions more than anything.

CHAPTER 19

Attorney Robert O'Shea hated opera. "Going to the opera is the most agonizing way I know of wasting precious time," he tried to convince the woman when she called him to set the meeting with her boss. But the latter insisted. Her principal had demanded they meet at Lincoln Center for the premiere of *The Tales of Hoffman*. His ticket, so he was told, would be waiting for him at the box office.

The theater began to fill with couples who saw the occasion as an excuse to flaunt their wealth. The lawyer stood with his back against the wall and his eyes scanning the gathering attendees. He couldn't help but admire the riches dangling from the necks of the women passing by. Each diamond could buy him his kind of woman's everlasting love. He had never understood why any man would invest a fortune in a single woman, only to be rewarded for his pains with jealous fits each time he dared to steal a glance at a young chick walking by. O'Shea had never believed in love. He was proud of his pragmatic approach to life and the financial means that allowed him to maintain it. Like his clients, he believed the healthiest relationships were of the give-and-take kind. One side pays money, and in return the other side provides the finest services it has to offer. His clients paid him large sums in return for legal protection. He, for his part, spent that money on luxury goods, which included the choicest escorts New York had to offer.

The sound of a bell accompanied by a call for the stragglers to take their seats echoed in the hall. Robert O'Shea glanced with concern at the two empty seats in the middle of the seventh row. One of them matched the ticket in his hand.

"Sir, I'm going to have to ask you to take your seat. We are about to start," he heard the usher's authoritative voice. O'Shea gave the young man an angry look, and the latter stared right back at him with insolent eyes. "Sir, if you're having a hard time finding your seat, I'll be happy to help."

Without a word, the lawyer began to make his way through the dozens of seated opera lovers by roughly pushing past their legs. His enjoyment in hearing their annoyed protests was far from enough to dissipate his anger. Darkness filled the theater and the opera began. The seat next to his remained orphaned. O'Shea was convinced that time had deliberately and cruelly slowed down its pace. The spontaneous outbursts of applause and "bravos" at the end of each aria, were conceived in his mind as malicious acts intended to further extend his agony and prolong the arrival of the wished-for intermission.

He kept looking at his phone, which vibrated in his pocket every few minutes, ignoring the hateful, indignant looks shared by a triple-chinned matron and the emaciated, hawk-nosed and bejeweled woman sitting next to the empty seat beside him. None of the text messages were related to the reason for his temporary incarceration in that damn place. Finally, after two tiresome acts, intermission came and brought, or so he hoped, an end to his suffering.

Robert O'Shea rushed up the aisle and into the lobby. Even the thought that he would have to inform his most dangerous client,

Arthur Bale, that the woman whose instructions he'd sworn to obey during their meeting in prison had not shown up, did not slow him down.

"Mr. O'Shea?" He felt a hand gripping his shoulder.

"Get your hand off—" O'Shea subdued his anger when he found himself looking into deep-green, catlike eyes situated slightly above his own.

Beneath those eyes were full, glowing lips, covered with a sensuous, glossy lipstick, and a swanlike neck adorned with a thin rose-gold necklace. A long and shapely leg showed through the high slit of her dress, and a black Salvatore Ferragamo handbag dangled from a curly gold chain on a shoulder as broad as a tennis player's. The woman was openly enjoying his admiring looks.

"I apologize on behalf of my manager, but an urgent matter requiring her immediate attention prevented her from spending an exciting night at the opera with you. She asked me to relay her sincere apologies." She curled her lips into a tempting smile.

"Please tell her I understand. I just received a call that unfortunately forces me to leave this impressive performance." His eyes remained glued to her pouty lips.

"Pity," she said with a velvety voice, "I was hoping we could watch the last two acts together."

"Well, let me try something, perhaps I can change my plans." O'Shea regretted his impulsive lie and fished the cell phone from his pocket.

"Oh, no." She placed long, comforting fingers on his arm. "I am convinced certain developments in your relationship with my boss will give us other opportunities to meet. And before I forget…" The girl opened her handbag and lingered a moment while examining her surroundings. It was only when she seemed convinced no one was looking that she took out a small white envelope. "Inside this envelope, you'll find a letter and an innocent-looking white pill. Memorize the contents of the letter, and tomorrow, while visiting Bale in prison, relay it to him word for word. It is important that you hand him the pill after he confirms the message in the letter. Goodbye and good luck with the emergency that prevented you from staying to see the rest of this amazing opera." She landed a light kiss on his cheek, turned around, and left, mincing her steps in a way that almost entirely concealed her limp and made all the men in the hall completely forget their female companions.

O'Shea watched her until she disappeared through the doors and then sat in an empty chair next to the table behind him.

"Excuse me, sir, can't you see that this table is taken?" He dimly heard the grievance of the man sitting by the table.

Without a word, O'Shea rose and slowly walked to the exit. The beauty's promise of further opportunities to meet suddenly sounded extremely unappealing. It was clear beyond a shadow of a doubt that a heavy pistol was the bulge he had discerned in her handbag.

CHAPTER 20

"I hope you've brought me some good news. For all your skill, I'm afraid we'll reach a point when you won't be able to postpone the trial date anymore," Bale confronted his lawyer as soon as the guard slammed the door behind them.

The sealed visitation room smelled of sour sweat, traces of the previous meeting that had ended just a few minutes before.

Robert O'Shea felt the remains of his breakfast rising up from his stomach and cleared his throat in an attempt to chase away the acidic taste filling his mouth. "Good news indeed. The lady informed me that the plan can commence." He unraveled a small thread from the lining of his suit jacket, took out the white pill and handed it to Bale. "The letter I received from her contained instructions for you to swallow this pill immediately. In a few hours, you will start feeling ill. Your condition will gradually deteriorate until they will be forced to take you to the prison infirmary. Once you're there, she will get you the additional material you'll need for the plan's success."

A repulsive smile rose to Bale's lips as he tossed the pill into his mouth and swallowed it with a grimace. "Anything else?"

"When will I know what the plan is?" O'Shea asked.

"When you need to," Bale answered irritably. "Is that it?"

"The lady asked me also to tell you she had received an update from her police sources. Apparently, Dr. Ronnie Saar, the Double N CEO, is pressuring them to investigate the information theft from his company. They say he is relentless and has even threatened to use private investigators. He sounds very determined to get to the truth. I don't know what this is about, but she's asked for your approval to make the problem go away."

Tension twisted Bale's face. "I'm not sure she's the right person to handle this threat. She's addicted to violence, and her compulsion sometimes clouds her judgment," he mumbled, then he straightened his shoulders and looked straight into O'Shea's eyes. "Remember the two professionals we used last year?"

O'Shea nodded. The pictures he'd received as proof that these "professionals" had successfully completed their task would remain etched in his mind forever.

"Contact them. Give them detailed information about this Ronnie Saar, and ask them to find out how much he knows and who he has working for him. Should they decide there's a problem that can't be solved in amicable ways" — another chilling smile rose to his lips — "they'll know what to do. If they talk about money, use the usual tariff. Am I clear?"

"Crystal," O'Shea assured him. He didn't really want to think about the "amicable ways" those two would employ.

CHAPTER 21

The courtroom was full to the brim. Those lucky enough to have arrived two hours before the beginning of the trial had filled every available seat. None dared leave for fear they would lose their place. Those optimistic enough to arrive at the last minute squeezed their way across the walls while elbowing their neighbors in a vain attempt to claim some territory for themselves. All was ready for the grand show. Arthur Bale's trial was about to begin. Over the past month, the press had constantly hawked the information fed to it by the police and the DA's office, presenting Bale as the most dangerous criminal America had known in half a century. Newspapers were selling like hotcakes. Now the hungry crowd was eagerly waiting for the main spectacle.

The defendant was sitting at the front of the courtroom. Next to him sat Robert O'Shea, his attorney, dressed in a Brioni suit stitched with white-gold threads. The suit was made famous in 1995, as it was worn by two celebrities — Donald Trump and James Bond. It seemed the attorney enjoyed basking in the same celebrity glory. Unlike O'Shea's glamorous and assured appearance, Arthur Bale sat with his shoulders hunched. His hair looked as if it hadn't been washed in days, and his face was adorned with tufts of stubble, shot through with patches of white. Even the stylish suit he wore failed to hide his miserable physical condition.

To their right, behind the prosecution table, which was almost buried by piles of thick folders, sat the prosecutor, Julie Wilson, dressed in a gray-striped pantsuit. Two young assistants sat next to her endlessly reorganizing the folders in front of them, failing to hide both their stress and their elation at the magnitude of the event.

"All rise!" the bailiff called as the judge, Glenn Morrison, entered through the heavy wooden door behind his elevated bench.

The judge straightened his robe, took his place, and instructed the crowd to sit down. "Before we begin with the jury selection process, do either of the parties have a statement to make?"

"No, Your Honor," the prosecutor answered quickly, instantly regretting her pronounced enthusiasm.

"Yes, Your Honor." O'Shea rose to his feet and threw back his shoulders. "My client's poor medical condition prevents him from remaining in the courtroom. I ask that this hearing be postponed one week to allow him some recovery time." Robert O'Shea looked around as if seeking the crowd's sympathy. He received very little of it from the annoyed crowd, who had been waiting over two hours for the show to begin.

"And what, if I may ask, is ailing your client?"

"Actually, my client's ailment isn't clear," the lawyer answered, arranging his features into a semblance of concern. "I ask the court's permission to present a document written by a medical expert who examined Mr. Bale along with the prison physician. These two distinguished doctors have signed a recommendation calling for Mr. Bale's immediate hospitalization for further super-vision and treatment."

"Your Honor, the prosecution objects to any changes in the

prisoner's conditions of incarceration," Wilson interrupted the defense attorney. "His life is in danger. Should he be removed from the 10 south wing, where he is detained today, the state cannot guarantee his safety."

"And why would you think the police will be unable to protect him from any threats against his life?" The judge furrowed his forehead with incomprehension.

"As the prosecution will demonstrate during trial, the defendant has murdered two members of the Green Gang. Their leader, 'Mad' Joe Murphy, has sworn not to rest until justice is done, no matter the cost. And when Murphy says 'justice,' he means murder. And if he is willing to sacrifice his own men, he certainly wouldn't hesitate to sacrifice the lives of innocent bystanders. Hospitalizing the defendant anywhere outside prison walls will put everyone around him, in or out of the line of duty, in dire danger."

"Your Honor..." the defense attorney began but stopped when he felt Bale's hand resting on his arm. He bent down to his client, and the latter whispered something in his ear. O'Shea's face flushed red, and he tried to answer, but Bale shook his head.

"I'm sorry, Your Honor, but my client asks to address the court directly."

A rustle passed through the crowd and the reporters readied their phones to record what was sure to become tomorrow's headline.

The judge took a quick glance at the prosecution table. Once he realized the prosecutor wasn't going to object, he spread his hands in invitation.

Robert O'Shea seemed to slowly melt back into his chair. Despite his attempts to appear in control, it was obvious that he had been just as surprised as the rest of the people in the courtroom by his client's request. A satisfied smile rose to Julie Wilson's lips as she watched the wriggling defense attorney. She hoped her decision not to object to the defense's strategy would soon prove to have been a brilliant move.

Arthur Bale heavily placed his hands on the table. He visibly strained to rise to his feet and set his eyes on the judge. Beads of sweat poured down his face and further dampened his already moist shirt.

"Mr. Bale, you may address the court while seated. I think that would save us all some valuable time." The judge waved his hand impatiently.

Bale collapsed back into his seat. "Thank you, Your Honor," he rasped. "I heard the prosecutor, and I agree with her. I don't want innocent blood on my conscience. Therefore, I agree to be treated in my jail cell, or anywhere else the prison doctors find suitable."

"Order in the court." The judge struck his gavel to try and arrest a deafening wave of mumbling that spread through the courtroom.

"I am also willing to waive my right to be present in the courtroom for the jury selection process. I don't want to delay the course of this trial more than necessary."

A heavy fit of coughing forced Bale to stop. He raised his hand, begging the judge's and the crowd's forgiveness. The coughing fit stopped, but Bale's breathing continued to be heavy.

"Still, I'd appreciate it if the court would approve two minor improvements in the terms of my incarceration and medical care. The first is to allow my personal doctor to participate in the process of my treatment, or at least serve as an advisor to the prison doctors. At this stage, the prison doctors do not have the faintest idea what the cause of my condition is, so I presume they would appreciate any help. My personal doctor has access to medical experts all over the world. I've instructed him to spare no expense while attempting to get to the bottom of my condition. My second request, which may sound strange to Your Honor, is that I be allowed to shower several times a day. This sickness causes me to suffer from constant perspiration. I'd also like to be allowed to use the same soap and shampoo that I regularly used at home. I feel this small concession will at least allow me to feel like a human being instead of a caged animal. After all, even I, despite the terrible way in which the media has been portraying me, am considered innocent until proven guilty. I thank the court for allowing me to speak." Arthur Bale wiped the sweat constantly trickling down his forehead.

"Your Honor," Julie Wilson began, rising to her feet, but she stopped when she saw the judge's face.

"Ms. Wilson, please sit down. In light of the defendant's pragmatic approach to this matter, I instruct the prison authorities to comply with his request and allow his personal physician to take part in the process of maintaining his health. Nevertheless, those in charge of the prisoner's health will continue to be the prison authority's doctors, and their ruling will be the determining and final one in any medical issue that may arise. Furthermore, I instruct that the defendant be allowed, so long as he is incapacitated, to shower up to four times a day. I don't see any reason to prevent the defendant, over the course of his hospitalization and as a temporary exception, from using his personal toiletries." The judge stopped speaking, making sure his ruling had been understood by both parties.

"I trust the prison authorities," he continued, "to meticulously examine the products brought to the prisoner and make absolutely certain that his doctor does not smuggle any unapproved medical drugs between the prison walls. Any deviation from the court's instruction will bring about an immediate cessation of these two benefits. I ask the guards to accompany the defendant out of the courtroom, so we can proceed with jury selection."

Not a member of the herd of journalists rushing outside the courtroom noticed the woman walking beside them with a nimble step while dialing her cell phone. "The judge has accepted the defendant's request. We begin," she issued the update with no expression whatsoever and hung up the call.

CHAPTER 22

Thunderous laughter sounded in the conference room.

"I've heard, Derek, that the Tesla Model S you bought has a bioweapon defense mode. That must be important to you," a foppish hipster chuckled at the person sitting next to him.

The man, about fifty-five with a mane of gray hair, dressed in a butterscotch-yellow polo shirt, a faded brown blazer, and matching tailored cotton pants ignored him.

"What do you need that mode for, anyway? I would think a vehicle that can accelerate from zero to sixty in two point five seconds could easily outrace any bacteria or virus," a young man butted into the conversation with mock surprise on his face.

Everyone in the conference room burst into a fresh round of laughter.

The door opened, and Ronnie Saar walked in the room. He glanced at his watch and smiled. "Thank you all for coming a little early. I'm happy to find you all in good spirits. I suggest we start the board meeting right away."

Everyone turned serious, nodded their agreement, and took their places around the conference table. Ronnie opened the laptop in front of him, and the meeting agenda appeared on a screen mounted on the wall. "As you can see—"

The chairperson raised his hand, interrupting him.

"Yes, Wyatt?" Ronnie asked with a frown.

Wyatt Robinson represented the company's biggest investor. The seven million dollars his fund, RK BioMed Investments, had invested in Double N, had paved the way for an additional ten million dollars in funding from the three other funds represented at the table. Their money was added to the three million dollars Ronnie had invested from his own pocket.

"Before we delve into your presentation, I think we're entitled to an update on the aggravated assault on Dr. Simon Fine."

The simultaneous inquisitive stares aimed at him from around the conference table made Ronnie realize that the question had been discussed among the investors and the ambush planned. The sudden sensation that he was trapped sent a sharp pain through his chest.

"Of course." Over the next few minutes, Ronnie recited all the known facts surrounding the attack and the current state of the police and the FBI investigations.

"Thank you, Ronnie, but we could have learned all that by reading the newspaper." Wyatt pinned him with another unwavering stare. "What interests me, and I believe it interests the rest of the investors as well, is the question of whether intellectual property was stolen from the company, and if so, what was the extent of that theft?"

Ronnie felt the circle of staring eyes closing in on him. "If the information in Simon's computer has fallen into the hands of genetic experts of the highest order, then most of our company secrets have been exposed. I must admit that even though the police are convinced the attack was unrelated to corporate espionage, I have reasonable grounds to believe someone tampered with Simon's computer before it was discovered in a trash can."

"What do you mean by 'tampered'?" asked the youngest of the investors, blinking nervously.

"The files we found on the computer had been opened the day following the attack on Simon," Ronnie answered weakly.

"Then obviously, the information has been stolen!"

"All I know is that someone opened the files following the attack." Ronnie took a deep breath. "But I can't understand why, after having stolen the information, they would make an effort to return the computer. That—"

"Unless Simon himself is somehow involved in the theft," Wyatt interrupted.

A heavy silence followed that suggestion.

"If you'd seen what he looked like after the attack, you wouldn't suspect him." Ronnie struggled to maintain an unemotional, businesslike tone.

"Perhaps that's what he wanted you to think," the chairperson persisted.

"I trust my own people. Your theory sounds completely illogical. If Simon wanted to sell company information, all he had to do was copy the information to a memory storage device and send it to the buyer. I don't see why he would roam about with the computer in some back alley, get beat up, and then return it just so he wouldn't be suspected. If you have a logical explanation for all that, I'd love to hear it."

"Allow me to tell you how I see the situation." Wyatt's face hardened. "In my world, the world of risk management, when doubt arises, one must always assume the worst possible scenario. In our particular case that would be the assumption that all materials are now in the possession of a competitor. If that is true, Double N's value has nullified. You couldn't possibly sell the company without disclosing to potential buyers your concern that competitors might have all the knowledge for which they are being asked to pay.

"Unfortunately, since we have yet to register a patent, you have no way of proving the information was actually stolen from your company. Therefore, none of the people gathered around this table will invest a single cent more in the company. Regrettably, you will not be able to raise new money, money that you need in order to turn what has so far been developed into a certified and approved product. Therefore, as much as it pains me to say this, the next obvious step is to close and liquidate the company and recover the money that we still have in the bank."

Ronnie felt as if his brain had frozen. "I'm sure you've all read the preparation material I sent you last week. You must realize that our latest breakthrough has turned us into a company that could easily be worth billions in the not so distant future. Stopping everything and rushing to close the company just because of a concern that some information might have been stolen makes no sense. It's shortsighted. Suicidal, even." Ronnie decided to go on the offensive.

"How much money have you wasted on this company to date?" Wyatt changed the course of the discussion.

Ronnie felt the blood pounding in his temples. "Zero. All the money taken out of the company account has been used solely for research purposes," he said icily.

Wyatt was doing his best to maintain his composure, clearly annoyed by Ronnie's tone of voice. "And how much money has been invested for positive purposes to date?"

Ronnie looked at the paperwork in front of him. "Four million, three hundred and seventy-two thousand dollars. It's all in the reports each of you has."

A smile touched the corners of Wyatt's lips, but his eyes remained stony. "If you truly believe in what you say, you can simply add to the three million dollars you have already invested in the company another one million, three hundred—" he paused, then added with exaggerated pathos "—and seventy-two thousand dollars. That should cover all of the money wasted" — that last word was accompanied by a mocking smile — "and return us our investments. Otherwise, I call for you to close the company and pro rata distribute the money remaining in the bank among the investors. I'm sure you know that, in such a case, you will be prohibited from making any future use of the knowledge developed with our money without our explicit consent."

"David? James? Derek? Do you all support Wyatt's demand to liquidate the company?" Ronnie looked from one investor to another, but none said a word.

"I suggest we put the matter to a vote," Wyatt interrupted the silence that followed Ronnie's question. "All those in favor of liquidating the company and distributing the remaining money among the investors, please raise your hands."

Three hands were raised. "Derek?" Wyatt turned to the oldest person in the room.

"I'm not really convinced this is the right decision. I need more time to consult with my partners before I can provide you with a firm answer. I understand that the three of you are in agreement. The way I see it, you have the majority on the board of directors as well as among the shareholders, and therefore you don't really need my vote. For the record, I ask that the minutes reflect my abstention. I assume Ronnie Saar will be voting against this decision. Furthermore, I want the resolution to include the right of the company to return the full amount invested by the funds leaving the table and continue to operate independently."

"Agreed. Then this decision is now affirmed." Wyatt gritted his teeth. "As of this moment, Dr. Saar, you are forbidden to make any expenditure or committing to any future expenses. I'm sorry to have to end our mutual adventure in this manner."

"I think you are making a big mistake. We will soon register our patents. After that, anyone showing up in the market with products that we suspect are based on our technology will be sued." Ronnie made one last attempt to turn things around.

Wyatt rose, and the two investors who had supported his decision immediately followed. "You won't have money to file any lawsuits," he said dismissively. He gave one last look at Derek, who remained seated, shook his head with open disappointment, and without saying another word left, accompanied by the two younger board members.

"Derek…" Ronnie started, his voice rough with emotion.

"Hold it, Ronnie, I'm on your side. I've already received approval from my partners to stay on board. I didn't like that stunt Wyatt pulled behind your back. I suggest we return their money in full and keep running the company ourselves. I'm sure we can reach an agreement regarding the compensation our fund deserves in light of its support. Once we return their money, we'll have a little over two and a half million dollars in the bank. That should suffice until we find out who is behind this plot. I think it goes without saying that you operate on a shoestring budget during this period of time. It's important that we don't bleed unnecessary funds."

"Thank you, Derek. I believe you deserve to be handsomely rewarded for sticking with the company in such a difficult time. I intend to put a million more dollars of my own personal money on the table, matching your investment. I promise you won't regret your support."

"Don't make any promises you might not be able to keep. Right now, the main thing is that you keep overseeing the business development aspects of the company. I promise to keep all of my commitments. Let's hope the police do their part and arrest whoever's behind this very soon."

CHAPTER 23

"How are you?" Gadi heard Ronnie's voice from the other end of the line.

"Considering that you woke me up at one in the morning, not so great. Talk to me!"

"A couple of hours ago my board of directors decided to liquidate Double N. They—"

"What? Are they completely out of their minds?"

"They claim the stolen information has nullified the company value, and they want to at least recover their share of the money left in the bank."

"And what, if I may ask, made them think the information was stolen? I thought the police were convinced it was an unfortunate mugging turned bad."

"I informed them that such a possibility exists." Ronnie tried to maintain a level tone.

"Are you fucked up in the head? Do you have a death wish? Why the hell would you do that?"

"Because I couldn't possibly lie. I truly believe the information was stolen."

"Great. So you just called me to brag about your impeccable sense of integrity?" Despite the harsh words, Ronnie heard sympathy in his friend's voice.

"For the time being, I am lucky to have the support of one of the investors and Double N continues to operate. Also, I committed to investing some additional money of my own. I have no intention of letting the company fail. But we won't be able to operate for long without raising additional funds. In order for that to happen, I need your help in finding who is behind this. Unfortunately, the NYPD isn't exactly on track, and if I rely on them nothing will ever happen. If you're busy, I'll just hire a local private investigator, but—"

"Quit whining. It'll take me a couple of days to sort things out with my company, and then I'll fly over. Nobody messes with my best friend. Now I'm pissed off too."

"Thanks, Gadi. I'll send you a ticket departing the day after tomorrow. Business class, of course, as befitting a mastermind detective such as yourself." Ronnie finally sounded more like himself.

"That's what I like about you. You are so generous when it comes to business. Speaking of generosity, do me a favor and don't be a penny-pincher when choosing a hotel."

"Promise."

"And, Ronnie, don't you worry about Liah. I'll have one of my employees watching over her at all times. And now with your permission, I want to go back to sleep." Gadi yawned loudly and disconnected the call.

CHAPTER 24

Ronnie and Sam were sitting at a corner table in the Ramini Espresso Bar on West 37th Street, when Gadi came in and joined them. Ronnie was convinced that the coffee shop, owned by an Israeli man named Rami, was the only place in Manhattan serving genuinely strong, delicious coffee.

"I took the liberty of ordering for you too," Ronnie told him. Three cups of cappuccino and three almond croissants sat on the small table.

Gadi ignored him. He was facing the glass wall, partially concealed by miniature palm trees in wooden pots, and intently scanning the crowded street.

"Hey, what's with all the spy stuff? Why couldn't we meet in my office?" Ronnie stared at his friend with curiosity.

"Just a precaution," answered Gadi. "I waited for you by your house this morning. I guessed you'd come here on foot. I wanted to see if you were being followed. Sure enough, I spotted at least two guys taking turns tailing you. When you met this gentleman" — he gestured with his chin at Sam — "they took pictures of you. Now one of them is talking on the phone across the street. These guys are pros. I was pretty sure they'd discover our connection at some point, so I decided to cut to the chase and expose myself."

"Oh, I'm sorry for my poor manners, Gadi. Please meet Sam.

Sam is my cousin who's been living in America for many years. On the way here, he told me he'd decided to invest half a million dollars in Double N. His money, along with the money I brought from home, and the money from the investor who insisted on staying with us, will give us enough run rate to raise funds with no pressure."

"Well done, cousin. If I know Ronnie, and I know him pretty well, this will turn out to be your best investment ever."

An amused smile spread on Sam's face. "Yes, I know. And I'm delighted to finally meet Ronnie's very own Sam Spade. Pleased to meet you. I hope you'll be able to solve this mystery quickly."

"You bet your ass I will." Gadi's eyes continued to scan the area.

"If I know you, you probably think it'd be a mistake to tell the police anything about this surveillance thing." Ronnie interrupted their exchange.

"And what would we tell them? That you have a strange feeling somebody's watching you? I think we need a little more proof if we want the police to take us seriously."

Ronnie took a sip of his coffee and considered their options. "So what are you suggesting?"

"I suggest you let me enjoy my coffee and croissant while you explain why you think they are following you, and whether you think there's more information they might be after." Gadi stuffed the croissant into his mouth and bit off half with gusto.

Judging by the expression on Ronnie's face, it was apparent that the same question had been bothering him for some time. "I wish I knew. There are so many possible reasons and motivations for the information theft that I can think of.

"In any event, even though filing a patent application at such an early stage of development is not in Double N's best interests, at least strategically speaking, work on filing such an application is now in full swing. No company — assuming a company stole our information — could manage to file a similar patent application before we do. Therefore, I believe if any company tried to come out in the market with a product based on our algorithms, it'd have a problem. This doesn't mean we'd have an easy time proving it, but I find it hard to believe any legitimate company would get involved in such a thing, especially since it could tie them to an aggravated assault that nearly ended in murder.

"On the other hand, a private individual would have a hard time developing anything at all with this information. The knowledge necessary for understanding our technology, not to mention the vast amounts of money necessary for developing new drugs based on this information, is too much for a single person, no matter how rich or smart he is, to handle on his own."

"And still, someone has invested a lot of effort to steal this information from you," Sam spoke up.

"You know, everybody working in the field of genetics in the past few years, as well as the various authorities, are mainly concerned with the question of how close we are to the programming of human beings and how that would affect humankind. And they are right. It all boils down to the intentions of the ones who have this technology in their possession. As I've already explained to Gadi, if the information is in the wrong hands, the dangers are unimaginable."

"Yes, I still remember your story about the mosquitos," Gadi recalled, speaking around his pastry.

"There's more to it than that. While it's true one of the reasons we developed this technology is to replace damaged genes with healthy ones, the contrary action is also possible. Let's suppose this technology is used to turn the male population of an entire nation sterile. In a couple of generations, that nation would be wiped off the face of the earth. That's a dreadful example of how scientific racism could be applied."

"And since we don't know who actually has the technology, we also don't know what they're planning to do with it," Gadi summed up with a desperate sigh.

"Precisely. The people in possession of our algorithm had no qualms about nearly killing Simon, and now they are following me. So, either we are dealing with one of the three-letter federal law enforcement agencies with which this country is so abundantly blessed, or we are faced with a sophisticated criminal organization with endless financial resources allowing it to form, in one way or another, a team of experts that can understand this technology."

"Looks like it's going to get interesting." A warm smile rose to Gadi's lips. "Glad I came on board."

Ronnie seemed concerned for a moment. "Maybe we should involve the police after all?"

"Maybe. But…" Gadi's eyes wandered behind Ronnie's shoulder. "There's a mirror behind me. Carefully look at the hottie who just went to the bar. The moment she came inside the coffee shop, she quickly scanned the place. I could have sworn she froze for a millisecond when she saw your face in the mirror. If I hadn't watched her from the moment she came in, I would've missed that. Maybe it's a coincidence, but the man who was standing on the other side of the street is gone. I think we're up against some serious pros here. Luckily, they don't know I'm quite good myself. Like I said, this is going to get interesting." Gadi burst into laughter, patted Ronnie's shoulder, and left the coffee shop.

CHAPTER 25

The Houndstooth Pub across the street was still closed. Gadi leaned against the grey marble entryway, holding up at a Manhattan street map, doing his best to look like a tourist. From time to time he looked around with a lost look and then lowered his eyes to the map in his hands. Finally, the woman emerged from Ramini's and turned toward Seventh Avenue. Ronnie and Sam were still engaged in an animated conversation at their table. Gadi slowly folded the map and returned it to his back pocket. Ignoring the honking cars, he ran across the street and began to follow her east. Considering the walking stick, she moved at a surprisingly brisk pace. She was talking into her cell phone, busy with what seemed to Gadi a heated discussion. Upon reaching Fifth Avenue, she turned left and walked uptown. When the woman finished her call, she glanced nonchalantly around and immediately started a new call.

Gadi kept his distance, making occasional sudden stops and constantly looking at the shop windows. By the time they crossed the fourth block on Fifth Avenue, he was convinced that he was not being followed. Furthermore, there was also no sign that the woman had noticed him.

After fourteen blocks, she turned and entered a high-end office building. Gadi hurried after her and stood behind the small crowd that was anxiously awaiting the elevators. The leftmost elevator of the three arrived, and the people hurried to squeeze inside. Gadi managed to see the woman pressing the button for the thirty-sixth floor before the doors closed on the crammed elevator. A couple of minutes later the doors of the middle elevator opened. He stepped inside, pressed the button for thirty-six, stepped to the back to make room for other passengers, then watched the doors close. After several stops, the last on the thirtieth floor, he was left by himself. The doors slid shut, and the elevator kept climbing. Gadi took out his wallet and withdrew a bundle of dollar bills and one, crisp hundred-dollar bill. He folded the bills so that the hundred was on the outside, Benjamin Franklin plain to see.

The door of the elevator opened silently, and Gadi stepped out to the hallway. A quick glance at the Plexiglas sign told him that three companies occupied the floor. He took a picture of the sign and walked to the door of the company at the far-left end of the corridor. The name ASSA was printed on the milky glass door. Gadi pressed the golden doorbell. A buzz sounded, and he pushed the door open and peeked inside. Behind a heavy wooden desk sat a woman of about fifty, a blue hijab wrapped around her head and a loose, long-sleeved dress covering her body.

"Excuse me, I'm looking for a tall blonde woman, dressed in a gray, tailored suit and using a walking stick. She was in the elevator a few minutes ago and must have gone up to this floor. When she took a folder out of her bag, she dropped this." He waved the money in his hand. "I couldn't stop the elevator in time," he added and panted a little.

"I can assure you, young man, that no woman answering your description has come into our office today. Well done for your effort. Most people would simply take the money for themselves.

Really, well done." She gave him a sincere look.

"Thank you." He smiled shyly and left.

In the other office he was welcomed by a young woman of about twenty-five with auburn hair. Gadi repeated his story.

The receptionist's eyes flared with suspicion. "I suggest you give the money to the guard at the entrance. If the lady you are describing has really lost such a large amount of money, she'd come looking for it."

"I don't trust him. Who says he won't just take the money for himself? I'd rather give it to her directly…" Gadi pretended to hesitate. "If you know her, I'm willing to leave the money with you. You seem like an honest person." He looked at her with utter seriousness.

"If I tell you I'll give her the money, you'd simply hand it over to me and leave?" she asked with disbelief.

"Yes. Why not?" he asked with feigned confusion.

The receptionist chuckled. "You're really cute. Unfortunately, we don't have anyone answering your description. But since you're so sweet, I'll try and help you anyway. I've seen a lady with a walking stick entering the office located to the right of the elevators a couple of times."

"Thanks. Now I have to run and get this over with. I've already wasted a lot of time as it is. My boss is going to kill me."

Gadi buzzed the third office and was given entry immediately. He stepped inside, and his heart skipped a beat. The woman he had been following could clearly be seen in the glass-walled conference room behind the reception desk. There were four other people in the room; they all seemed immersed in a slideshow presentation projected on the large screen at the end of the room.

"May I help you?" the receptionist addressed him.

Gadi turned his head to her. "Is this ASSA?" he asked with an embarrassed look.

"Sorry, no. ASSA is the company at the other end of the hall." She sounded like she said that a lot.

"Thank you. So sorry." Gadi hurried to leave.

The woman in the conference room immediately rose from her seat. "Thank you, Mr. Greenzweig, for allowing me to join this meeting on such a short notice." She placed a gentle hand on the arm of one of the participants. "It's been very interesting, but I'm afraid I must leave now. Prior commitments, you know." She smiled briefly and left the room, aware that the eyes of all the men were following her, stripping her in their minds.

CHAPTER 26

"Who is it?" the man barked.

"It's me, Pete Rogers," a hesitant voice answered.

"How'd you get my number?"

"I just dialed back the number you called me from last time."

"I hope you have a damn good reason to call."

"Well, I couldn't sleep worrying about whether DHS traced my systems breach. So, I've spent the past week engineering a new hacking system that will prevent any possible exposure of my identity and my whereabouts, and… I hacked into the DHS computer system again."

"Are you nuts? I specifically told you not to get anywhere near their computers ever again. What wasn't clear about this simple instruction? Do you have a death wish?"

"I know, I know. But you have nothing to worry about. They're not onto me."

"So why are you calling me? To brag?"

"No, but if you let me talk for a second, I'll tell you." Pete mustered all his courage.

"Talk," the man spat.

"I found out that Gupta is dead. The cause of death was a systemic failure that brought on irreparable circulatory collapse. And then…" Pete hesitated, searching for the right words.

"And then?"

"To avoid contradictions in the postmortem results, I thought I should probably restore all of his original genetic and retinal information. Sunil Gupta is back to being the man he used to be…" Pete stopped for a moment then added, "Just slightly deader."

The man's lips stretched into a cold smile. He must speak with Young and order some more of the solution he'd used to get rid of Gupta.

CHAPTER 27

"Welcome back. Come on in," Ronnie greeted Simon, who was standing in the doorway of his office. Ugly bruises showed through the bandages covering his face. Ronnie extended his hand, then changed his mind and gave Simon a hearty hug. "I'm so happy to have you back." He examined him from head to toe. "How do you feel, Simon?"

"Pretty well, all things considered. I guess I was born under a lucky star. My life could have ended in that alley, or I could have suffered permanent brain damage. Still, the doctor who treated me said he found it hard to believe this was the work of some random homeless person. According to him, whoever roughed me up was careful not to cause irreparable damage. Each of the blows landed in a sensitive area and any of them could have resulted in my death. Apparently, the assailant pulled his punches."

"Come, sit down." Ronnie led Simon to the small sofa in the corner of his office and sat in the armchair facing him. "You're saying the doctor thinks these were not blows caused by rage, but calculated ones dealt by an expert? What do the police have to say about that?"

Simon's lips twisted into a pained smile. "The police completely disregarded the doctor's conclusion. They think human beings in our world are divided into two groups: those who are lucky, and those who are no longer with us. McCarthy, whom I think you've already met, went as far as suggesting that I donate some money to my church. I guess his investigation has been so exhaustive that he couldn't even unearth the fact that I'm Jewish."

"By the way, Simon," Ronnie said casually, "why do you have a sticker on your laptop with a quote from Paulos?"

It seemed Simon had been caught off guard. He looked briefly confused before he stammered out his answer. "He's a genius. I admire him."

Ronnie dragged his armchair closer to Simon. "Where's the logic in sticking a password clue on a laptop containing the company's privileged information?"

The embarrassment on Simon's face blossomed into a deep blush. "There are countless possibilities for a password derived from what you are referring to as a 'clue.' Would *you* have been able to discover the password?"

"No, but I'm not a hacker. Also, in light of what you've told me about the physician, I want to be honest and share some of my other thoughts with you. From the moment I found out what happened, I thought this was an attack intended to steal our intellectual property. I must admit" — Ronnie looked straight into Simon's eyes —"that I've had my suspicions about you. I thought you might have been behind the theft and that a last-minute dispute with your accomplices brought about the violent end. If the doctor is right about those people beating you in a way that wouldn't cause any permanent damage, you are right back on my suspect list."

"I may be the one who got whacked in the head, but you are the one who's not thinking clearly!" Rage and incredulity flared in Simon's eyes. "Are you crazy? If your suspicions are correct, why would I have told you about what the doctor said in the first place?"

"Because you know I'm in contact with the police, and I'd probably end up finding out about it from them. If you hadn't told me about it first, you would have had a hard time explaining why you withheld such important information from me." Ronnie's cold gaze did not leave Simon's face for an instant.

"If I wanted to sell privileged company information, why would I go to a dark alley, get beaten half to death, lose the computer, and have you find it later? Had I been involved with a group of shady criminals, would I have arranged to meet them in a dark alley and trust their professional integrity? Wouldn't it have been simpler to contact them over the phone and email the file from some untraceable internet café?"

"I thought you didn't know the first thing about computers," Ronnie said sharply.

"You don't need to be a computer whiz to know how to email files anonymously." Simon shifted uncomfortably on the couch. "Ronnie, you don't really suspect me, do you? This is surreal."

"Simon" — Ronnie's voice softened — "I don't know who to trust anymore. Someone has stolen the information. What I really don't understand is how could they have known you have such detailed information on your computer. How could they have tracked you to that precise time and place? I have to admit I don't have answers to all the questions, but I promise you one thing, when I have the answers, someone is going to pay for this. Dearly."

"I had the same exact thoughts after my talk with the doctor." Simon fidgeted and seemed to be considering his next words carefully. "Can I be frank with you, Ronnie?"

"Anything you tell me stays in this room."

"If you are ready to suspect everyone, I won't be telling you anything new by saying all the company employees knew I was leaving to work from home, just as they knew I'd be taking all the material necessary for the design review presentation. Remember, they all popped into the hallway to watch like it was some kind of freak show? The self-satisfied faces of those who thought they deserved to lead the design review? And then, anyone who knows Manhattan could have guessed what route I would choose to take and ambush me on the way. The only thing I don't get is why they would beat me up. I'm no hero. If they had simply threatened me and demanded I give them the backpack and get the hell out, I would have done so without the slightest hesitation. And since they decided to beat me up, why would they take pains to keep me alive?" Simon sighed and looked about him.

"What are you looking for?"

"Something cold to drink. I feel dizzy." He leaned his head against the cushion and closed his eyes.

Ronnie opened the door. "Two large bottles of water and two cups of coffee, please." Michelle rose from her chair and hurried to fill his request.

"Quite a few people in the company told me I should work from home. Some just teased me for needing my work environment to be as quiet as a graveyard in order for me to be able to hear myself think, others were genuinely concerned for me and wanted me to be able to get my work done. At least that's what I thought till now." Simon sounded thoughtful. "When I think back to the day of the attack" — a shiver passed through his body — "I remember that even Michelle had come to my office and told me everyone was talking behind my back about how stressed I looked. She said she thought I'd feel much better if I went home to finish my work on the presentation. I remember being surprised that she knew who I was, let alone what I was working on." The water had helped Simon regain his composure.

Ronnie smiled. "Yes, Michelle has made it a habit to know just about everything going on in the company. In her job interview, she told me her inspiration comes from Donna, the legal secretary on the television series *Suits* who knows everything and can fix anything, no matter how complicated. When we found out about your attack, she was the first to come to her senses and went to visit you with a huge bouquet of flowers. She felt it was important you knew you were on our minds the moment you woke up."

"Yes, I can only dimly recall her visit. I remember how she handed me a glass of water and asked me a million questions about the assault. She was more determined to get to the bottom of the mystery than all the police investigators combined."

"You think someone in the company might be involved?"

"I don't know what to think. But I do know that I have nothing to do with this. The only part I played in this terrible affair is that of the victim." Simon smiled weakly. "The questions you've asked are relevant and important. If someone in the company is involved, find him and maybe he will provide the answers you are looking for and perhaps tell you why they decided to spare my life."

Silence settled in the room.

"All right, let's keep this conversation between us. Not a word of it should get outside this room, even to the police. I don't need the company's activities to be further disrupted. You'll find a new computer waiting for you on your desk. I'll keep the old one with me. Prepare the design review presentation and keep up the good work."

"Thanks, Ronnie. I know I'll stay on your suspect list until you find out who was behind this theft, so I'd like to sincerely thank you for giving me this opportunity of proving I'm not the one behind this unfortunate affair."

He left the room, followed by Ronnie's thoughtful gaze.

CHAPTER 28

The fourth day of Arthur Bale's trial was about to begin. The jury was seated and stared at the defendant with curious eyes. Contrary to the colorful descriptions filling the front pages of nearly every newspaper in the country, Bale was far from looking like a lethal killer or the dangerous leader of a ruthless crime organization. He appeared lost in thought, and it seemed as though the uproar surrounding him did not interest him in the least.

"All rise!" The bailiff's voice was heard above the chatter.

The judge sat and began to detail all the legal technicalities going forward, preventing the lawyers from interfering in the process. Bale continued to show a pronounced lack of interest. Occasionally, he sipped some water from a small bottle in front of him. The rest of the time, he simply stared at some random point in the air, ignoring everything, including his harried lawyer.

The procedural part finished, Julie Wilson, the prosecutor, slowly rose, adjusted her skirt, and smiled at the jury, exposing two rows of enviable, snow-white teeth. She knew from experience that the sooner she gained the jurors' trust, the better the chance they would subconsciously want to help her. Her famous smile was a weapon that had proven its effectiveness more than once.

"The state will prove that the defendant, Mr. Arthur Bale,

committed three acts of murder. The victims: Patricia Roberts, twenty-nine years old, the defendant's companion for two years until the time of her disappearance; Aiden McGrath, thirty-five; and Sean O'Sullivan, forty-two, both members of the Green Gang. According to the word on the street, their rivalry with the defendant has already caused significant bloodshed. The prosecution will prove beyond a reasonable doubt that the defendant was present at all three crime scenes and was also the one who actually pulled the trigger and ended the victims' lives." Wilson stopped speaking and gave the jurors a long, knowing look, nodding slowly. Two of them nodded back. "Thank you." Wilson smiled, as if including them in a secret, and returned to her seat.

Robert O'Shea rose confidently and gave his client a reassuring smile, despite the latter continuing to ignore him. He moved to the other side of the defense table and sat on it, half turning to the jury members, who seemed mesmerized by the courtroom theatrics.

"I hope you'll excuse me, but I'm about to give you a little spoiler about the end of the story my esteemed colleague is about to concoct for your benefit. Mr. Bale is innocent. The prosecution intends to base its claims on two facts and two facts only. The first is the testimony of a known felon, who will earn his freedom in return for testifying he saw my client shooting the three people the prosecutor just mentioned in her compelling speech. The second, and the main one —" the lawyer gave the prosecutor a wide, fatherly smile "—DNA evidence found at the crime scenes." O'Shea got down from the table and calmly walked toward the jury box. When he reached it, he rested his hands on the railing, leaned toward them, as if about to divulge some great secret, and announced in a stage whisper that could be heard in every corner of the courtroom, "But they're lying. They are deliberately lying in both cases."

The murmuring in the courtroom ceased, replaced with silence.

"Your Honor…" the prosecutor protested.

"Forget about the objection." O'Shea waved a dismissive hand at her. "Seeing as how tomorrow I will prove my claim, I agree that my last statement be stricken from the record. I withdraw it, just for you." He gave the prosecutor a little bow and flailed his arms dramatically.

"Your Honor, the prosecution objects…" the prosecutor began to shout again.

"The defense is finished." Robert O'Shea returned to his seat and looked at his client. Bale responded with indifference.

"I instruct the members of the jury to ignore the defense attorney's last remarks. Mr. O'Shea, I would like to remind you that this is a courtroom and not a theater. Next time you repeat this kind of disrespectful behavior, you will be charged with contempt of court. Are we clear?"

"Yes, Your Honor, very clear."

"We're coming up on the weekend." The judge glanced at the large clock above the entrance door. "We will adjourn and reconvene on Monday, when we will begin hearing the prosecution's case. I wish you all a pleasant weekend."

Bale took one last sip from his bottle, brought his wrists together, and extended them to the guard, who handcuffed him and led him toward a distant side door. O'Shea slowly packed the papers resting in front of him, while the prosecution representatives and the viewers hurried to leave the courtroom.

The attorney followed his client with his eyes until Bale disappeared behind the door. Only then did O'Shea gather all the belongings on the desk, place them in his briefcase and leave the room.

Only the empty defense table was left behind, clean and polished.

CHAPTER 29

It was almost 10:00 pm. Pete Rogers lolled contentedly on the white leather sofa. The back pillows, upholstered with rolls of leather stuffed with soft foam, filled him with a sense of tranquility. For the first time in a long while, he felt happy. The nightclub, The Top of the Standard, was on the roof of the hotel in which he was staying and afforded a breathtaking view of Manhattan. The money flowing into his secret account had made it possible for him to finally start living the high life. At least his version of it.

A few hours earlier, without giving it any prior thought, he'd headed downtown and rented a corner room at The Standard. The hotel rooms' glass walls gave the guests the feeling of intimacy with the city. He had spent the next few hours shopping on Bleecker Street, enjoying the envious looks of passersby staring at the impossible number of shopping bags he was carrying. Now, while holding a cocktail glass in his hand, he examined the crowded nightclub with satisfaction. He could see his own image reflected in the window. The designer clothes he wore flattered him. Even the new haircut, he had to admit, emphasized his square features and gave him an air of sophistication. Out of the corner of his eye, he saw a tall blonde in her thirties examining his face with curiosity. He tried to catch her eye, but she quickly lowered her gaze and slipped out to the patio. From afar, he could see her slowly sipping an orange drink from a tall glass garnished with a lemon slice while observing the city through the tall glass rail. Pete rose from the couch, cursing at the sight of his drink spilling and staining the front of his trousers. He hoped the relative darkness outside would hide his disgrace.

"Good evening. I noticed you couldn't keep your eyes off me, so I decided to make things easier on you and approach you first." Pete smiled, hoping his nonsense would not chase the beauty away.

The blonde turned and gave him a shy smile. "I was hoping you wouldn't notice. Sorry if I embarrassed you." Her eyes glinted at him with an emerald sparkle. He guessed they were colored contact lenses, but that did not detract from the hypnotic effect of her eyes.

"No... no." His cheeks turned red. "It's really quite all right. It's actually flattering to have such a beautiful woman even notice me." He felt he was gradually regaining his confidence.

The woman tilted her head back and burst into a long, throaty laugh. "How could a man like you be so insecure?" She placed her hand on his arm. "You are an attractive man, a fact I'm sure you are aware of. I came out here because I had assumed women bother you all the time. Like men always bother me. I decided not to do unto you what I don't want done unto me, as they say. Nevertheless, I'm glad you followed me out." She glanced at her watch, and a sense of panic overcame Pete.

"I hope you don't need to leave so soon?"

"Oh, no. I'm just hungry, and I think they're about to close the kitchen. Excuse me for being forward, but I'd love you to join me for dinner." She rested on his arm without waiting for an answer. "Please excuse me, I have this nagging tendon injury from working out too hard at the gym. My foot is killing me. I hope you don't mind if I lean on you on the way to the table."

"Certainly." He was unable to hide the relief in his voice.

"I'm very hungry. If you don't mind, I'll go straight to the main course. I'll have prime ribs with polenta and a glass of red wine. Feel free to order an appetizer. You're a man and need more food than I do." She bit her lower lip and gave him an apologetic look.

Pete felt he was falling in love. He had never dated such a beautiful and classy woman. "I'll start with the main course too. I'll take the Colorado lamb. But with your permission, I suggest we order a nice bottle of wine. Between the two of us, I'm sure we'll be able to finish it."

"Only if you promise me you don't need to drive at the end of the evening."

"I just need to take the elevator. I'm staying in this hotel."

Her smile lit up the room. "Excellent. Me too. Then by all means, order a bottle. Malbec?"

"Malbec is perfect." He raised his hand to flag down the waiter.

The conversation between them flowed easily, and Pete felt as though he had known the girl his entire life. She told him she was a partner in an accounting firm, and her specialty was software companies. That such a beautiful woman found the computer world to be fascinating was a refreshing novelty. Throughout his life, he'd managed to form relationships either with weird hacker girls who spoke computer coding more than they did English, or girls his friends had introduced to him with a strict warning they would end the date the moment he started blabbering about technical subjects.

Time passed and the place emptied out. A restless waiter had already begun to walk about their table, hinting that the restaurant had already closed. They both rose, swaying, from the table, with Pete insisting on having the meal added to his room bill. An awkward silence settled between them when they reached the elevator. The door opened, they squeezed together into the empty elevator and simultaneously sent a finger toward the eighth-floor button. The touch of her finger on his hand made Pete shudder.

The elevator silently descended. The door opened and they both exited. "Good night." The girl leaned forward and planted a gentle kiss on Pete's cheek.

"Good night," he answered and turned to his room a little dejected.

The sound of footsteps close in his wake reignited his hopes. He looked back and saw his companion wobbling after him.

"My room is also over there." She pointed a finger in the direction they were both headed and lost her footing. He grabbed her hand and helped her to gently lean on him as they continued on their way.

They stopped in front of room 811. "Well, this is me," said Pete, "but I think you need some help getting to your room."

"Very funny," she said and tittered drunkenly. "I'm the one in room eight eleven." She drew out a small cardboard envelope containing the magnetic card and waved it in front of his eyes.

"You're in room *nine* eleven." He smiled at her. "But perhaps you subconsciously wanted to sleep in room eight eleven tonight." He opened the door and gestured with his hand in invitation.

"Only if you promise I can shower in your room." She looked at him and batted her eyes comically.

"Promise." Pete gently closed the door after her with a triumphant smile.

CHAPTER 30

"You come all the way to New York only to disappear on me for a few days after a single date?" Ronnie grumbled theatrically at Gadi, who was standing on his doorstep with a smile on his face.

"Aren't you going to invite me in?" Gadi pushed the door open, stepped inside, and sprawled on the living room sofa. "Grab me a beer, will you? But a good one. Keep the cheap ones you buy at Costco for yourself."

Ronnie, already on his way to the kitchen, looked over his shoulder and smiled. "I can't tell you how much I've missed your overdeveloped delicacy."

"After I left you in the coffee shop," Gadi said after his first sip of beer, "I decided to follow that beauty. She never bothered to check if someone was tailing her. It looked like she was in a real hurry, but who knows? Here in New York, everyone always looks like they're five minutes late for the most important appointment of their life." He laughed at his own joke and took another sip. "She went into six fifty Fifth Avenue and took the elevator to the thirty-sixth floor."

"How do you know? Did you go up the elevator with her?"

"I didn't have to; I got lucky. From where I was standing, I was able to see the elevator keypad. I waited a few minutes and went up after her. There are three offices on the thirty-sixth floor. Two of them are occupied by investment groups; the third tenant is an accounting firm. Thinking investment firms might have something to gain by stealing Double N's intellectual property, I tried them first. The girl wasn't there, so I—"

"How can you know for sure?"

"Because she was at the accountants. As soon as I walked into their reception area, I could see her through the partially transparent glass walls of the conference room, engrossed in a business presentation with several other people."

"You're saying you followed the wrong person?"

"That's what it looked like, but I wouldn't entirely rule out her involvement just yet." Ronnie frowned, but before he could utter a question, Gadi continued with an explanation. "You know how I am. The idea that I might have been wrong drove me crazy. I was convinced the girl recognized you in the coffee shop. Since I couldn't really believe that woman was one of your ex-girlfriends, I decided to dig a little deeper into who these tenants on the thirty-sixth floor are."

"And why exactly couldn't she be one of my ex-girlfriends?" asked Ronnie with feigned offense.

"She'd eat a nerd like you twice before breakfast, but let me finish. What I ended up finding on the internet was scary. Turns out the Alavi Fund, which owns the building, and the ASSA Fund were recently in the news after being indicted on money laundering for the Iranians. It seems, at least according to the media, that the ASSA Fund is a shell company that operates for the Ayatollah regime in Iran. I think the building has been seized by the authorities and will probably be sold soon."

"But don't you think you're getting ahead of yourself and jumping to conclusions? Even if the woman you followed works on the same floor as these two problematic funds, I'm pretty sure an office building that size holds a few dozen — maybe even a few hundred — companies. I'm not saying I don't believe you, but I will say I hope you're wrong."

Gadi snapped his fingers. "Grab me another beer. It's time for a short, tension-building commercial break. And I'd love a bite to eat too. Just order something if you don't have anything in the fridge. I'm famished."

Ronnie handed Gadi a can of beer and placed another on the table. "Pizza's in the oven."

"Pizza? What can I say? Yours is a life fit for a king." Gadi snapped the tab of his beer can open, when his face suddenly turned serious. "If the Iranians are really involved—" he took a sip and gave his friend a worried look "—then this is way out of our league. I suggest we drop this whole thing. If something happened to you because of my investigations, I'd never be able to forgive myself."

"I can't just 'drop this whole thing.' I have employees who believe in me and rely on me. As you know, I've poured a lot of money into the company, and Sam recently invested money in it too. I can't just let everyone down."

"From which hole did you drag this Sam from? I don't know why, but I really can't stand him."

"Great, Gadi. Now's the perfect time to act like a jealous wife. I assure you, my relationship with him doesn't mean that I love you any less."

Gadi shrugged. "Just saying… But let's get back to the topic at hand. I understand your responsibility, but if the Iranians are truly behind this theft, then we are now in unfamiliar territory, where the only known rule is that there aren't any."

Ronnie chewed his inner cheek, narrowed his eyes, and tried to digest this new information.

"If you're too stubborn to drop this whole thing," Gadi interrupted the silence, "why don't you tell me what you were able to find out? But first, I suggest you take the pizza out of the oven before you burn down the whole building."

Ronnie jumped from the couch and rushed to the kitchen. A few moments later, he returned with a smoking tray and placed it on the table.

"All my culinary dreams have finally come true!" Gadi burst out laughing. "Burnt pizza and cheap beer. I guess that's what you get when your best friend can change humanity with a scientific patent but has a hard time tying his own shoelaces."

"Finest incinerated pizza in Manhattan," said Ronnie with a smile. Then he described his conversation with Simon down to the tiniest details. "I must admit," he summed up with a sigh, "that I haven't the faintest idea whether Simon or any of my other employees are involved in the theft. If they are, I can't understand how an Iranian investment firm would even hear about them. Few people in the genetics world can even guess at what we're doing, let alone people from outside the industry."

"Give me some time to dig a little deeper and get to know them better." Gadi stretched and gagged dramatically. "Sorry, I think my body is putting up roadblocks to stop this gourmet pizza from reaching my stomach."

"Try pushing it in with another slice." Ronnie fondly patted his friend's back. "Seriously now, about a week ago, per your request, I sent you a list of every company in the market that might have had something to gain by obtaining our stolen IP. Have you done your homework?"

"Yes." Gadi turned serious. "One of my employees is a computer whiz. I asked him to develop a web crawler for me. He designed it to fish out any information on the internet containing one or more of the names you gave me. I was hoping we could find out something by observing unusual activity changes."

"And?"

"I was overwhelmed by information that I can't really analyze. I'll send it for you to study. The only thing that grabbed my attention, although I can't understand how it is related, if it is related at all, is the following small news item." Gadi searched his cell phone for a moment and then handed it to Ronnie.

Pete Rogers, 35, a computer expert at G-Pharma, has been found dead in the shower of his room at The Standard hotel. There was no sign of forced entry into Mr. Rogers' hotel room. Witnesses claim to have seen Mr. Rogers leaving the hotel restaurant accompanied by a tall blonde woman. Police suspect the woman had arrived at the hotel with an accomplice, whom she later admitted into the victim's room and together, these two robbed and murdered Rogers.

CHAPTER 31

Robert O'Shea was panting heavily. He hated anything that even remotely reminded him of physical activity. The thought that he was late for the trial's opening session terrified him. With sweat pouring down his face, he burst into the courtroom and rushed toward the defense table. The judge's and the jurors' eyes followed him with dismay. His client gave him a chilling look and then turned away, his body bristling with pent-up rage.

"I apologize for being late, Your Honor. There was an accident on Broadway, just before Canal. The police blocked the roads, and I had to run the rest of the way. I'm sorry, Your Honor, this won't happen again." The lawyer opened his briefcase, took out a water bottle and set it on the table. Arthur Bale extended his hand, opened the bottle, and sipped with indifference. The lawyer looked at him quizzically, hesitated for a moment, then took out another water bottle and took a sip before placing it on the table.

"If you're quite finished with the drinking ceremony, I suggest we allow the prosecution to start."

"We would like to call Sergeant Joshua McNeal to the stand," a call was heard from the prosecution table.

A man of about thirty-five, wearing crisp khaki Dockers and a blue button-down shirt with an open collar took his place on the witness stand. After being sworn in, he looked expectantly at the prosecutor, who stood in front of him with her arms crossed.

"Sergeant McNeal, please tell the court about your education and current employment," she instructed pleasantly.

"I hold a bachelor's in forensic science and a master's degree in biomedical forensics from Syracuse University. I have six and a half years of experience working in the FBI's forensic laboratories. For the past year, I've been managing the DNA casework department, which provides DNA-based forensic services to all branches of the FBI and other law enforcement agencies." The calm with which the witness spoke held the jurors rapt.

Wilson seemed pleased with the jurors' reactions. "Before we get to the convincing evidence, could you try and explain to us laymen" — she looked about her apologetically — "how the genetic matching process is conducted and what makes us so certain the results of such testing are reliable?"

"I'll try to explain it as simply and clearly as I can. Please stop me if I dive too deep," McNeal answered with a smile. "Contrary to common belief, only fifteen percent of the genome chain contains the genetics needed to build us. Until recently, it was believed the remaining eighty-five percent contained nothing but genetic trash, but today…" McNeal stopped when he saw Wilson clasping her hands with exaggerated mock patience.

"In any event," he continued with a contrite smile, "research has shown that much information is hidden in that mysterious eighty-five percent. In forensic identification, we use a method called STR — short tandem repeats. Without getting into too much unnecessary detail, we look for certain markers in the hereditary material. In layman's terms, a genetic marker is a DNA sequence that repeats itself seven to ten times. We have discovered that when observing twenty-two chromosomes, several genetic markers can be traced in each of them. When we find a genetic sample, a hair including its root, for example, or sperm cells, a little spit, or flakes of skin — we are able to isolate these markers and compare them to the DNA taken from a suspect. If the samples are an exact match, we know with certainty that both belong to the suspect."

"I am sure," said the prosecutor, "that not everyone here was able to understand why such an identification process is infallible. Perhaps you could elaborate on this point a little further?"

"Of course. When discussing homogenous populations, the chance that two people having the same number of repetitions in a particular chromosome is about ten percent. In other words, one out of ten people might have the same repetition group or the same markers as the suspect's in a single chromosome. But the odds of two people having identical markers in two chromosomes are down to one in a hundred. In three chromosomes, one in one thousand, and so on. The odds of an exact match in twenty-two chromosomes are as low as one to ten raised to the power of twenty-two, or one divided by one and twenty-two zeroes, which is probably the closest number to zero you are likely to encounter. Allow me to describe it a different way. There are seven billion people living on this planet today. Let's even say ten billion. Ten billion is one followed by ten zeroes. The number I mentioned earlier is a hundred billion times larger."

"What you are saying is that the chances of an erroneous identification are zero?" the prosecutor came to the jury's aid.

"Exactly."

"And what did you find in the DNA samples we had you examine: three sets from the various crime scenes and the fourth belonging to the defendant?" She pointed a finger at Bale, who still appeared completely uninterested in the proceedings.

"I received seven samples from the crime scenes. Four from the crime scene where Patricia Roberts' body was found, two from where Aiden McGrath was found buried, and one from Sean O'Sullivan's. We have duplicated each of the samples hundreds of times and examined them all. In all seven cases, there was an exact match between the DNA taken from the field and the suspect's DNA."

"The prosecution asks to enter the criminal forensic report into evidence as exhibit one." Wilson took a massive document from her desk and handed it to the judge.

Judge Morrison examined it briefly and handed it to the bailiff. "It is my understanding the defense has no objections to the exhibit." The judge looked at O'Shea, who waved his hand in approval.

The judge's face clouded. "I would like to actually hear your answer."

"The defense has no objections," O'Shea answered, enunciating every syllable.

"I have no further questions for this witness," Wilson said and returned to her seat.

O'Shea stood and walked to the witness stand. "Sergeant McNeal, what you are saying, if I understand correctly, is that the samples you received from the crime scenes are an exact match with the sample belonging to the defendant, Mr. Bale?" he asked, scratching his chin and cocking his head.

"Correct."

"And what samples did you get, exactly?"

"All the samples I received were of human hairs, including the root."

"Sounds like someone has a serious hair loss problem. Any genetically enhanced treatment you could recommend?"

"Objection. The defense is badgering the witness," Wilson protested, rising quickly to her feet, exposing her shapely legs.

"My apologies. I withdraw the question," O'Shea replied with a small smirk, then added, ignoring the judge's angry look, "Do you happen to know if the same investigation team was handling the three cases?"

"To the best of my knowledge, there were three separate teams."

"Interesting. That means my theory about a corrupt cop on a one-man crusade to incriminate my client is not going to work here, huh?" O'Shea turned to the witness as if asking for his help.

Sergeant McNeal did not answer.

"No, no, it's not going to work. How can I save my client, then?" O'Shea scratched his head theatrically, as if considering some weighty dilemma.

"Objection. The defense continues to badger the witness." The prosecutor jumped up, immediately drawing the attention of the male jury members, who were hoping to get a second glimpse at her long legs.

"Mr. O'Shea, please get to the point or I will release the witness!" It was obvious that the judge's patience had reached its limits.

O'Shea began to pace across the courtroom, continuing to scratch his head, when suddenly, he turned around and moved hurriedly toward the witness stand. "Unless, of course, someone tampered with my client's DNA records in the police database. What do you say? Wouldn't that explain everything?" He spread his hands as if he had just found the solution to the world's most pressing problem.

"All I can say is that there is an exact match between the samples from the crime scenes and the one supplied to me for comparison."

"And if that sample for comparison had been taken from another man, then that other man is the vicious murderer and not Mr. Bale. Am I correct?"

"Determining who should be brought to trial is the work of the prosecution. But in that case, hypothetically, I would agree that there wouldn't be any proof confirming the defendant's presence at the crime scenes."

"Your Honor" — O'Shea turned to the judge, who suddenly seemed alert —"law enforcement authorities have been after my client for years without ever being able to find a shred of evidence. I wonder—"

"Objection, argumentative," the prosecutor cried, her face flushed with anger.

"Sustained. Get to the point," the judge instructed.

"Yes, Your Honor. The expert witness has spoken about statistics. This made me wonder about the likelihood of the police and the FBI suddenly finding such conclusive evidence of my client's presence at various crime scenes, as if he were the lowliest of neighborhood bullies. The only explanation that comes to mind for all this serendipity is that the DNA sample to which the seven others have been compared does not actually belong to Mr. Bale. Therefore, I ask that the court order a new sample to be taken from my client. I further ask that the sample, from the moment of its retrieval until the moment we receive the examination results, be in the hands of a law enforcement agent accompanied by a defense representative, who will make sure it is not tampered with throughout the process.

And before the prosecution objects, I agree that all testing will be conducted in the police or the FBI laboratory." O'Shea turned to the witness. "Am I safe in assuming the results of such a test must be identical to the ones you conducted?"

"Absolutely."

"How quickly could you bring a team to take the DNA samples from the defendant?" The judge turned to McNeal, who seemed utterly fascinated by O'Shea's proposal.

"About an hour."

"And how long will it take you to bring your expert?" the judge asked O'Shea.

"He is sitting outside the courtroom." O'Shea worked hard to maintain a straight face, thrilled that his gambit was about to pay off.

"The defendant will remain in a side chamber under supervision. This court will reconvene in one hour."

A deafening noise rose in the courtroom as a multitude of journalists simultaneously reported the unexpected developments to their respective editors.

CHAPTER 32

Despite the late hour, Henrik Schmidt, G-Pharma's CEO, looked as if his clothes had just been starched and ironed. His coal-black hair was neatly gelled and slicked back. He leaned against the cushion of his high back chair and gave the man who had just entered the room a curious look. It was Sean Young, the company's founder and CSO. Young dragged a chair from the conference table on the other end of the spacious room and sat stiffly in front of the man he had chosen to run his company.

"All right," Schmidt began, "there's a rumor running around that you and your development commando team have been locked up in your out-of-bounds laboratory for several weeks. Perhaps it's time for you to let me in on the matter and tell me what you people are actually involved in." Schmidt's face emanated a firmness sharply at odds with his polite tone.

Young frowned, searching for words that would precisely communicate the message he wanted to convey. "I am in possession of an algorithm able to map various types of bodily tissues with a high level of accuracy. To be more precise, based on each tissue's unique role in the body, the algorithm is able to describe it in a simple mathematical way that will later enable accurate delivery of medication or any other treatment to it. We'd been experimenting with the concept of genetic marker-based targeted delivery for about eighteen months. In that time, we were able to define the characteristics of a single particular tissue, that of the kidney, for which we are currently developing a drug. The algorithm we are now secretly developing, and I am sure you understand the reason for our discretion, produced the same result within minutes. Additionally, the algorithm has been able to correctly predict the properties of quite a few other types of tissues. We are now confident that the accuracy of the algorithm is above ninety-seven percent. In other words, we have found a way to significantly shorten production times and save the company hundreds of years of research." Young's eyes sparkled with fervor.

"How does something that is not a hundred percent accurate help us, exactly?"

"It helps in two ways. One — when it comes to therapeutic drugs delivery, even ninety-seven percent accuracy is marvelous. Worst-case scenario: a small dose of the drug would reach other organs. Today, in most cases, drugs are injected into the bloodstream and are delivered equally to every organ in the body. Two — even if we insist on reaching a hundred percent level of accuracy, our current starting point is ninety-seven percent, which is better than zero by far."

Schmidt's face lit up. The realization that they possessed a goose that would soon be laying golden eggs took hold, quickly leading to calculations regarding the value of his company shares. "When do you think you can bring me a detailed budget for the next phase of developments, so I can get further funding from our investors?"

A grimace briefly appeared on Young's face. There was nothing he and his team loved more than hefty development budgets. But Young knew that at that particular point in time, the fewer people exposed to the knowledge in his possession, the more latitude he could have.

"Right now, I am working on two ideas. The first involves improving the drug we have been developing for kidney cancer. The second, and the more important one, focuses on the question of how we can quickly develop, based on the kidney cancer cure, additional drugs for various types of cancer. My initial attempts involve seeking a cure for pancreatic cancer. A successful outcome of this experiment would serve as proof that our idea can be expanded with relative ease."

"And when will I know if your idea works?"

"There is no question that it will work, but I need a few more months to determine the best way of achieving it."

"How many months? Three? Thirty?"

Young scowled. "We're wasting time now. Let me get back to work and you'll have your answer. We share a common interest — quickly finding a treatment that will write our name in the pages of history as the company that eradicated cancer. Now, with your permission, I'd like to go back to my laboratory to resume my work. When the time comes, I hope you will see to it that I receive adequate funding." Young abruptly pushed back his chair and left the room.

Schmidt frowned with concern as he watched the door to his office slam shut. From experience, he knew that whenever Dr. Young started working on a new idea, one of the first things he did was demand more money for the development group. But now, though working on the most innovative idea the company had ever had, Young showed no interest in discussing the potential of new funds. Something about his behavior was off. Schmidt had long ago learned to listen to his instincts. Right now, every ounce of his being was screaming, "Trouble!"

CHAPTER 33

"I miss you. How are you hanging in there?" she whispered into the receiver, while her eyes nervously darted around, examining her surroundings. She heard his heavy breathing whistling in her ear, and it broke her heart. "Talk to me, please. I've proven to you more than once that I am willing to do anything for you." She was practically whimpering.

"I asked you never to call me again. It's over between us." His voice sounded distant, estranged.

"I know you love me, and you should know better than anyone that I'll love you forever. So why are you being so cruel to me? I understand that we can't meet right now, and I'm willing to wait as long as it takes before that is possible again. But don't you think I deserve some compassion and consideration? I've never done anything to you. Why are you being so distant?"

"I'm sorry that you feel that way. We've had this conversation countless times. Being apart is hard for me too, but it is the right thing to do. Please, leave me be and go on with your life. You are young, beautiful, and brilliant. There are countless men who would give anything to share their lives with you. I really cherish the time we've spent together, that you were even willing to be with me, but now it's over. Over!"

Insult was replaced with a stinging feeling of betrayal. "I have information I think you will find very interesting. If you'd like to hear more details, you'll need to call me." She hung up and hurried to take out the small compact she always carried in her bag. The face looking back from the small mirror emanated a deep sadness.

"Is everything all right, Michelle?"

"Not really. I've just received some troubling news from my mother," she improvised, angry at herself for losing her self-control. "Sorry, but I'd rather not talk about it," she added and wiped her eyes with exaggerated distress.

"You can take the day off if you need to." Ronnie looked at her with genuine concern.

"I'll be all right." She regained her composure. "As much as it pains me, I can't help my family with their problems, and I know how much you need me here. I'm staying."

"Thanks, Michelle," he said fondly, "I really appreciate your loyalty."

CHAPTER 34

Three New York State court officers blocked the corridor leading to the courtroom where the next session of Arthur Bale's trial was about to begin. The complaints of the latecomers who had to remain outside fell on deaf ears. The officers remained standing motionless with their hands clenched and placed on their hips, barring the entrance door. Their body language left no doubt regarding their determination, and no one dared challenge them.

Inside the stifling courtroom, those lucky enough to have entered on time fidgeted anxiously. Judge Morrison took his place, and the constant murmuring was replaced by the rhythmic creaking of the ancient ceiling fans.

"It is my understanding, Ms. Wilson, that you have the results of the second set of DNA testing." Judge Morrison got straight to the point.

Julie Wilson's face spoke of distress. "Yes, Your Honor, but before presenting the results, I would like to present one more piece of evidence."

"Objection." Robert O'Shea remained in his chair and appeared smug and comfortable. "There are two possibilities. Either the DNA belongs to my client, or it doesn't. We shouldn't waste the court's precious time on insignificant details."

The judge gave the prosecutor a questioning look. "On the face of it, it seems there's logic behind the defense objection."

Julie tried her hardest to maintain a matter-of-fact demeanor. "Extracted DNA or biological evidence can be analyzed aid solving criminal cases in many different ways. I would like to refer the court to State v. Jose Alvarez (Jr), a North Carolina case involving a double homicide. That case proved the reliability of DNA phenotyping, or in other words, the ability to predict a suspect's physical appearance using his DNA sample. The prosecution would like to discuss this subject before presenting the results of the second DNA testing, conducted according to the instruction of this esteemed court. We believe that the test results we received will play a major role in the outcome of this case."

O'Shea snorted contemptuously.

The judge glared at the defense attorney. "I will approve the prosecution's request," he said, "but I expect you, Ms. Wilson, to make your point quickly."

"Thank you, Your Honor. The prosecution would like to recall Sergeant Joshua McNeal to the stand." The prosecutor's voice had regained some of its earlier confidence.

After the judge admonished the witness that he was still under oath, he gestured for the prosecutor to begin.

"Will you explain to the court what DNA phenotyping is?" Wilson asked the witness.

"Gladly." McNeal leaned forward, but immediately moved back in his chair in an attempt to demonstrate ease. "Each DNA fragment contains all the necessary instructions for creating a complete human being. Therefore, years ago, a scientific theory evolved regarding the possibility of reconstructing a man's face based on his DNA sample. Today, there are several companies around the world that are able to successfully perform such reconstructions. The technique they use is called DNA phenotyping."

"Is there any legal precedent for the use of this technique in a court of law?" Wilson looked around the room, taking great pleasure in watching O'Shea's mien change from smug to alert.

"The most famous case involved the French family murders in North Carolina. The murderer had accidentally cut himself and left a drop of blood at the crime scene. Using that drop of blood, the criminal forensic laboratories were able to reconstruct his face. Based on the reconstruction, the man was positively identified as Jose Silvano Alvarez, Jr., who was known to the police. At his trial, Alvarez admitted to the murder. Currently, we are working with Snapshot and Identitas, two of the leading companies in the field of reconstructing facial features and body structure based on DNA samples."

The prosecutor went to a computer that had been prepared in advance and pressed a key. The witness' face appeared on the screen from several angles. "Could you explain what we are seeing here?"

"These are my facial reconstructions. They are based on a DNA sample I voluntarily provided."

"Well, there's certainly a striking resemblance." The prosecutor smiled at the jurors.

"I can only agree with you regarding the headshot. I have no idea what my profile looks like." Laughter spread through the courtroom but immediately died as the judge glared at the spectators.

"Have you performed a similar test using the defendant's DNA?"

"Yes. Per your request, such a test has taken place."

Four images appeared on the screen, all closely resembling Arthur Bale. "Were these images produced by using the defendant's

DNA?"

"Yes." The witness' affirmation was immediate and confident.

"No further questions." The prosecutor returned to her seat.

"Don't get into this whole facial reconstruction business," Bale whispered into his attorney's ear, clenching O'Shea's arm so tightly that the knuckles of his fingers whitened.

"Does the defense have any questions?" The judge turned to O'Shea, looking at the defendant's hand with interest.

"Yes, Your Honor." O'Shea forced his way up, shaking off his client's grip and ignoring the furious look in Bale's normally sharklike eyes. "Did you conduct the same test using the second DNA sample?"

The witness started rummaging through the papers before him, and a triumphant smile rose to O'Shea's face. "What's the matter? Can't you remember?" he asked sarcastically.

McNeal let go of the paperwork. "Oh, I remember it well. I conducted the test twice, once with the first sample and once with the second sample. Both images in the upper row are from the first test and the lower two are from the second test."

O'Shea paled. It was obvious that Wilson had used his arrogance to lure him into her trap. "Does this mean that both DNA samples you used are identical?"

"In many regards, they are indeed alike," the witness answered.

"Alike? Not identical?" O'Shea recovered.

"Similar." Traces of defeat could be heard in the witness' voice.

O'Shea was quiet for a moment while everyone in the courtroom held their breath in anticipation. They all knew what O'Shea's next question would be.

"Did the tests you conducted with the DNA sample taken from

the defendant here in this courtroom yield a different result from the one you provided in your initial testimony?" The defense attorney's voice thundered in the courtroom.

"Yes."

"I couldn't hear you. Would you please repeat your answer aloud, so the jurors can hear it?" The color had returned to O'Shea's face.

"Yes." McNeal raised his voice with marked defiance.

"Based on this second test, are you able to determine beyond doubt that the DNA found at the crime scenes belongs to the defendant?"

"No, I cannot."

"When you first came up to the witness stand, you gave us a fascinating lecture about odds and probabilities. Could you please tell me, what is the probability that it was the defendant's DNA that was found at all three crime scenes?"

"Infinitesimal." The answer was met with a loud rumble of murmuring from the spectators.

"Order in the courtroom!" The judge slammed down his gavel. It was apparent that he too had been surprised by the witness' answer.

O'Shea now looked like an orchestra conductor waiting for the impressive finishing chord to sound. "Would I be wrong in translating your words into layman's language and saying that the DNA traces found at the crime scenes, the samples that led to my client's prosecution, do not actually belong to him, and therefore there was no justification for this trial?"

"All I can say is that based on all the tests we have conducted, the new samples are significantly different from the ones that led to the charges against Mr. Bale."

"Your Honor, I ask that my client be immediately released.

Furthermore, I ask that this court award him ten million dollars' compensation in light of the deterioration in the state of his health caused by this false arrest and malicious prosecution."

"Your Honor," the prosecutor cried out, "I must admit that I do not understand the results of this last test, but the facial reconstruction yielded the same exact result in both cases — the spitting image of the defendant. Also, we have the testimony of a witness who saw Mr. Bale at all three crime scenes."

"A witness who would say anything in order to avoid life imprisonment. Wouldn't you testify that the world is flat if you were in his shoes?" O'Shea turned to the prosecutor with marked contempt.

"I ask permission to further question the witness." The prosecutor raised her voice more than she had intended to.

"By all means," answered the judge, while sending a paralyzing glance at the defense attorney who was about to rise and voice his objection. O'Shea sat back down.

"What are the odds of two different DNA samples yielding the same image of a suspect's face?"

"Same as the odds of two different people having an identical face."

O'Shea jumped from his seat. "Then find the person who has the same face as my client. Perhaps he was the one your witness saw."

"Mr. O'Shea, this is most definitely your final warning." The judge turned to Wilson again. "Does the prosecution have any further questions for the witness?"

"The prosecution is finished," answered Wilson with a shaky voice.

"The court will now take a one-hour recess, following which I will announce my decision on the defense motion to dismiss the charges." The judge rose to leave the courtroom.

"If your arrogance leads to any result other than my freedom, you are a dead man," Bale whispered with his hand crushing his attorney's arm.

CHAPTER 35

Thoughts raced through Gadi's mind. The idea that hostile countries might be involved in the theft gave him no rest.

He reached the Omni Berkshire Place hotel at Madison and East 52nd Street, nodded to the desk clerk and went up to his room on the seventh floor. He inserted the key card into the slot activating the electricity, and the room flooded with light. Facing him, he saw a stranger sprawled in the armchair at the far end of the room. A pistol with a long silencer attached to it was clutched in the stranger's hand, aimed directly at Gadi's chest. He recognized the weapon as a Beretta 92FS, one of the most precise weapons ever manufactured.

"Are you from room service, or did my mother send you to make sure I don't let the bedbugs bite?" Gadi slowly moved toward the pistol-wielding stranger.

"A comedian. Great, I just love comedians."

"You've come to the right room, then." Gadi continued to advance.

"I suggest you stop and take a seat on the sofa. You and I are going to have a serious talk."

Gadi kept moving forward. The rustling whisper of a bullet passing next to his left ear made him stop in his tracks.

"On the couch, Bozo. The next bullet will add a nasty, asymmetric hole in your head."

Gadi looked back and saw a hole in the wall above the door. The man had avoided tearing a hole in the door itself, averting any unwelcome attention from passersby in the hallway.

"All right, I'll sit down, but first, you have to promise that you'll pay for the damages." He followed the barrel of the pistol with his eyes while his mind desperately sought ways of escaping the awkward situation.

"Tell me what you know." The intruder's voice turned colder.

"About what? I'm a real Renaissance man. Unless you're a little more specific, we'll really need to call room service, this could take a while." Gadi positioned his legs in a way that would allow him maximum momentum should the opportunity of a counterattack present itself. The man in front of him had so far made only a single mistake: He was sitting with his spine against the back of the chair with his legs sprawled, demonstrating a smug confidence. Should Gadi decide to initiate an assault, the stranger's posture would not allow him a quick response. Gadi could only hope that the intruder wouldn't decide to shoot him first.

"All right, I'm sick of your wisecracking. Next smart comment, I'll shoot your right shoulder. Then I'll move on to the left and after that, I'll just need to improvise." The look in the hoodlum's eyes made it clear that he wouldn't hesitate to live up to his promise.

"I assume you are referring to the robbery a few days ago involving the theft of a computer containing valuable information."

The man just stared at him.

"We think the Iranians are involved," Gadi spat out.

His interrogator reacted with an involuntary blink. "Go on."

Gadi noticed that the tip of the silencer had begun to drop down toward the floor. He knew the new angle would translate to a few more critical seconds that could play to his advantage should the opportunity to attack present itself.

"You must be dying to know how I came to that conclusion." Gadi maintained an amicable tone.

"Talk." The man leaned his elbow on the armrest. The weight of the silencer began to have an effect on the position of the gunman's hand.

"Your surveillance work is nothing to write home about. I recognized you and your friend when you followed Dr. Ronnie Saar. At one point, we switched roles and I followed the limping hot babe. She went inside an office building at six fifty Fifth Avenue, then up to the thirty-sixth floor. I looked at the directory in the lobby and saw that two famous Iranian funds were on the floor. I put two and two together and suddenly got a very clear answer."

The man smiled. "And…?"

"That's it. That's all I've been able to find out. So, what are you going to do with me? When my body is discovered, or if I vanish from the hotel, the police will realize the robbery was connected to the information theft and start to investigate." Gadi slightly shifted his legs, allowing increased blood flow into the muscles.

"You got me real scared now." The hoodlum grinned, exposing a missing front tooth.

A knock sounded on the door. The eyes of the thug instinctively moved toward the source of the noise. That was the moment Gadi had been waiting for. He rolled toward the table separating them with one hand outstretched and the other bent, causing his body to divert from its course and reaching the right side of his opponent, close to the hand holding the pistol. The man tried to slip away to the left, but that proved to be a mistake. Instincts aren't always right. It would have been better for him to fire a blind shot than to move. Gadi sent a leg up and dealt a mighty kick that landed right on the man's chin. The sickening sound of a breaking neck followed. The battle was over before it had even begun. The man dropped lifeless to the floor.

"I'd like to see Bozo perform such a neat trick," muttered Gadi while disarming the dead man.

Another knock sounded at the door.

Gadi took a small towel from the bathroom and wrapped it around the pistol handle. He went to the door and looked through the peephole.

A wide-shouldered man was standing in the hallway, impatiently shifting his weight from one foot to the other. Gadi quickly opened the door and pressed the gun barrel into the man's right eye. "Get inside slowly. Move too fast and I'll have your eye saying hello to the back of your skull." Gadi moved back, and the man followed him inside.

"Close the door."

The door slammed shut.

"Be a good boy, take out your gun slowly and drop it to the floor." Seeing his unwanted guest hesitate, Gadi aimed the pistol straight at his head. "Now!"

The stranger slowly moved his hand toward his gun.

Gadi stepped back, keeping his eyes on the man in front of him. The involuntary eye movement a split second before the hoodlum's brain could send an instruction for his arm to quickly draw his gun was the sign Gadi had been waiting for. The man's arm continued to move, its muscles straining to fulfill the order they had just received, but the bullet that pierced his skull left them no chance of accomplishing their task. The man was on his way to hell even before his body reached the floor.

Gadi cleaned the pistol and placed it back in its owner's hand, pressing the corpse's hand to the grip with his index finger wrapped around the trigger.

Then he left the room and hung the *Do Not Disturb* sign on the door handle. After a brief search, he found the cleaning staff's storeroom. There, he tossed the towel into the laundry basket and took a new one. When he returned to his room, he neatly placed it in the bathroom. He looked about him carefully, taking in the smallest details. Finally, pleased with what he saw, he went to the telephone on the nightstand and dialed.

"Nine one one. What is your emergency?" the answer sounded clearly from the other end of the line.

CHAPTER 36

Gadi sat in the hotel corridor with his hands wrapped around his bent legs and his forehead submissively pressed against his knees.

"Let me see your hands," a shout came from the end of the hallway as one male and one female police officer came into view with their weapons drawn.

Gadi raised his hands and turned his eyes to them. They seemed frightened. The door to one of the rooms down the hall began to open.

"Police. Get back inside your room and lock the door," the female officer screamed with a high-pitched shrill that cracked and abruptly died into a nervous silence. The door immediately slammed shut and the rattling sound of a security chain followed.

"Get up and stand with your face against the wall. Hands behind your head." The female officer did her best to sound authoritative.

Gadi slowly rose and obeyed the officer's instructions, making sure his hands were in plain view at all time. Seconds later, he felt the cold touch of metal handcuffs locked on his right wrist. Both hands were pulled behind his back, and his left wrist was cuffed as well. The officers performed a quick body search. When they were convinced he wasn't armed, they instructed him to sit back down on the floor while the female officer continued to point her weapon at him.

Wouldn't it be something if I managed to escape professional killers only to die from an accidental discharge fired from the pistol of a hysterical cop, thought Gadi, careful to keep his face lowered at the floor. The second officer, once he was convinced the situation was under control, pushed the door open with his foot and stepped into the room. Seconds later, Gadi heard him reporting two dead bodies on the radio. Static followed, then the officer answered, "Ten-twelve," confirming that a suspect was in custody.

The officer emerged from the room but remained standing in the doorway with his grim face focusing on Gadi. Time passed slowly, until the sound of heavy footsteps finally sounded from the far elevators. Gadi remained motionless in his fetal position.

"Hello. My name is Detective McCarthy, and I'm taking charge of this crime scene," the detective addressed the two uniformed officers, while pushing the half-open door with his foot. "Has anyone else visited the crime scene?"

"Me," the male officer spoke up. "I wanted to make sure there was no one in the room in need of assistance. When I saw both victims lying lifeless on the floor, I immediately exited the room. No one has been inside since."

"And who is he?"

"This is the man who called the police. We've searched him, and he was unarmed. He was sitting here waiting for us. We cuffed him and waited for you." The officer's voice was bursting with pride over that he had managed to follow procedure.

"Great. But if this man was sitting here waiting for you, why was it so important to cuff him? Did he show any signs of resistance? Did he attempt to escape?" McCarthy examined the officer's face, which immediately flushed pink.

"I thought it was better to be safe than sorry." The officer tried to justify his actions.

"All right." McCarthy kneeled in front of Gadi. "Do you mind standing up? My knees are killing me."

Gadi shrugged and struggled to his feet. "Now, since I'm being so considerate, would you mind returning the favor and removing these handcuffs? You guessed right, I have no intention of running away."

The detective rose to his feet, his face twisting with pain. "Uncuff him."

The female officer obeyed the order with marked reluctance. Gadi rubbed his wrists, and only when he felt the blood returning to his hands did he direct his eyes to the detective. "Thanks."

"At this stage, I won't be arresting you, but I'd be very interested to hear exactly what happened while everything is still fresh in your mind. Nevertheless, I'd like to stress that you are not obliged to speak with me without the presence of an attorney. Of course, if you choose the official way, I will simply read you your rights and we'll continue this conversation down at the station."

"The lawyer can come when he wants. We can start now as far as I'm concerned."

"Great. Describe to me, in your own words, what happened in the room. It looks like a slaughterhouse during rush hour."

"About an hour ago, I came back to rest from touring the city and before meeting with some friends this evening. I went into the room, put the card in the electricity slot, and to my astonishment, saw a man sitting in the armchair and holding a gun with a silencer. He instructed me to slowly come into the room. I tried to understand what he wanted from me, but he demanded that I walk into the room. When I was close enough for him, he told me to stop. I heard another voice behind me. I turned my head and saw another man coming out of the bathroom and blocking the door. That man had no gun in his hand, so I returned my attention to the man I thought I should neutralize first."

"Neutralize? Most people would crap their pants if someone pointed a gun at them."

"I guess you're right, but I'm a martial arts expert, specializing in Israeli Krav Maga. I've had to make use of my skills more than once in my life." Gadi paused when he saw the curiosity in McCarthy's eyes and added, "I served in a special unit in the Israeli military police."

"All right. Go on."

"The man with the gun ordered me to sit down and kept exchanging meaningful looks with his partner, who was comfortably standing by the door, waiting for the show to begin. All I needed to do was wait for them to exchange another long glance. When this happened, I attacked. I kicked the man in the head, but to my surprise, he did not lose consciousness immediately. We struggled over the gun. I knew I didn't have much time before the other hoodlum would interfere in the struggle or draw a gun of his own. While we wrestled, two shots were discharged. I think one of them hit the man standing next to the door, but the situation prevented me from being certain. Attempting to end the struggle as quickly as possible, I broke the gunman's neck. I turned around to face the other one, but then I saw him lying dead on the floor with gun beside him. I guess I was lucky."

"Two shots, you say?"

"That's what I remember, but I might be wrong."

"Are you willing to go into the room with me and show me where you and the gunman sat?"

Without a word, Gadi walked into the room and pointed at the place where the first criminal had sat and the place where his accomplice had stood. McCarthy rubbed his chin and began to walk around the room. Finally, he seemed satisfied and returned to Gadi. "There is a bullet hole in the wall above the door, all right."

Gadi said nothing.

"If I check your hands, do you think I'll find gunpowder traces on them?" he asked with an indifferent tone that did not fool Gadi.

"I assume there is a chance you'll find some, or maybe none at all. After all, we were grappling with the gun when the shots were discharged. I'd be happy to let your forensic team examine my hands."

"I must say, you're being awfully cooperative. You said you were expecting your lawyer. Could you explain why you called a lawyer if you had no intention of using his services?"

Gadi knew that the next few moments would lead the investigation in one of two directions. Either he would be charged with murder, or the police would start helping Double N locate the criminals who had stolen their information.

"I didn't call a lawyer. My friend, who is the CEO of a genetics firm here in New York, called him. I didn't think it was necessary, but he disagreed." Gadi gave him an apologetic look.

"What is your friend's name?"

"I don't see what that has to do with your investigation."

"Indulge me."

"Ronnie Saar."

"The Double N CEO?"

Gadi looked at him with astonishment. "How did you know?"

"I investigated the case involving the assault of his employee. Do you think the two cases are related?" The detective tensed.

"I don't know. I thought this was a case of mistaken identity, and these guys had simply entered the wrong room. But now that you mention it, perhaps the two cases are related. Ronnie and I are childhood friends. One of his employees was attacked, now I was attacked too. This seems like more than a coincidence."

"Stop talking," a voice sounded from the door behind them. They both turned their heads to look. A burly man dressed in a luxury suit and holding a fine leather briefcase stood in the doorway. "My name is Mark Goldman, and I represent Mr. Abutbul. You will be talking with me from this moment on."

Gadi and the detective exchanged glances. For a moment, they both seemed amused, as if sharing a good joke.

"I'd like to hear your opinion about how these two cases are related." The detective ignored the lawyer.

"Would you like to discuss it over coffee down in the lobby? I'd love to hear your thoughts about it too." Gadi gave the open-mouthed Goldman a reassuring look.

"Guard the room until the forensics team gets here. We'll be down in the hotel bar if they need us," McCarthy ordered the two officers and turned to the elevator with Gadi and his attorney close behind.

CHAPTER 37

Liah and Juanita emerged from behind the frosted glass doors and looked around the airport arrivals area, becoming concerned when they did not see Ronnie waiting for them. They stopped in their tracks, ignoring the complaints of passengers marching behind them.

"Hi, Liah," a familiar voice surprised both women.

"Sam! What are you doing here? Where's Ronnie?"

"Ronnie asked me to pick you two up and take you to my place in Keyport. Come with me, I'll explain everything on the way."

Liah did not move a muscle. "Explain first!" she demanded.

"If we continue to stand here, the departing passengers will probably end up trampling you to death with their carts. Don't think the fact that you're in the last months of your pregnancy would stop them. Come, please. I'll explain everything on the way. I promise."

With pronounced hesitation, the two began to follow him, refusing his offer to take their baggage carts for them. Sam stepped toward the exit door and flagged the driver of a limousine parked a few yards away. The vehicle crawled toward them, and Sam opened the back door for them. "The driver will take care of your suitcases."

The two women slipped into the fancy limousine, and Sam took his place on the opposite seat. He reached back a hand and closed the partition separating the passenger area from the driver. Liah and Juanita followed his actions with a bit of worry in their eyes.

Sam took a cell phone from his pocket, hit a speed-dial button, and switched it to speaker mode. "Ronnie," he began, "I have Liah and Juanita in the car with me, and we're on our way to Keyport. Liah is about to murder me any minute now, so I thought you might want to talk to her."

"Hi, Liah, honey. How was your flight?"

"Cut the 'Liah, honey' bullshit. What's going on here?" Liah snapped even while her face paled with concern.

"Gadi and I are fine, but—"

"What do you mean 'Gadi is fine'?" Juanita interrupted. "Why wouldn't he be fine?"

"If either of you would let me talk for two seconds, I'll tell you everything. Last night, when Gadi returned to his hotel room, he was surprised by two burglars who were waiting for him there. They were both armed and probably wanted to interrogate him about what he and I know regarding the stolen know-how. The only thing they didn't take into account was that Gadi is a martial arts expert. Now they're both lying dead in the city morgue. Gadi was unharmed. Last time I spoke to him, he and the attorney I'd hired for him were talking to the police. I don't know who sent the intruders, and I've no idea what their intentions were, so I decided you two would probably be better off staying with Sam until this whole thing clears up. Gadi and I will come visit as soon as he is released."

"And what if they won't release him?" asked Juanita, her trembling voice threatening an impending storm of tears.

"According to his lawyer, this is a classic case of self-defense.

He is convinced the police are aware of that and won't even charge him. I have to go now."

Sam disconnected the call, took two other cell phones from a hidden compartment in the limousine and handed them to Liah and Juanita. "These are prepaid and untraceable devices. Please give me your phones and don't call anyone unless it's an emergency. Gadi's, Ronnie's, and my numbers are stored in the cell phones' memory. I promise that we will call you several times a day from unlisted phones."

Liah and Juanita exchanged glances before finally handing their personal cell phones to Sam. He switched off the devices and tossed them into his briefcase.

The limousine got very quiet.

"You're aware you are treating us as if we were children." Liah's face darkened.

"You're pregnant, and Ronnie isn't willing to take any chances. He tried to get hold of you in Israel to dissuade you from coming, but I guess you had already boarded the flight. Ronnie isn't treating you like a baby, but to be completely honest, you are acting like one."

"You—" Liah began to reply with fury.

"Let's not argue about it, please. Ronnie and Gadi need time to think, and knowing that you two are safe means that they have one less thing to worry about."

Juanita gently placed a soothing hand on Liah's lips. "Her pregnancy has nothing to do with this," she said while widening her brown, tilted eyes. "We're here because we're concerned about our husbands and feel safer next to them. Besides—" she paused and bit her upper lip "—I'm pregnant too, and Gadi doesn't know about it yet."

"What?" Liah's anger instantly vanished, and she covered Juanita with kisses.

"When did you find out?"

"Two days ago. Gadi will kill me when he hears about it."

"You're a nutcase." Liah chuckled, momentarily forgetting all their troubles. "Gadi is going to lock you up in a room wrapped in cotton wool. Then, after the baby is born, he will simply put it in there too. He'll go crazy once he hears the news. It's settled, then. I have no problem staying with you, Sam, until you let us know everything has turned out all right."

Sam leaned his head on the headrest and shut his eyes. Liah and Juanita chatted about pregnancy and birth.

Two pregnant women. What a mess, he thought, a split second before he fell asleep.

CHAPTER 38

Following several unexpected delays that further frayed O'Shea's already ragged nerves, the bailiff finally announced the session's resumption.

"Counsel, do either of you have anything significant to add before I announce my decision?" Judge Morrison addressed the tense attorneys.

"Your Honor" — the prosecutor rose to her feet — "I think it appropriate that the prosecution be allowed to call the eyewitness to the stand before this court announces its ruling."

Bale's death grip kept his attorney in his seat. He leaned and whispered into O'Shea's ear, "I made the mistake of not murdering that little cockroach. I won't repeat the same mistake with you. I don't want to hear his testimony." Bale eased the pressure on O'Shea's arm.

"Mr. O'Shea?" the judge impatiently addressed the defense attorney.

"Your Honor, we mustn't waste this court's precious time. I am willing to stipulate that the witness would testify seeing my client shooting the victims. He might even say he saw my client insulting their grandmothers, so what? Mr. Bale does not know the witness, has never seen him, and was definitely not in his company at the time these three murders took place. This is the testimony of a convicted felon with a criminal record the size of the Bible. He'd be willing to say anything to regain his freedom. Until the next time he's in prison, that is. It's the word of a convicted felon against that of my client, who has never been convicted of a crime in his life. Your Honor, after learning the authorities tried to frame my client by tampering with his DNA samples, whom do you believe?" O'Shea smoothed his suit and sat back down, refraining from looking at Bale.

"In that case, I ask that the record reflect the witness' statement that he saw the defendant firing at the victims in all three cases. It should also mention that the defense confirmed the existence of this testimony." The prosecutor desperately attempted regain some dignity.

O'Shea waved both hands contemptuously, affirming her request.

Judge Morrison cleared his throat and all murmuring ceased. "I agree with the defense that even if the eyewitness' testimony had been given in court, it would have eventually been the witness' word against the defendant's. As for the DNA tests, I have no recourse but to rely on the only test currently accepted by the courts of law of this state and agree with the defense that the DNA sample taken from the defendant in the presence of a court official is not enough to place him at the scene of the crime." The judge looked almost humble by this point. "Furthermore, in light of the reasonable suspicion, brought to our attention during testimony, that the DNA samples presented over the course of this trial had been tampered with and changed, the same samples that had initially brought about the charges against Mr. Bale concerning three murder cases, I hereby dismiss the case and order the defendant's immediate release. Members of the jury, I thank you for your service. You are excused."

Bale rose, headed toward the exit door, and disappeared before O'Shea had the chance to react.

CHAPTER 39

Bob's Bar on the ground floor of the Omni Hotel overlooked East 52nd Street. Two businessmen sat on tall bar stools and spoke in whispers. They held martini glasses and occasionally picked a peanut or a green olive from one of the small bowls in front of them. At the end of the counter stood a bored barman, monotonously polishing long-stem wineglasses before hanging them on a rack behind the bar. Gadi and his lawyer, Mark Goldman, sat at the far end of the room on a blue leather bench with a tall back. McCarthy sat opposite them in a wood captain's chair, looking miserable. His oversized hand dangled off the chair arms and he spread his long legs, trying to get comfortable.

"Shall we switch places?" the lawyer suggested.

"Gladly." McCarthy rose and went around the round table separating them. He waited until the two men had taken their seats and then sprawled on the bench. "Sorry, my knees are killing me," he apologized offhandedly.

"Can I ask you a question that's been bothering me?" Gadi said as soon as they were all settled.

"Mmm…" the detective hummed.

"I'll take that as a yes. When you went into my room, you took a brief glance at the two victims and didn't seem too broken up. Who were they?"

McCarthy pulled himself up. "Moment by moment, I'm becoming convinced you are a pro who could have fixed the crime scene to suit your cover story."

"You're right. I could have if I needed to. In this case, I didn't. I'm sure you realize if I wanted to murder two strangers, I wouldn't have dragged them to my hotel room and killed them there. Who were those two guys?" Gadi repeated his question.

"Don't you think you're getting a little mixed up? As far as I remember, I'm the detective and you're the suspect."

"Look, Detective, I couldn't have been more cooperative. I hid nothing from you. I believe you've already realized I'm a professional who can help you. Now's the time for you to decide — am I a murder suspect or a civilian whose skills saved him from certain death?" Gadi gave him a cold look.

The geniality instantly vanished from McCarthy's face, and his words became clipped. "You are in no position to dictate terms. If you prefer, we can continue this conversation in the interrogation room at the police station. Now, please tell me why you think the two cases are related."

Gadi said nothing and looked at his lawyer. Goldman rose from his seat and motioned for Gadi to follow him. "Detective McCarthy, is Mr. Abutbul under arrest? If he isn't, please excuse us, but we need to leave. My client needs to find another hotel room."

Gadi stared into the detective's eyes and slowly got to his feet.

"Those two dead men were hired killers who were on the most wanted lists across the country, although we've never been able to convict them of anything. Now sit back down."

Gadi squinted and shook his head, confused. "And they don't belong to any criminal organization?"

McCarthy shrugged. "No, they were hired guns who worked for anybody who paid them. And they got paid a lot. Rumor has it they charged over half a million dollars for every solved problem. I guess someone really wanted you to leave this world."

"How come you were never able to catch them?"

"We've never located any of their victims' bodies."

Gadi slowly sat down. Goldman's glowering left no room for doubt; he considered Gadi's continued presence at the table to be a grave mistake.

"Perhaps you could solve a riddle that's been nagging me," the detective continued. "What's the connection between you and Dr. Simon Fine?"

"I don't know…" Gadi stalled, thinking of the best way to get the detective's help without telling him about his various exploits in New York. "Double N is dealing with developments in the field of genetics. Groundbreaking developments. Any company or country in the world would give anything to get its hands on this information. Perhaps a competitor hired the services of these hoodlums to rob Simon. Perhaps it was a foreign country."

"A foreign country?"

"Based on what Ronnie explained to me, every new breakthrough in the field of genetics has the potential to cure terminal illnesses, improve the quality of life, and many other fantastic things. At the same time, it could also bring about the development of deadly viruses, terrible biological weapons, and other disasters we don't even want to imagine. There are quite a few countries that would be delighted to put their hands on such doomsday weapon technologies. Perhaps these two worked in the service of such a country."

A thoughtful silence settled around the table. Even the lawyer seemed shocked by what he had just heard.

"But you're not a scientist. Why would they attack you?"

"They couldn't have known that. Perhaps they followed Ronnie and saw us together. They put two and two together and got five. The question is what will their employers do next? Will they continue with their attempts to kill me?"

McCarthy looked pensive. The new angle Gadi had presented bothered him. "This is way beyond my pay grade. I'll have to share your theory with the FBI. We may want to talk to you again." He turned his head and looked at the attorney. "Currently, Mr. Abutbul is not a murder suspect, but I'd appreciate it if he would leave his passport with me. I want to make sure he doesn't leave the country without my permission."

"You're asking him to stay in New York, where it's highly likely another attempt will be made on his life?"

The detective turned his head to Gadi and raised his eyebrows in question.

"I'll stay," said Gadi with a smile. "Shall we order some coffee?"

CHAPTER 40

Sean Young was sitting in the shadows, gently holding his wife's sinewy hand as she lay motionless in bed. Only her eyes seemed alive, pleading with him.

"Let me go." Her lips moved as well, in a whisper.

Sean felt his eyes moisten. "I'm in the possession of information that can help cure your cancer. I just need more time. I'm working around the clock to find you a cure. Give me more time. Please, my love."

"What do you mean by 'in the possession of'?" she muttered. The sudden fire in her eyes reminded him of the gifted scientist he had married.

"I've been given access to an ingenious algorithm that helped me develop the next level of targeted drug delivery systems. The price I paid for the information was steep, but I don't care. The only thing that matters is finding a cure for your cancer. The entire team at G-Pharma has been working with me day and night for several weeks. I'm positive that we'll make it. The injections I've been giving you were supposed to take care of the metastases in your kidney. I'm close to being able to treat many other affected areas. I just need you to be strong." He was begging now.

She smiled sadly. "I deserve better than being a lab rat for your latest developments." Her voice had steadied. "We both know that even if tumors in my body vanish, I have already suffered severe damage to all my bodily systems and would be condemned to a life of misery."

Something cold crawled into Sean's eyes. "I have to try and save you. Without you, I'm better off dead. I have no intention of giving up on you." He cleaned the skin of her hand with an alcohol pad, took a syringe from his bag, and injected its contents straight into the vein protruding from the back of her emaciated hand. Then he drew a blood sample from another vein. "I'll never give up on you." He ignored the wince of pain that tightened her face and turned to leave the room.

"I know you too well, Sean," she whispered. "You are motivated by ego, not by love."

Sean pretended not to hear. In his pocket he carried another syringe, and the burden of that hidden needle felt as heavy as his wife's suffering.

CHAPTER 41

The atmosphere in the G-Pharma conference room was optimistic. The board of directors had just heard an overview from Sean Young. The breakthrough he had presented fired up their imaginations. It became clear to them that their investment in G-Pharma was close to putting their names in the Midas Touch Hall of Fame.

"Although we do not need further funding at this stage, I'm sure you all realize an additional fifty million dollars could help us set up parallel development teams. This would allow us to simultaneously go to market with several drugs and become the world's leading company in the field of cancer treatment." Young was determined to take advantage of the board members' excitement.

Someone at the far end of the room raised his hand. Young looked at the man questioningly. He had never seen him before.

"Allow me to introduce myself, Dr. Young, as you weren't present at the beginning of this discussion. My name is Wyatt Robinson, and I am a managing partner in the RK Biomed Investments fund. I am filling in for my partner, Roland King, who was unable to attend this meeting due to personal reasons."

"Welcome to the board of directors," Young greeted him with cold disdain. He had always had a deep dislike of arrogant moneyed men.

"It is not every day that one comes upon such an ingenious

breakthrough." The investor ignored the hostile tone of Young's greeting. "Perhaps you could share with us the inspiration that led you to the discovery and development of this idea. After all, we all sit on the boards of several companies. If there's something we could learn to the advantage of our various companies — on the principle level, of course, without getting into specific details — we'd love to hear it."

"This is a problem my staff and I have been grappling with for close to a year. There was never a single Eureka-like moment of discovery. It was merely the result of arduous Herculean work and an attentiveness to the minutest of details."

"Very interesting. I've never encountered such inspired genius that resulted only from hard work." Wyatt feigned naïveté.

Young bit his lip, holding himself back from simply leaving the table and the conference room. "When brilliant minds work hard together I guess they end up getting results."

"And when exactly did you know you were in the possession of the solution you've just introduced to us?"

"About three months ago," Young answered flatly.

Wyatt pursed his lips in mock surprise. "And it's only now you see fit to update us?"

All pretense of civility was gone from Young's face. "I preferred to test the effectiveness and accuracy of the solution several times, not wanting to give rise to false hopes among the esteemed members of this group. Now, if you'll excuse me, I should be heading back to my laboratory to continue the work for which you have invested in this company." Without waiting for a response, Young rose and left the room.

"I'm new here," said Robinson, "but what just happened seems highly unusual. I hope the company has adhered to all fiduciary duties in the development of this impressive new technology." The satisfaction he derived from putting on that little show made Robinson miss the CEO's searing look.

"We have always adhered to a strict transparency policy as well as any other fiduciary duties, for good or ill. But I have to admit I fail to understand the nature of your questions. If you have reason to believe the information Dr. Young has shared with us is not accurate, we all would love to hear from you." Schmidt's tone took Wyatt aback.

"Absolutely not." Wyatt recovered and asked innocently, "Do you?"

Something here stinks to high heaven, and this is not the first time I've had this feeling, thought Schmidt. He studied the room for a short while and then, in a matter-of-fact tone, addressed the board members. "I suggest we terminate the discussion at this stage. I believe we all have much to think about following this meeting. I'd be delighted to answer any questions that might arise. Thank you all for coming."

The attendees rose and began to leave until finally, only Wyatt and the CEO were left in the room.

"You didn't answer my question." Wyatt's eyes bored into Schmidt's.

"I believe I have already given you my answer. If I had any hesitation about the genesis of this development, I would never have presented it to the board of directors in the first place."

"Exactly what I was hoping to hear," Wyatt said and left the room without another word.

CHAPTER 42

The atmosphere in the Double N design review meeting was tense. The enthusiasm over the technology, so characteristic of the team, was tainted by the concern that, as they spoke, it might be in the hands of a rival company. At one point, Derek Taylor asked permission to address the group. Everyone fell silent, curious to learn what he had to say. It wasn't customary for an investor to participate in technical discussions.

"I know you are all concerned about the company's financial future. I am attending this meeting in order to reassure you that my fund and I will continue to support Double N as long as you all, its most precious assets, continue to believe in it. I am not doing this because of Ronnie's beautiful eyes, but because I believe we have some groundbreaking technology here. Should a competitor go to market with technologies related to the stolen material, I know more than a few lawyers who'd be happy to crucify it.

"I've been listening to you for the past two hours. Right now, I'm even more convinced that my decision to continue to support this company was one of the best I've made in my long and illustrious career." Taylor smoothed his gray hair with theatrical exaggeration and was rewarded with smiles from all around the conference table. "Recently," he continued, "I have been approached by several funds I've been cooperating with for many years. They were all scrambling for an investment opportunity in your company. At this stage, I have rejected their offers, claiming the company does not need any further funding. I believe the moment we file our patent applications, the company's value will hit the two hundred million mark. And in general, playing hard to get raises the price people are willing to pay in order to get inside your corporate pants." Taylor smiled, and the attendees joined him in some much-needed laughter. Ronnie was nodding at him appreciatively, when he noticed Gadi waving at him from beyond the conference room's glass wall. "Excuse me, but I need to leave for a few minutes. Please continue the discussion without me." He went out and warmly placed his arm around his friend's shoulder, aware that everyone in the conference room was staring at them. "What's up?"

"I need to talk to you." Gadi grabbed his arm and pulled him to the end of the hallway, out of sight of the conference room. "I've been thinking about everything that has happened since the theft. I'm still bothered by the theory that the Iranians are behind this, and the two stiffs were working for them. But this theory gives rise to quite a few other questions. For example, why would a country with an army of security forces need to utilize the services of an accounting firm to attack a civilian and steal his computer? Why are you still being followed? And why was there an attempt on my life? If I were them, I'd simply vanish with the technology without a trace. And to be honest, life tends to be simple, unlike the complicated plot I've fabricated."

"So, what do you have in mind?"

"I've decided it's time to shake the tree a little. Before I do that, I want to make sure you understand the risks and are willing to take them. Because if I'm right, then this shaking might bring about two possible results — could be the fruit will drop straight into our laps, but maybe the whole tree will collapse on our heads."

"I agree with you that it's time to take the initiative. I only have one request — share all your plans with me in advance and let me help where I can. Don't take all the risks yourself. The investor sitting in the conference room has been telling the staff some pretty stories. But I suspect that unless we gain some sort of breakthrough in our understanding of who else is in the possession of our technology, and what they plan to do with it, I don't think those promises will actually hold water."

"Be ready to hear from me soon, then." Gadi gave Ronnie a warm hug and left.

CHAPTER 43

Kate was sitting at the last booth in the row. For some strange reason, Clinton Station Diner, off I-78 was a favorite of the person she was meeting. She had never understood why a man in his position was so enamored of a diner built in a railroad car. A half-empty plate sat on the table in front of her. She reached out and picked at what was left of her hamburger and ketchup-drowned fries. Nothing like basic food, she thought, wiping her mouth with a white paper napkin from the dispenser at the end of the table. This wasn't the first time she'd arrived early for one of their meetings. She liked to eat quietly, before his scornful eyes watching her ruined her appetite. Despite believing Bale to be an emotionless psychopath, for some reason she couldn't quite understand, she felt much more afraid of the other man. She knew nothing about his role in the organization, and it was no secret that even Bale respected him.

She knew him as "Mr. Brown." That was how he had introduced himself to her. He had never mentioned his first name. She suspected this wasn't his real name, but when she had tried to ask Bale about it, she'd found herself looking straight into the barrel of a gun aimed right between her eyes.

"Meddle into Mr. Brown's affairs again, and you're as good as dead," was the clear message she had received. Obviously, she had not asked any further questions.

When Mr. Brown had brought up the idea of trying to outwit the authorities by tampering with DNA samples of suspects who had been convicted following forensic tests, Bale had immediately taken up his suggestion and allotted him unlimited resources. Kate was fascinated by the way those two were able to communicate. A mere few words and minimal gestures she was unable to decipher, were enough for Bale and Mr. Brown to exchange complicated ideas. She knew he thought of her as a lowly creature and hated him for it with every fiber of her being. One day, so she hoped, she would get to strangle Mr. Brown with her bare hands. The mere thought of it sent warm ripples of pleasure up and down her body.

The door opened, and he stepped in. As usual, he completely ignored her and slowly walked down the aisle, inspecting the model trains on display with childish delight. He held a stuffed backpack in one hand. Kate followed him with concern. Whenever he was around, she felt as if a black widow spider were crawling up her back. Suddenly, he turned and smiled as if noticing her for the first time. As always, he approached her with a clumsy step and gallantly kissed her hand before sitting in the spacious green banquette.

"The usual," he told the waitress.

Kate knew he wouldn't touch his food and would enjoy letting her pay for it. Her filthy rich employer, Bale, would refuse to cover the expense as well.

"These are the last bottles our mutual friend needs to use." He pushed the bag toward her with his foot. "And as a token of my appreciation for your cooperation, you'll also find a personal gift from me inside the bag." The smile that accompanied his words failed to reach his eyes.

Kate did not respond.

"A life of violence has taken its toll on you." The spine-tingling sound he emitted sounded more like a bark than actual laughter. "The blows you've received to your hip over the years have resulted in trochanteric bursitis, in other words, an inflammation of the bursa at the lateral point of the hip. You thought you were tough enough to take it and didn't take care of it in time, so the inflammation has turned chronic. Furthermore, from the way you cringe in pain from time to time, I understand your greater trochanter has also been injured. You may not understand my words, but you can definitely sense the worsening pain. As I see in you a potential partner who can help me in solving further problems in the future, I've prepared a concoction that will eliminate the inflammation and help in your recovery. I personally wrapped your vial and added a pink touch to it." He broke into another fit of hollow laughter. "Drink half today and the other half tomorrow."

"Thanks. Pink is my favorite color." She gave him a wry smile. "Now to the business at hand." She turned serious. "Arthur Bale wants to offer services, similar to those he received from you, to other people. He thinks we could have them in our debt for life and at the same time, make millions off your invention."

The man gazed at her impassively. "The fewer people who know about the idea, the safer we are. A few million dollars isn't worth it to me. If it was discovered how Bale avoided conviction, all the money in the world wouldn't help him. He'd spend the rest of his life behind bars. After all, we both know he's a sick murderer."

Kate ignored his last remark. "Mr. Bale thinks we could charge ten million or more to keep people out of the electric chair. He's willing to pay you a million dollars for every client we are able to save. Since he guessed you would react poorly, he told me you have his word that your name will never be mentioned, unless you want it to be."

The man looked at his plate, poking his fork into the cooling piece of meat resting on it. "Tell Bale I agree. But I have one condition," he said without taking his eyes off the food. "I want five million for each customer." He rose without saying another word and left the diner.

Kate opened the bag he'd left on the sticky floor. It held three soft drink bottles and a small vial wrapped with a pink ribbon. A shiver passed through her, and she was afraid to open it. Finally, the darts of stinging agony through her hip helped her overcome her fear. She tore off the ribbon and opened the vial. The transparent liquid was odorless. She hesitated for a moment, closed her eyes, and swallowed half of it down.

CHAPTER 44

The sound of the door as it rubbed against the thick carpet sent an involuntary tremor down Kate's spine. She sat up straight in her chair and eyed Bale as he entered the small conference room. Other than some fatigue wrinkles at the corner of his eyes, there was no trace whatsoever of his former poor medical condition.

Bale examined the room until his dead eyes settled on Kate. "As you can see, I'm a free man again. You've had quite a lot to do with that."

Kate maintained a tense vigilance.

"Now's the time to tie up all the loose ends. That's why I called you here. But before we agree on our next steps, I'd love to hear your assessment of the current situation. Namely, what are the potential risks you see in the immediate future?"

Kate remained silent, organizing her thoughts, and carefully selecting her words before beginning her report.

"Speak!"

She flinched, and pain shot through her bad hip. "The plan worked exactly as you had foreseen before your arrest. The scientist we found was true to his word. Mr. Brown thinks it would be useful for you to keep using the substance for a little while longer, but you can soon stop using it altogether." She smiled at him uneasily.

Bale smiled back and nodded his understanding. "I've missed

you, Kate." He reached out and stroked her cheek. Kate pressed his hand with hers for a brief moment and then removed it from her cheek. "We'll have all the time in the world later."

Bale's gaze immediately turned cold and pragmatic. "Go on."

"The only problem we have remaining is the Double N CEO. I don't think he will let go. Word on the market is that all his investors, save one, have requested their investment money back. That motivated him to go on a quest to find whoever stole his intellectual property. He hired an Israeli private investigator, who has already started rocking the boat. I must say, I was impressed by him. One morning, when I walked into the Ramini Espresso Bar, our eyes met for a brief moment. That was enough for him to realize I had identified one of the people with whom he shared the table. He decided to tail me. He even dared to come inside our offices under some pretext."

"If you knew he was following you, why didn't you shake him off?"

"If I had done that, he'd have known he was onto something for sure. Instead, I joined a meeting with some customers in the transparent conference room. I've successfully used this trick several times before. When he walked into the office, he simply saw me attending a meeting. I believe this made him ask himself whether he had followed the right person. But that is the least of our problems."

"What now?"

"Two men I am not familiar with tried to assault that private eye in his hotel room. I don't know what happened in there, but they were both found dead. Do you know anything about that?"

"No. And I forbid you to go anywhere near that guy or Dr. Saar. Any more to-do around that goddamn genetics company could bring me right back into the spotlight. Right now, we need to keep a low profile. Let those clowns do whatever investigating they want, just let me know if you think they're onto us." Bale waited for Kate to nod her understanding before he continued.

"Now let's move to another subject. As I'm sure you already know, the million dollars I promised to transfer to your account was wired yesterday. What I don't understand is why the money vanished from your account moments after it was processed." His eyes took on the look of a deadly snake's, seconds before biting its prey.

"We agreed that the money would be mine and mine alone. I knew you wouldn't be able to help yourself from accessing my bank account. I earned that money fair and square. Don't try to find it."

A thick silence ensued, finally broken by Arthur Bale's sinister laughter. "No other person in the world dares to talk to me like that. Perhaps that is why I love you so much. You spice up my life."

"So I'll see you later tonight, Arthur?" She gave him a seductive look.

"I'm afraid not. You have some more important work to do." He surprised her with the unexpected answer. "Throughout the trial, O'Shea's behavior verged on recklessness. His arrogance nearly brought about my downfall. He defied my strict instructions and questioned a witness. He is no longer reliable and, unfortunately for him, he knows far too much. I ask that you permanently solve this problem as soon as you can. Tonight, if possible. Make it look like an assassination carried out by a frustrated client. No one would suspect me. After all, the poor bastard got me off. And besides, it wouldn't hurt for the police to have one more thing to occupy their donut-starved minds."

Kate slowly approached him, reached out with both hands, and pressed his face against her chest. Bale groaned, and his hands crushed her buttocks. Suddenly, he let go and slapped her injured hip. Kate pulled his head back and pushed him away wildly. Bale lost his footing but soon managed to regain control. He raised his hand menacingly but stopped when faced with her teasing smile. Slowly, he let his hand drop. Without another word, he exited the room, leaving Kate on her own.

You are not fooling me, Arthur Bale, she thought. *I know you sent those two killers after the private investigator. Which makes me wonder, when will it be my turn? And whom will you assign the task of killing me?*

CHAPTER 45

It was 6:30 am when the phone woke Ronnie up. "Hello, Wyatt," he answered without a hint of warmth. "How can I help you?"

"I must admit your quick response time impressed me. I saw that our investment in Double N has already been returned, and the money was wired into our bank account yesterday. I always knew you were efficient."

Ronnie glanced again at his watch. It was a little early for Wyatt to be calling.

"Ronnie?"

"Yes, I hear you," he tried to conceal his curiosity.

"The more I think about everything that happened at that board meeting, the worse I feel about the outcome."

Ronnie maintained his silence. He had no intention of making it easier on the man who had, until recently, chaired his board of directors, and then, at the most inopportune of moments, decided to jump ship, driving out most of the other investors.

"As you know, our fund portfolio comprises nineteen investments in genetics-related areas. I still believe Double N is at high risk because of the information theft, but if you can assure me you will register your patents in the near future, my partners and I believe we can convince one of our companies to purchase yours."

"Our company is not for sale." Ronnie pulled himself up into a sitting position.

"I think you are being too hasty. I suggest you take some time to think about my offer. I assume it would only be decent of you to consult with Derek Taylor, the sole investor who stuck with your company," said Wyatt with a gradually cooling tone.

"I don't think you're in any position to be preaching to me about decency." A vein in Ronnie's forehead began to throb. "Besides, we already have another investor."

"It would be a pity to turn a business offer into a struggle driven by a personal vendetta."

"Why should I have a personal vendetta? After all, this is strictly business." Ronnie paused for a moment. *Let him stew*, he thought. "Do you have an estimate of how high an offer you could get me?"

"I believe both you and Derek could triple your initial investment at the very least." Hope resounded in Robinson's voice again.

"Hmm… Well, I believe I could easily do that on our next fund-raising round. But, I accept your recommendation and will consult with Derek. I promise to get back to you soon. Have a nice day."

"Hold on, Ronnie." Wyatt seemed suddenly solicitous. "If it's only a matter of price, I can try to improve the offer."

"I have to say that I find this entire conversation more than a little weird. Just a few days ago, you claimed our company had lost any real value, now you are negotiating its price?"

An embarrassing silence ensued.

"All right, I'll wait for your answer," Wyatt finally replied.

"Thank you, Mr. Robinson. I promise to get back to you as soon as I can. After all, you just praised my quick and efficient administrative skills."

"All right, Ronnie, I'll wait, but the deadline for my generous offer is tonight." Robinson sounded hostile again.

"I'll do my best to give you my answer before that. Have a great day, Mr. Robinson." Ronnie disconnected the call. The temptation to tell the investor who had conspired against him to go fuck himself was almost beyond what he could handle. But Ronnie knew that decency called for him to consult with Derek first.

It was still early in the morning, and Ronnie decided to take advantage of the unexpected wake up and go out for a run. The cool air that greeted him outside filled him with energy, and he quickly headed off, trying to clear his head of the disturbing thoughts that had not ceased to bother him over the past few weeks. Gradually, he progressed to a steady running pace, enjoying the feeling of fresh perspiration covering his body. Since Simon had been attacked and Double N had fallen into financial difficulties, he had found no time to run. His leg muscles began to signal that they needed more oxygen than his heart had been providing, but Ronnie just kept going, determined to finish the three-mile course he used to regularly run. The echo of his heartbeat throbbing in his ears served as a metronome regulating his pace. He continued to ignore the burning sensation in his muscles and accelerated, slaloming his way between pedestrians. His apartment building appeared around the final turn, and he covered the remaining distance with renewed energy.

Following a cold shower and a light breakfast, the time had come for a conversation with the only investor who had stood by him.

"Yes, Ronnie," Derek answered after a single ring.

Without a moment's delay, Ronnie described in detail the call he had received from Wyatt Robinson. "I wanted to hear your opinion about it," he summed up.

"I think it's more important to understand what you think about this offer." Derek put the ball back in Ronnie's court.

"I think the offer is insulting. If it were up to me, I'd reject it. But I see you as a full partner, whose opinions I deeply respect."

"Hmm… First of all, thank you. I really appreciate your consideration. Actually, I'm rather disturbed by the conversation you described. This doesn't sound like Wyatt at all. He is an aggressive man who rarely admits to a mistake. Based on what you just told me, he must be under enormous pressure. And I can't even imagine what or who could have gotten to him like that. Unless he's heard that your company was about to be acquired for a hefty sum. Something like that would make his decision to forgo his assets seem stupid beyond belief."

"I suppose if that were to happen, I'd know about it too," Ronnie interrupted him.

"Not necessarily. If you knew about it, it would be too late for him to try and buy the company at a bargain price. His excuse of feeling uncomfortable with that stunt he pulled sounds disingenuous, to say the least. What I can't understand is why he didn't try to initiate such a move while still on the board. What has he discovered that he didn't know a few days ago?"

"I don't know, but I think we are in agreement that we should reject his offer," Ronnie finished Derek's line of thought.

"Yes, it definitely seems that way. I only hope we won't live to regret it."

"Some wise old man once said, 'Don't waste time regretting the things you didn't do, you'll have plenty of time to regret the things you did.'" Ronnie laughed, relieved to have Derek on his side again.

"A wise man indeed. But let's not forget, even wise men sometimes make mistakes. Good day, Ronnie, and good luck."

The next call was a brief one.

"Hello, Mr. Robinson, I promised you a timely reply. After giving it some further thought, I've decided to reject your offer. Thank you, but at the moment, this just doesn't seem like the right choice for the company and its investors."

"I was afraid your emotions would get the better of you," Wyatt snorted in contempt.

"I assure you this decision was dictated strictly by business considerations."

"In that case, I hope you will soon discover what a grave mistake you've made by having me as your enemy rather than your partner."

Ronnie placed the phone back on the table, lost in thought. Derek was right. It appeared something much larger loomed behind Wyatt's offer.

CHAPTER 46

Ronnie leaned on the reception counter at AE and Partners Accounting, while Gadi wandered nonchalantly toward the aisle leading to the firm's offices.

"Hi, my name is Ronnie Saar. I have an appointment with one of the senior partners."

"Do you know which one?" asked the receptionist, nervously following Gadi's movements.

"No, I don't. I set up the appointment only this morning and was told I could meet with whoever was available."

"Just a moment, please. Let me see if I can help you." The receptionist gave Gadi another look and the latter turned around and returned to the reception area. "Have a seat, please," she pointed at two dark-blue leather sofas.

Gadi and Ronnie sank into the soft cushions. Gadi leaned back, closed his eyes, and clasped his hands behind his neck. "I could easily fall asleep in no time."

"Mr. Saar?" A raspy voice sounded to their right. Ronnie turned his head, quickly rose from the couch, and shook the extended hand of the impressive woman standing in front of him.

"Kate Frost. Pleased to make your acquaintance. I'm the company's customer relationship manager. Is the gentleman over there comfortably napping with you?" She smiled mischievously.

Ronnie gave Gadi's leg a light kick, and his friend rubbed his eyes and uprooted himself from the soft comforts of the sofa. "Sorry, I haven't had a chance to get any sleep lately. My name is Gadi Abutbul, and I'm Dr. Saar's personal advisor."

"Come with me, please." Much to Gadi's surprise, Kate wasn't limping. She walked with an assured, steady gait toward the glassed-in conference room. Upon entering, she gestured toward the chairs at the near side of the table. Gadi and Ronnie sat with their backs to the transparent wall separating the conference room from the reception area. They were blinded by the sunlight coming through the bare window. Kate sat at the other end of the conference table, and the sun's brilliance outlined her with a golden halo. "And what is your particular expertise as an advisor, if I might ask?" She turned to Gadi with exaggerated interest.

"Security and many other areas."

"Such as?"

Gadi steepled his fingers and said nothing.

"I understand. Correct me if I'm wrong, but you look familiar, Mr. Abutbul. Didn't I see you walking into our office a few days ago?"

"How flattering to have been noticed by such a beautiful woman, despite the fact that I was only here for a few brief moments."

Kate raised her right eyebrow.

"I came in here by mistake. I was looking for the fund down the hallway. As Dr. Saar will soon tell you, several investors have recently left our company, and I thought that philanthropic funds, such as the ones situated on this floor, might be interested in replacing them. I had an appointment scheduled with one of them. Unfortunately, it turned out our company's activities do not allow them to consider us as a philanthropic investment, legally speaking."

"So, what brings you here today?" She turned to Ronnie.

"As Mr. Abutbul mentioned, several investors left our company not too long ago, due to a concern that some important intellectual property had been stolen from us. The company's accountant had been recommended to us by Wyatt Robinson, our former chairperson. Despite the assurances we've received regarding the complete separation between the accounting firm's clients and the investment firm that originally recommended it, we have decided not to take any chances and fired our accountant. At first, we thought about signing a contract with one of the big three accounting firms but ended up coming to the conclusion we would be better off having a senior partner of a boutique financial firm handling our annual reports and tax issues rather than a junior employee of a famous name. We are in the process of interviewing about five firms of your caliber."

"And why would your investors suspect that important information had been stolen from your company? Normally, people know whether something was stolen or not."

"They are harboring suspicions, because I have suspicions of my own. The said information was stored on a laptop computer. This computer was taken from one of my employees in a violent robbery. The police suspect it was just a coincidence. I don't believe in coincidences, so I am operating under the assumption that the worse has happened. This was what I reported to my board of directors."

"It's refreshing to meet a businessman with your kind of scruples. But let's get back to the matter at hand. Unfortunately, our firm provides services to investment firms, not startup companies specializing in the field of genetics. Therefore, if you allow me some integrity of my own — we are most definitely not what you are looking for. On the other hand, if you are in need of further fundraising, I believe we could introduce you to some of our prestigious clients. Needless to say, we have excellent connections with many investors . Now if you'll excuse me." Kate stood up, indicating that the meeting was over.

"How did you know we are a genetics firm?" Ronnie looked at her curiously from his chair.

"One of our analysts ran a background check before you arrived," she muttered as she left the room, leaving behind her two guests, who had remained seated.

Ronnie and Gadi hurried after her.

"I'm glad to see your limp is almost gone." Gadi flashed his impish smile.

"Thank you," Kate answered without stopping.

"But I'm still bothered by one last little thing. If you ran a background check and knew we weren't suitable clients for your firm, why didn't you call to cancel the appointment?"

Kate stopped, brought her mouth close to Gadi's ear, and whispered, "The thing that killed the cat, Mr. Abutbul. Curiosity."

CHAPTER 47

Ronnie and Gadi walked down Madison Avenue, their eyes alert to their surroundings.

"How would you sum up the meeting?"

"I still need to process it. That chick made the hair on the back of my neck stand up. Not exactly the body part I'd expect to be affected by her. She reeked of danger."

"I saw the lady whispered in your ear before leaving."

"Jealous? She said she was curious to know what we're after. But what I find disturbing is that she didn't even bother to see us out. It was a kind of statement. She saw me checking out the place and wanted me to understand I wouldn't find anything."

"Well, what's wrong with that?" asked Ronnie as they turned west on 39th Street.

"Nothing of what took place in the meeting indicated a problem. Still, all my senses kept sounding alarms. That is why I decided to mention her limp. She didn't bat an eye. But unless she knew I'd seen her before or had followed her from the coffee shop to the office, she had no reason to think I knew she'd limped in the past. She must have noticed me, despite all my evasion attempts, and that was why she fell right into my trap."

"Or maybe she didn't. In any case, now she knows for a fact that you followed her."

"Excellent. Shaking the tree, remember? That was our original plan."

The two turned south on 8th Avenue. "I don't see anyone following us." Ronnie returned to the subject that bothered him most.

"Me neither. But it's not like we're hiding. You have an apartment in Chelsea and I have a room at the Omni. I suppose if anyone really wants to find us he'd have a pretty clear idea where we lay our heads at night."

Moments later, they entered the Edison ParkFast on Ninth Avenue, not far from West 36th Street, where Ronnie had left a rented car the night before. Ronnie's PayFast card allowed them a quick exit from the parking lot. The drive into the Lincoln Tunnel went smoothly and they began to get excited at the upcoming reunion with their wives.

Gadi called his office in Israel and began spitting out instructions. "I need you to find me the names of the companies serviced by AE and Partners Accounting Firm. Also, I need you to check if any technology-oriented companies are numbered among their clients and whether they have any known connections with foreign countries, especially Iran."

Gadi listened in silence to the barrage of questions that followed. "Do whatever you need to do to get the information. It's time for you to prove you're worth every dime of the fat salary I'm paying you." He blinked thoughtfully. "Sure, you can break into their computers, as well as the Pentagon's, the IRS, and wherever else you want, so long as you don't get caught."

The laughter from the other end of the line could clearly be heard in the car.

"What a character," Gadi sighed. "Why does every one of my

employees have to be a certified nutcase?"

"Because there's a high probability that you choose people who are just like you."

"My shrink told me the exact same thing."

"Have you been seeing a psychologist?" Ronnie's eyes widened as the vehicle slid onto 1st Street. The Atlantic Ocean could be seen between the houses.

"No," answered Gadi with utter seriousness, enjoying seeing his good friend shaking his head in despair.

"Well, we're here. This is number one thirty-five," said Ronnie while looking for a parking space. The rusty skeleton of a washing machine rested on the road. "Just like back home in Israel, people do whatever they need to in order to keep their parking spot safe," he sighed with frustration.

The phone in Ronnie's shirt pocket vibrated. It was a message from Liah. *You can move that piece of junk on the road. Sam put it there this morning before flying to the West Coast to make sure you could park out front.*

"I can't believe it," Ronnie muttered. "God help me, Sam has turned into your twin, Gadi."

For the first time since he had arrived in America, Gadi burst out into genuine laughter.

CHAPTER 48

The balcony in Sam's apartment offered a spectacular view of the Atlantic Ocean's sandy beaches. It wasn't for nothing that Keyport residents had nicknamed their town "Pearl of the Bayshore." The doorbell rang, and Juanita broke into a run toward the door with Liah wobbling behind her. Juanita opened the door wide and jumped on Gadi, locking her strong legs around his hips and her hands around his neck.

"Sorry, babe," said Liah with a smile, "but your son and heir prevents me from doing any jumping." She kissed Ronnie's lips passionately.

He gently hugged her and whispered in her ear, "I'm sorry I didn't come to the airport. Good thing we have Sam."

"That's right. And he is such a considerate man, too. He went off on a business trip, and since his wife is in Europe, the apartment is all ours." Liah kissed him again while leading him inside.

"Are you two coming inside?" Ronnie burst into laughter at the sight of Gadi trying to free himself from his wife's embrace. Juanita simply wouldn't stop covering his face with wet kisses. They walked inside, with Juanita still wrapped around Gadi.

Ronnie closed the door behind them. "How's the apartment? Are you two having fun?"

"This place is fabulous, and the BMW has a much smoother

ride than my Mazda. Juanita and I have decided we're staying. Tell Sam we've changed the locks and he should find himself another place to stay."

Gadi looked around. "It's nice enough, but not what I was expecting. I thought Sam's place would be more—"

"Don't be silly," Juanita said. "Sam doesn't live here. This is a rental he owns and since it was vacant, he decided to stay here while his condo in Short Hills was being renovated."

"By the way," Liah joined in, "you and Ronnie could come and visit, just be sure to let us know in advance. We have our eyes on some of the gorgeous men hanging around on the beaches here. We wouldn't want you to catch one or two of them here in the apartment."

Liah and Juanita exchanged a mysterious smile.

"Have you two been practicing that look?" asked Gadi.

"Yes, but for a good reason."

"Mmm. Can I have something to drink?"

"We've searched the apartment down to the last drawer. Come, Ronnie, I'll show you where your friend is hiding his best liquor." Liah forced herself into a standing position.

Juanita bounced on her feet lightly, and Gadi noticed her discomfort.

"What's going on here?"

"I've no idea, but I'm starting to get scared," answered Ronnie.

"It's nothing, really," answered Liah with an innocent look and led Ronnie to the adjacent room.

A gigantic aquarium was built into one of the walls, the water bubbling and the rich vegetation swaying from side to side. Ronnie approached it and took a closer look. "What's this? All the fish are dead?"

"Yes, when we got here we were shocked to see all the fish floating motionless in the water. Sam laughed it off and said he had tried a new diet for them, but it obviously didn't work. He promised he'd clean the tank before going away, but as you can see, he must have forgotten."

"I can take care of it." Ronnie appeared unduly disturbed.

"Forget it. Tell me, what's new with the investigation?" she asked.

"Let's go back to the living room, and Gadi and I will give you an update." Ronnie looked around the room. "Why did you drag me in here, anyway?"

"I wanted to give Juanita some privacy while she tells Gadi he is going to be a father."

Ronnie tensed involuntarily. "What? And you've kept it a secret from me until now? We should have an ambulance standing by. Gadi is going to go through the roof. Just to remind you, his reactions aren't always predictable even when he's in a normal state of mind."

"Whaaat?" A scream was heard from the other room.

"Here we go." Liah smiled. "Shall we take a peek?"

"By all means."

The two hurried to the door. Gadi was sitting on the sofa with his head in his hands. Juanita was sitting in front of him, examining him with a worried look.

"What's going on?" Ronnie quickly entered the room with Liah trudging behind him.

"I think Gadi is about to have a heart attack." There was a hint of concern in Juanita's voice.

The three looked at Gadi as his eyes filled up and a wide smile lit up his face. "I'm going to be a father," he whispered. "I'm going to be a father," he repeated the sentence, thrilled at the sweet taste and sound of the final word.

Juanita slowly approached Gadi and gently hugged him, breaking into a relieved fit of tears. "I was afraid you wouldn't want this child," she sniffled, half-laughing, half-crying.

"There's nothing in the world I want more." Gadi kissed her wet cheek, while brushing at his eyes with embarrassment.

Ronnie and Liah sat on either side of them and wrapped the couple with a loving hug.

Gadi extricated himself from the group hug and stood in front of Ronnie. "Thank you, Ronnie. If you hadn't stuck with me when we were growing up, I would probably be sitting in jail, instead of spending my days with wonderful people like you. But enough with this mushy stuff. Let's all agree that Ronnie will be the godfather, and let's raise a virtual toast to celebrate the occasion. After all, Liah and Juanita—" he stopped for a brief second and then joyfully screamed "—are pregnant!"

"We'll have at least seven more months to discuss this pregnancy, why don't we move on to discussing more urgent matters," blurted Liah. "It's time you tell us everything that's happened to you since Gadi was attacked. And don't you dare leave out a single detail."

CHAPTER 49

The sound of the doorbell made Robert O'Shea jump with a start. He looked at his watch. The small hand kissed the number eleven. "Get inside the bedroom." He grabbed the arm of the surprised call girl and led her toward the door. "And don't say a word." O'Shea pushed her roughly onto the bed.

He stood in front of floor-to-ceiling mirror and straightened his clothes. The doorbell rang again, and this time, the irksome person kept pressing the button over and over. How had he gotten past security? O'Shea scowled, annoyed. He made a mental note to reprimand the building superintendent in the morning and looked through the peephole. He drew in a sharp breath, which made him cough uncontrollably. This was the second time his behavior probably ruined his chances for a date with the captivating woman he had met at the opera. He opened the door, wearing a wide smile. "To what do I owe the pleasure?" The smile was instantly wiped off his face when he saw the pistol in her hand.

"Mr. Bale has personally asked me to give you his regards and to reward you for the wonderful job you've done in protecting him." The woman pressed the pistol against O'Shea's chest.

The attorney stepped back, all of his attention focused on the silencer screwed to her handgun. "If you've come here to thank me, what's with the…" He stopped talking when she slammed the door shut with her heel, never taking her eyes off him.

"Darling, is she gone yet?" The call girl emerged from the bedroom, and her mouth widened with shock.

"No, sweetie." Kate wrinkled her nose in imitation of the girl's coquettish manner. "But I think you've already figured out you're the third wheel here. What do you say? How about going home to catch some sleep?" She moved aside and cleared the way for the hooker to get to the door.

The call girl quickly collected her purse. "But he hasn't paid me yet," she said stubbornly.

"Pay her," Kate instructed the lawyer.

He fumbled in his wallet, fished out ten hundred-dollar bills, and held them out with a trembling hand.

"Thanks. I'll be going now and forget everything I just saw." The girl walked past Kate, gratitude on her face. She did not suffer. She was dead before her brain could register the muffled, crackling sound of the bullet that hit her head going 500 miles per second.

"W-why did you k-kill her? Why did you w-want me to p-pay her?"

"I thought she at least deserved to die happy," Kate answered dismissively. "Now let's move on to why I'm here. Well, that's pretty obvious, isn't it? To kill you. But I suppose you'd like to know why you will be saying your final farewells in a few seconds." She looked at him with open contempt.

Instead of answering, O'Shea tried to lunge at her and snatch her pistol. Years of physical inactivity left him with zero chance of success. Kate quickly drew the gun back then brought it down hard on his left cheekbone. He yelped, and his hand reached for his bleeding face.

"Bale warned me you don't know how to conduct a civilized conversation." Another soft blast and O'Shea collapsed to his knees. After a few seconds, while the physics of death determined which way his body would fall, he finally dropped flat on his face. Kate walked around the fresh body, stood behind it, and fired an additional bullet in the back of the neck. Then she repeated the procedure with the call girl. She surveyed the room, and when she felt satisfied, she went to the lawyer's bedroom.

Following Bale's instructions, she took a painting from Picasso's blue period, forged in China, off the wall and carefully placed it on the floor. Behind it, she found the recording device of the security cameras covering the apartment. Kate ejected the memory card, hung the painting back on the wall, and returned to the living room. She carefully examined the killing field one more time, nodded in satisfaction, and left the apartment.

The elevator arrived, and Kate stepped inside, ignoring the security camera mounted in the corner; she had removed the hard drive from the building's security system on her way up to the apartment. The elevator door silently slid open and she exited in the lobby.

"Goodbye." She waved to the security guard sitting behind the desk. The red stain spreading on his jacket explained why he didn't wave back.

CHAPTER 50

"Just so we're all on the same page, I'll start from the beginning."
Ronnie stretched his arms above his head until his back crackled
and popped.

Gadi was sitting opposite him, his hands not leaving Juanita's
belly for a moment, and Liah was walking around the room, trying
to get the blood circulating back into her numb right leg.

"About a month and a half ago, Simon Fine, a genetic researcher
working for Double N's advanced development team, was mugged
walking home from work. The attack was vicious, and it was only
by some miracle he survived. His backpack, which contained,
among other things, his laptop, was stolen. A passerby heard
Simon screaming and called the police. The police were already
on alert because of a serial killer, so they arrived immediately at
the crime scene, but unfortunately, the assailant was long gone. In
light of the findings at the crime scene, the police are convinced
it was not the serial killer who was behind the attack, but rather a
homeless person who saw in Simon an opportunity to make some
easy money.

"Despite the darkness in the alley, Simon managed to get a
look at his attacker. According to him, it was a tall person, skinny,
wearing a black coat, his face covered by a ski mask and his hands
clad with black gloves. Fibers of black wool that were found on

the assault weapon — a plank from a nearby crate —support at least that part of Simon's story. Contrary to what the police think, one of the doctors at the hospital who treated Simon's injuries is convinced this was the work of a professional who knew precisely where to strike and how to restrain his blows to make sure Simon wasn't killed."

"Or to make him suffer as long as possible," Gadi commented.

"Where did you get that idea from?" Ronnie looked disturbed by Gadi's suggestion.

"If the purpose of the attack was robbery, one precise blow would have been enough. I think this was the work of a sadist, and only the cops' timely arrival prevented him from finishing the job."

Liah gave Ronnie a questioning look. "So now we're trying to trace a sadistic monster?"

The brief moment of hesitation before he answered did not go unnoticed by his friends. "This is just a theory. One of many. Anyway, I'd like to continue the update."

Liah rolled her eyes and reminded him that this was not a business meeting.

"Two days later, Simon's backpack was found in the garbage behind a nearby restaurant. The restaurant was closed due to a death in the family, so the garbage container didn't have much in it and was not emptied by the garbage men the day after the assault. The detective in charge of the investigation believes that the assailant was startled by the approaching policemen and quickly got rid of the backpack.

"But when we checked the computer, which was encrypted and passcode protected like all the computers in the company, it turned out that someone had managed to read, and possibly copy, files from it the day following the attack. What's disturbing is that Simon had a sticker on his laptop with a favorite quote on it that could have inadvertently provided a hint to his password. When I asked him why he would do such a thing, he defended himself by saying he could not believe someone could guess the password based on the quote. I have to admit that I tend to agree with him. Whoever cracked the password must have been a highly sophisticated hacker." Ronnie sipped the remaining wine in his glass.

"Why did Simon take such important information home with him in the first place?" asked Liah, still roaming around the room.

"We were supposed to have a design review meeting. Simon was in charge of presenting our latest breakthrough. He claimed that the noise in the office and the questions of the other employees kept him from concentrating. I didn't see any problem with him working from home and approved his request."

"So perhaps he had nothing to do with the theft. Maybe Simon wasn't concerned about taking the computer with the information out of the office because he was convinced no information could be extracted from it, even if he did somehow lose it. Perhaps he believes this entire affair was just a cruel coincidence, bad luck." Liah paused in her pacing to see what he had to say.

"Perhaps. And if we follow that line of thought, then every employee in the company is a suspect. You don't need to be an experienced detective to conclude they all knew that once I finished my conversation with Simon, he would leave with all the sensitive information in his possession. On the other hand, if one of them wanted to sell the information, he or she could have easily copied it from the server and passed it on to the highest bidder. This whole so-called sophisticated approach of 'let's assault Simon and steal the IP so nobody will suspect me' doesn't seem likely to me although I must admit, some of these scientist characters have a strange mindset.

"In any event, after sharing my suspicions with the company's investors, all of them, except for one — Derek Taylor — decided the company's intellectual property must have been stolen and demanded to liquidate the company and distribute the cash among the investors. I decided to buy them out and keep the company alive. In order to do so, Derek invested an additional million dollars, and Sam came to our rescue with half a million. In light of their vote of confidence in me and the company, I thought I too should invest an additional million dollars." Ronnie looked at Liah, who nodded with approval.

He smiled at her lovingly and continued. "Assuming the intellectual property was indeed stolen, another, no less important question is — what was it stolen for? If it was a competitor, which seems most likely, it would force us to check any new product brought to market to determine whether our technology was used in the process of its development. At least that scenario gives us the small comfort of knowing the thieves used our know-how for a positive purpose. I don't believe, however that this is the case. Right now, my suspicions focus on the option of a government body being behind the attack, American or Iranian. The only question is—"

"Iranian?" Juanita and Liah cried out in a single voice.

"It's a long story. I'll get to that in a moment," Ronnie continued, downplaying his concern. "Like I told Gadi, and I'm sure you realize yourself, any technology can be used either for noble or devious purposes. It all depends on who has it. Our intellectual property could help in the development of groundbreaking medicines, but it could also be used to create weapons the likes of which humanity would not know how to handle."

Ronnie paused as he heard the quickening breath of the women in the room. He rose and hugged Liah.

"Go on," Liah mumbled and sat next to Juanita, who held her hand.

"Gadi traced some people who were following me. He tailed one of them, a woman, to a building on Fifth Avenue, where he discovered she works in an accounting firm on the same floor as two Iranian funds. These Iranian funds have been convicted by the American authorities with money laundering for the Ayatollah regime. Under the pretense of looking for a new accountant, Gadi and I paid a visit to her place of business and got the feeling they had a lot more information about us than they should have."

"What does that mean, exactly?" Liah interrupted.

"We don't know," Gadi said. "The woman who met with us didn't even try to hide the fact they'd agreed to a meeting despite knowing we weren't suitable clients. No serious organization would have wasted its time on a pointless appointment."

"Perhaps your assumption that she knew ahead of time is wrong, and she decided to look into Double N after the meeting was already set up," Liah suggested.

"During the brief conversation, she demonstrated impressive knowledge about our company's activities. I felt like nothing we said was new to her. I'm sure she gets many similar requests every month and turns them down flat. For some reason she invited us to her office, even after, according to her, one of her analysts had provided her with detailed background on our company."

"But if she wanted to keep an eye on you, wouldn't it have made more sense for her to offer her company's services at an attractive rate? That way, she could be in regular contact with you," Liah challenged his explanation.

"I thought so too, at first. But then I realized that would also have given us a reason to visit their offices now and then. If she or her company are somehow involved with the information theft, that's not something she would have wanted."

"I still think we're missing something." Furrows traced themselves in Liah's brow.

"You're being Gadi now?" Juanita joked, trying to ease the tension.

"I must have always been Gadi. That explains why Ronnie fell in love with me in the first place. Now let's suppose that this woman, does she have a name, by the way?"

"Kate."

"Let's suppose Kate is somehow involved. She probably doesn't have any knowledge of genetics, so she can't make any personal use of the information. She must be selling it. Assuming that's what's going on, why would she keep following you? I'd keep a low profile if I were her. If she had, you never would have been able to track her down. Did she strike you as stupid?"

"No!" the two men answered simultaneously.

Liah and Juanita exchanged meaningful glances then nodded to each other.

"What?" asked Gadi.

"She's hot," answered Juanita. "She's obviously hot."

"Smoking hot and smart too. But how is that relevant to the subject at hand?" Gadi smiled, all innocence.

"Oh, it's not. It's just interesting," Juanita teased him with a smile that emphasized her high cheekbones.

"Go on, Liah," Ronnie seemed curious.

"I don't understand how she could have known that what you are doing is worth a lot of money. You would need in-depth knowledge of genetic research for that. And why would a senior employee of an accounting firm be involved in such criminal activities in the first place?"

"You've touched all the points that have been bothering us as well," Ronnie answered slowly, "and that is why my conclusion is that she is working for someone else. Someone with a lot of money."

"The Iranians?"

"That is one possibility, but not the only one. It's obviously someone who is familiar with the world of genetics. Maybe someone who heard us presenting at some scientific convention or someone we know. The problem is that someone that knowledgeable would realize we will soon register a patent. The moment he introduces a product on the market using our technology, he exposes himself to a patent infringement prosecution and becomes an immediate suspect in the attack on Simon. Something here doesn't quite fit. That's why I think the information was stolen for more sinister purposes, purposes that do not require any patent registration or other form of legal authorization.

"Was it the Iranians? I don't know. Perhaps it's just a coincidence that the accounting firm is on the same floor as those two Iranian funds. But even if it isn't, the people currently in possession of our technology are far from ordinary."

A disturbing quiet settled on the room. Liah returned to pacing back and forth, lost in thought. Ronnie followed her with his eyes, while Gadi wrapped his arms around Juanita, who in turn rested her head on his chest.

Liah stopped and faced them. "They are still following you because you are closer to solving the mystery than you think. There must be some piece of information right in front of you, one you just haven't noticed yet. Until we know what it is, we won't be able to figure this out."

CHAPTER 51

The Three Sins nightclub was closed for a private event. The name of the club faithfully described the behavior that regularly took place there, although many guests did not limit themselves to the number of sins advertised in the venue's name. Topless waitresses roamed among dozens of men, who devoured them with their eyes. Quite often, a hand reached out to caress exposed buttocks or tuck a folded bill into a thong. That a female companion was hanging from the arm of each guest did not prevent them from treating the other women in the room like playthings.

The outbursts of raucous laughter indicated that most of the guests were already royally drunk. Bale and Kate stood in the corner of the room apart from the hubbub and examined the guests with barely disguised contempt. The party was in honor of Bale's release from prison, and he used the occasion to stuff his guests full of the finest cuisine and alcohol the state of New York had to offer and satisfy all their earthly needs, no matter how extreme those might be. He regarded it as a demonstration of his power. A clear statement to all those who had doubted his ability to wriggle out of three murder charges: *I am here, and I am above the law!* Invitations to the party had been handed out with one single condition — no weapons of any sort were allowed. Four burly men stood at the club entrance to ensure the rule was followed. The abundance and variety of weapons left by the guests for safekeeping in a storeroom would not have shamed a commando unit armory.

"Look at them," said Bale, "dressed in the finest designer clothes, driving luxury cars, living in houses worth more than the whole neighborhoods they came from, but nothing can change their essential nature. They have always been criminals and will forever behave like ones. You can't erase their nature with money."

Kate Frost gave Bale a mischievous look, amused that he excluded himself from that observation. More than once she had seen him berate people simply because they had misinterpreted his wishes or had not shown him the respect he thought he deserved. Bale ignored her raised eyebrows. He continued to examine the crowd, one hand always on her hip, making sure she remained glued to him. Each time his dead eyes settled on one of the guests, the latter quickly nodded, then humbly lowered his eyes to the floor.

The hierarchy in the club was very clear-cut. Most of the guests refrained from approaching and conversing with him. Occasionally, one stepped over to him, without his companion, muttered some clichéd congratulations and quickly retreated. They were all business associates who came to him for financial advice, money laundering, or for solving problems, a service that often included making the "problem" vanish forever from the face of the earth. They all paid him good money for his services. And they were also scared to death of him. They knew that if it served his needs, he wouldn't hesitate to expose secrets that would bury them in prison for the rest of their lives, not to mention his proven ability to arrange a more permanent burial for his opponents.

As if responding to some cue, the music died and the commotion in the club instantly died with it. Bale let go of Kate's hip and climbed on a small stage. Two dancers, dressed like Eve before the apple, hurried off.

"I wanted to thank you all for making the effort to come here tonight," he opened, knowing perfectly well, as did his guests, they'd really had no choice. "I don't intend to bore you with speeches. After all, you came here to have fun. But I do have one important thing to say. I want to thank all those friends who remained faithful to me in my time of trouble. And to those who were quick to turn their backs on me — I'll see you in the afterlife. Cheers!" He raised his glass.

"Cheers," echoed the crowd with a roar.

As Bale slowly stepped off the stage, his attention was drawn to the sound of a disturbance coming from the entrance. A SWAT team poured into the club and took up positions around the walls. The door opened again, and a tall police officer stepped inside, accompanied by Julie Wilson, the prosecutor from his recent trial, her head held high with self-importance. They stopped in front of him.

"I don't recall inviting you, and I certainly didn't invite your friends," Bale's voice oozed with loathing.

"Mr. Bale, you are under arrest for the murder of Robert O'Shea. Anything you…" the voice of the detective reading him his rights dimmed in Bale's ears. Ignoring the world around him, he craned his neck, a vein threatening to pop right out of his forehead, and gave Kate a chilling look. His eyes did not leave her for a single moment as he was led to the entrance.

The door opened, and Bale and his escorts were flooded with bright camera flashes and blinding lights directed at them by the numerous television teams and journalists waiting outside.

Undoubtedly, someone had leaked the news of his arrest to the media.

The triumphant smile on Julie Wilson's lips left no room for doubt regarding the identity of that someone.

Bale ignored the furor around him and continued to look back, his eyes still set on Kate, who had stopped next to the club door. He knew she had both planned and executed the murder, which should not have pointed to him in any logical way. Had she purposely planted evidence to frame him? And if she hadn't, what could have caused the police to be in such a hurry to arrest him?

He knew with certainty that he would quickly be released from custody. After all, the deputy mayor, with whom he had spent a long evening at Del Frisco's Steakhouse, discussing the rehabilitation of Bronx neighborhoods, as well as the generously tipped waiters, would provide him with a perfect alibi for the time of the murder.

CHAPTER 52

The man who stormed into the police station hurried right to the duty officer's desk, ignoring those sitting quietly and waiting their turn. With a British accent imperious enough to forestall any protests from the crowd, he announced, "My name is Martin Gibbons and I am Mr. Bale's attorney. I demand to see my client this instant."

The duty officer looked at him indifferently, impressed neither by Gibbons' expensive suit, nor by hearing Mr. Bale's name. "Have a seat. I'll let the officer in charge know you're here."

"Now look here, sir, I don't have time for your dillydallying. I…" The attorney stopped the flow of his speech as the desk sergeant rose from his chair with clenched fists.

The policeman leaned on his hairy knuckles and said slowly, with perfect enunciation, "I'm not going to say this more than once, and I definitely don't intend to put up with the bullshit you're stupid enough to think is some sort of power demonstration. Now sit your ass down until the officer in charge of the investigation is available, or go find a judge who will authorize you to see your client without following NYPD procedures to the letter."

The attorney sat down reluctantly among those waiting their turn to file a complaint or visit a family member in custody. His body language screamed distress. He could still recall how Bale had shown up unannounced in his office the day before.

"I suppose you know who I am," Bale had said, as he sat in the visitor's chair and propped both of his expensive shoes on top of the surprised attorney's desk.

Gibbons nodded, deliberating whether he should ask his visitor to take his feet off the polished mahogany.

"For quite some time I've been following your short, yet highly illustrious career. About an hour ago, I was told that my attorney of the past several years was murdered, and I am interested in retaining your services."

"Gladly." Gibbons recovered his senses. "Could you please tell me what this is about?"

Bale's rolling laughter surprised him. "This isn't *about* anything. I want to retain your services on a permanent basis. I'll need you to be available twenty-four hours a day, seven days a week for any demand or whim I might have. I am willing to pay generously, of course."

"I'm sorry, Mr. Bale, but I have obligations to other clients—"

"No, you don't. You no longer have any other clients. I've spoken to all of them, and they were happy to release you from any agreement you think you have with them," Bale interrupted him. "If you are considering rejecting my offer, just know that your chances of preserving your clientele, or getting new clients anytime soon are slim to none." Bale removed his dark glasses and gave the astonished attorney a withering look. "I, on the other hand, am willing to pay you a retainer of one million dollars a year, in addition to doubling your current hourly rate. Do we have a deal?"

"Could I possibly take some time to consider your generous offer and give you my decision in a few hours?"

"You've got two hours. Goodbye." Bale rose and walked out without waiting for an answer.

The calls Gibbons made to his clients quickly made him understand the full extent of his new client's influence. The contract between them was drafted and signed that evening.

"Mr. Gibbons?" he heard his name called from the desk, startling him out of his reverie. He hurried over to the police officer who'd called for him and together, they silently marched toward the interrogation room where Bale sat handcuffed, watched over by a uniformed officer.

"I'd like to talk to my lawyer in private," Bale barked the moment they entered. The officers shrugged and left the interrogation room.

"I expect you to respond more quickly next time." Bale's voice was venomous.

"But I got here as—"

"Shut up and listen. They arrested me on suspicion of murdering Robert O'Shea." Bale paused when he saw Gibbons' eyes widen with shock. "Don't worry, I didn't kill him, and I have the deputy mayor as my alibi. It's important that I find out why they believe I killed him. That's why I haven't told them that I have a solid alibi. If they have some sort of proof, then obviously someone is trying to frame me. As much as I have a low opinion of the police, I don't believe they are the ones fabricating the evidence this time. Certainly not after having been so recently caught in the act."

Martin Gibbons shifted in his seat. He seemed relieved to learn his client wasn't in the habit of murdering his attorneys. He went to the door and signaled to the officer standing outside that they were done.

The officer, accompanied by a man in civilian clothes, entered the room. "You are free to go," the civilian surprised Bale and his attorney.

"I think my client deserves some sort of explanation, not to mention an apology for this harassment by the police on the very same day he was celebrating his release from yet another one of your illegal arrests."

"You have the department's apologies." The officer looked like he had just drunk some rat droppings with his coffee. "We received information tying Mr. Bale to the murder of Robert O'Shea. The information wasn't properly verified, and the officer responsible has been reprimanded."

"And what exactly was this information that caused you to deduce with such certainty that my client was guilty and hurry to arrest him as though he were some petty criminal?"

"The information was wrong, so the details are not important. Have a pleasant evening." The officers left the room.

"In my thorough review of your last couple of courtroom successes," Bale said, smiling weakly, "I realized you couldn't have won those cases so easily without having someone on the inside feeding you information." Bale raised his hand to silence any attempt on the part of his new lawyer to deny the information. "Use your source again to find out what made them think I was involved. Now, I'd love for you to join me in the party that was so rudely interrupted. I'm willing to bet not a single guest has left the club."

The two stepped outside the police station. The few journalists who had followed Bale to the station had already gone. Only one woman in her mid-twenties stood outside the police station with a scruffy cameraman close by. Bale marched right up to her.

"I assume you're waiting for me." He smiled to see the fear in her eyes. "Who do you work for?"

"I'm an independent journalist." She held her head high, as much as her courage allowed her to.

"Well, let's help you make some money, then. You can ask me two questions and record my answers." Bale stood in front of the camera. The blinking light above the lens betrayed the fact that it was already recording.

"Mr. Bale, why were you arrested, and how is it possible that you were released from custody so quickly?"

Bale subdued a smile. "Is that one question or two?"

"One. The subjects are interrelated," the interviewer answered, sticking out her chin in defiance.

"Unfortunately, my lawyer — who did such a great job in exposing police attempts to falsify evidence during my trial — was murdered. The police, for reasons known only to them, immediately arrested me as their prime suspect. Anyone with a little sense in his head would have realized I would be the last person on earth interested in the murder of Robert, my dear friend for the past fifteen years. I assume that as soon as word of my arrest got out, the police received a call from the deputy mayor, who told them we were dining together at the time of poor Mr. O'Shea's murder. Luckily, I'd spent the time of the crime in the company of a man whose integrity is beyond reproach."

"Do you have any idea who murdered Mr. O'Shea and who tried to frame you?"

"How could I possibly know? If I knew who killed Robert O'Shea, my longtime friend, I promise you I'd turn him over to the authorities. Such a man deserves to be punished to the full extent of the law. Thank you." Bale turned to leave.

"And who tried to frame you?" the reporter shouted after him, as the photographer tried to release the camera cable and hurry after him.

Bale stopped and turned his head toward the camera. "Perhaps the same people who tried to frame me during my trial. Who knows?" He turned around and stepped inside Gibbon's Aston Martin, which drove off with a screech of tires back to The Three Sins.

CHAPTER 53

Liah and Juanita whispered together in the living room corner, while Gadi made himself comfortable on the couch. He propped his feet on the coffee table between the cardboard containers of the Chinese takeaway they had just finished eating. His fingers ceaselessly tapped on the remote, and boredom was written all over his face. "I can't believe the number of channels available here. It's just driving me crazy. And the movies? Boring as hell. Does anyone remember on which channel one can catch the news?"

Liah rose, rolled toward him, and snatched the remote from his hand. Seconds later, a newscast appeared on the screen.

A financial correspondent talked about the recovering automotive industry. When he was done, a handsome female anchor appeared and leveled a sincere gaze at the camera. "We have just learned that Arthur Bale has been arrested again. Bale was taken by the police from The Three Sins nightclub, where he was celebrating his recent courtroom success. The reason for the arrest remains unclear." In the background Bale was being led out of the nightclub by two uniformed officers and a woman whose body language virtually screamed victory.

"Who is this Bale character?" Gadi asked Ronnie, who had just entered the room holding two beer bottles.

"I don't know exactly. If I'm not mistaken, he's some arch-criminal the police have been trying to nail forever and have failed time and again."

The image on the screen changed to the weather forecast. Ronnie handed one of the bottles to Gadi, who completely ignored him and continued staring at the screen.

"What's up? The weather is so interesting?"

"Not really. I don't know. Something is gnawing at my subconscious. As if I just remembered something or saw something important. Problem is, that 'something' is slippery and I can't quite put my finger on it. And I know what's going to happen next — now this shit won't leave me alone until I figure it out." Gadi rose from his seat. "Anyway, I'm dead tired." He hugged Juanita and whispered in a voice loud enough to reach Liah and Ronnie, "Are you coming to bed?" Then he bent and kissed Juanita's belly. "I'd only take you, but at this stage, we have to take your mama with us too."

CHAPTER 54

It was 9:00 am when Gadi and Juanita finally emerged bleary-eyed from their bedroom. Liah and Ronnie were sitting in each other's arms on the balcony overlooking the ocean, Liah's head resting on her husband's shoulder. The remains of the breakfast they had just finished were scattered on the table in front of them.

"Couldn't you have waited for us?" Gadi growled and threw himself into an available chair.

"We could have, but we didn't really want to. Right, Ronnie?"

"What? So now romance is more important to you than friendship?" Gadi strained to look insulted.

"Stop being such a pain in the ass," Juanita told him. "Leave them alone. What would you like me to prepare for you?"

"Whatever they had. A doctor and a scientist must know what the perfect breakfast should be. Right?" He hugged them both and kissed their foreheads fondly.

"Be strong," Juanita blurted melodramatically. "Since he found out he is going to be a father, he's gone completely off the rails."

Gadi got up. "I don't need romantic ocean views to prove to my beloved that I love her. Juanita and I will eat in front of the television. Right, mummy?"

Juanita blinked her eyes and gave him the "Oh, yeah?" look she had perfected at the tender age of seventeen. "You got only half of it right, Gadi. We'll both eat: you in front of the television and I on the balcony with my friends."

Gadi sighed. "Women. No matter how nice you try to be, they'll always find reasons to get mad at you."

The sound of the television emerged from the living room. Seconds later, Gadi's tense voice called out, "Ronnie, come here!"

Ronnie hastily rose and joined Gadi in front of the TV. "What's the—"

"Shh… Look."

Bale's interview with the young reporter was on the screen.

"Do you have any idea who murdered Mr. O'Shea and who tried to frame you?" the reporter asked Bale, who stood in front of her, calm and brimming with self-importance.

"Oh, come on—" Ronnie started, when Gadi shushed him again.

"Just look how he loves being in the spotlight."

"Gadi, we have enough troubles of our own. What's up with your obsession with this Bale character?"

"Look," Gadi snapped at Ronnie and pointed at the screen.

"Earlier that evening, Mr. Bale was arrested at the nightclub where he was celebrating his acquittal in his murder trial. The police…" the reporter was heard describing the sequence of events. Gadi turned down the volume.

"I would expect him to run straight to the cameras at the moment of his arrest and voice his opinion about the police, just as he did now, after being released. But during the arrest, he looked like he refused to move. He kept looking back, as if he wanted to relay a message to someone there."

Gadi went right up to the screen and took a closer look at Bale. Then he froze. Kate Frost emerged through the club door.

"Fuck. So that's what's been bothering me. My subconscious saw her but refused to share it with me."

"Saw who?" Ronnie was losing patience.

"Kate, the chick from the accounting firm."

The report ended, and Gadi began to feverishly zap through the various news channels. He stopped when he reached Fox News, where the same report was being broadcast.

"Take a good look at the front door of the club." Excitement filled Gadi's voice.

"I can't believe it. Kate," Ronnie muttered and sat on the sofa, looking puzzled.

"The breakfast you ordered," Juanita announced in her best waitress voice, but she paused when she saw the look on the men's faces.

"What now?" She placed the cups and plates on the table in front of them. "Liah," she called her friend, "they've flipped out again."

Gadi was the first to come back to his senses. "We have enough computers here to find all the information published about Bale's trial and about his past. Girls" — he turned to Liah and Juanita, who exchanged glances — "we just discovered there's a connection between this Bale character and Kate Frost. It might be just coincidental, but maybe we've found the thread that will lead us to solving the mystery of who stole Double N's technology and why. I suggest you two focus on doing background research on Bale, while Ronnie and I try to figure out what exactly happened at his trial."

"Finish your breakfast first," said Liah. "Ronnie and I will bring in the computers and start working. The sky won't fall if you take another ten minutes to join us."

Gadi stood, but Ronnie's hand pulled him back down. "Liah's right. Take it easy, eat your breakfast. Join us when you're done."

After about three hours of strenuous work, interrupted occasionally by Gadi's enthusiastic or frustrated cries and howls, the four reconvened in the living room.

"I have to say," Liah spoke first, "we weren't able to find out much about the man. There are quite a few rumors and a lot of speculation about his involvement in the underworld, but nothing, except for this recent murder trial, has ever materialized into actual criminal charges. We found quite a few articles discussing his money laundering. Those reports almost entirely ceased after Bale sued a newspaper for libel and won two and a half million dollars. There was also an article crowning him as the head of a criminal organization, serving as a sort of supreme judge and arbiter in underworld disputes, but the subject quickly disappeared from the media and has never resurfaced."

"So, we are dealing either with a sophisticated criminal or with an innocent man harassed by the authorities," said Ronnie.

"Generally speaking, Bale owns a consulting firm," continued Liah. "We needed to do some extensive digging to find out who his clients are. We weren't able to find many. Most of them are shell companies registered in tax havens like the Cayman Islands, Bermuda, and Jersey."

"Jersey? Since when is New Jersey a tax haven?" Gadi sputtered.

"Not New Jersey, just Jersey, you dope. It's a tiny island off the coast of France. Its small size stands in stark contrast to the amount of money hidden there. Experts estimate the banks have about ninety billion dollars deposited in them. That's two billion dollars for each square mile. It is the El Dorado of tax evaders."

Liah paused, allowing the information to sink in. "His company doesn't have a website, he doesn't advertise, and it seems his services are discovered only by word of mouth. All we were able to find was the information reported to the New York State Division of Corporations and some details regarding the extent of his businesses, information that Bale himself provided in the few interviews he has agreed to give. The data we were able to unearth sounds too perfect. Like an alibi Bale formulated in order to provide the tax authorities a feasible explanation for the financial sources supporting his lavish lifestyle."

"And here I was thinking I was the one who found something important," Gadi said wistfully. "I read all the reports published about Bale's trial. The gist of the story is very simple. Bale was accused of murdering three people and making them disappear — two organized crime figures and one woman, who, according to the district attorney, was his girlfriend at the time of the murder. A man claiming to be Bale's soldier at the time and to have seen him committing the murders, led investigators to the three graves. Traces of Bale's DNA were found at all three crime scenes. The way I figure it, if he was truly the one who murdered them, he must have been positive the bodies would never be found, which was why he wasn't worried about leaving any traces behind.

"The trial came to an abrupt end after his lawyer claimed the police had tampered with the DNA evidence. He demanded that Bale's DNA be tested again in the presence of witnesses on behalf of both the defense and prosecution. When the test results came back, it turned out that the DNA found at the crime scenes wasn't Bale's and he was immediately released and the charges dropped. Supposedly, this served as proof of his innocence."

Gadi rose from his seat and began to pace in the room. "Throughout his trial, Bale was kept in isolation for fear of his life. Two of the victims belonged to a murderous Irish gang. The question that has been bothering me from the beginning is why this gang would think Bale murdered its men. If he truly has no connections to the underworld, they would be the first to know it and would simply wait for the outcome of the trial. There are few known cases, if any, involving a civilian attacking and murdering gang members, then burying them in an unknown location. My only conclusion is that Bale must be a serious criminal who got involved in some kind of dispute with the gang leader, making his prosecution very logical in their eyes. So, if he truly is a dangerous criminal and is somehow associated with Kate, the next question is whether she is just his current chick, or if she's a member of his organization.

"Also, I was bothered by his behavior when he was arrested for his lawyer's murder. The only explanation I can think of is that Bale knew Kate was involved in the murder, and he suspected she might have framed him. I found the video of his arrest on the internet. The look on his face changed from incomprehension to accusation and anger. Therefore…" Gadi covered his face with his hands and heaved a great sigh.

Liah and Juanita held their breaths. After what seemed like an eternity, he sighed again and said, "I wouldn't be surprised if it was Kate who murdered O'Shea."

"Don't you think you're jumping to conclusions?" Juanita remarked. "What do you say, Ronnie?" She turned to Ronnie, who seemed lost in thought.

Ronnie slowly raised his head and looked at them as if he had just noticed their presence. "Excuse me?" he asked with embarrassment.

"What are your thoughts about Gadi's conclusions?" Juanita repeated.

"I haven't been listening to everything Gadi was saying, but I trust his instincts. I believe Bale and Kate are somehow connected and that they both have something to do with the theft."

The three turned their faces in unison and looked at him with curiosity.

"And how exactly did you reach this conclusion from what Liah and Gadi have been telling us?"

"Like I said, I haven't been paying close attention, but I do believe I've solved the riddle of how Bale was able to get away with murder."

CHAPTER 55

Ronnie stretched up, laced his fingers behind his neck and examined his friends' faces through narrowed eyes. All three waited patiently.

"Before I explain why I believe Bale was behind the theft of our technology, and what he did with it, I would like to begin with an in-depth explanation that will give you some insight into the CRISPR-based technology we developed at Double N."

"Cris what?"

Ronnie nodded at Juanita with understanding and launched into an explanation "The world of science views CRISPR as a genetic editing tool. It is a tool that enables us to cut out a fragment of a DNA strand, usually a damaged one, and replace it with a healthy one. Just like the 'cut and paste' option in a word processing program."

"So, your company is dealing with this CRISPR thing?" asked Juanita.

"Yes, but—"

Gadi interrupted before Ronnie had a chance to continue. "If CRISPR can be used to swap out genes, does this mean you could change a living person and make him a 'better' one by your standards" — Gadi made the air quotes — "biologically speaking? If so, how do you plan on preventing people from programming their unborn babies or countries having their populations go through a reclamation process? Do you really want to play God, Ronnie?" Gadi crossed his arms on his chest while biting his lower lip.

"The ethical aspects are indeed highly complicated, but Double N is a minor part of the problem. The principle of genetic editing was invented by several organizations long before we started our research. It was only in February 2017, following a three-year legal battle, that the American courts ruled CRISPR to be the property of the two organizations that simultaneously invented it — Harvard and MIT. Today, there are already rumors regarding Chinese scientists utilizing CRISPR to change fetal cells and create genetically programmed babies. There are rumors of sperm and egg cell programming intended for the selection of eye color, muscle strength, and various other preferences for the next generation. In a few years, drug tests in the Olympics games and such will become obsolete. The competitors will have been programmed to be super athletes while still in their mothers' wombs.

"Abusing the ability to implant specific genes is much easier during the fetal stage, before the cells divide into specific types. There have been a number of committees established around the world with the aim of addressing this subject. Governments are also well aware of the vast potential, both for good and evil, inherent in this field. I agree with you that there will always be governments, as well as wealthy individuals, perhaps, that would use this technology in a misguided way. But I suggest that for now we put the ethical aspects aside. I will get back to that once I start explaining what I think Bale has done."

"All right," Gadi drew out the last word, obviously confused. "Who the hell thought of inventing this CRISPR thing, anyway?"

"Actually, it was nature. Did you know that for every type of cell in the human body, there are about ten various forms of viruses? Some of those viruses are the most dangerous form of predators that exist in nature. In order to multiply, they must insert their own DNA into the cell of a living organism and use its reproductive mechanism to reproduce themselves. Our immune systems destroy most of them, but researchers believe that given enough time, new forms of viruses will emerge, ones that the body does not recognize, or cannot cope with, such as the Zika virus." Ronnie paused to allow his listeners to digest the information.

"Great, but you didn't answer my question," Gadi snapped.

"The type of cell," continued Ronnie with a measured tone, ignoring his friend's jittery impatience, "that has been attacked most often by viruses since the earliest days of creation, is the bacterium. When a virus attacks a bacterium, the bacterium has a very brief period of time to stop the attack before the attacker uses its nucleus in order to duplicate itself and extinguish its host in the process. Bacteria have developed an immune system whose attributes are very similar to those of CRISPR, only edgier. The moment a bacterium senses a virus has entered its guts, it launches a mechanism very much like CRISPR that tears the virus to shreds."

"But isn't it too late by then?" Gadi was starting to show interest.

"Good question. Sometimes it is. This is why, when the CRISPR-like mechanism annihilates the virus, it takes a DNA sample from it and stores it in its memory, as it were. Think about it as building a virus library or database. From then on, every time that particular virus comes anywhere near the bacterium, the CRISPR-like element recognizes it based on the sample it possesses and destroys it. Over time, it develops a library able to recognize thousands of types of viruses, which enables it to quickly react to any malicious attack."

"Sneaky little devils, bacteria…"

"You don't know the half of it. Bacteria are no less dangerous than viruses. On the contrary, we use antibiotics to wipe them out. Unfortunately, bacteria have found a way to rapidly mutate. The moment they develop an antibiotic-immune mutation, they multiply at record speed and cause infections in the entire body. This is what we call a flesh-eating bacterium. The only way we can destroy such bacteria is, once again, by using a CRISPR mechanism that would penetrate their cells and implant a self-destructive gene. Science aims to fight bacteria by utilizing the same system they brought into the world."

"Amazing. But what does any of this have to do with your company?"

"We've developed a library of predatory bacteria, as well as one of violent viruses, and tried to send CRISPRs equipped with that recognition knowledge to destroy such bacteria and viruses in infected human bodies. A kind of auxiliary force intended to help the body's own immune system. While it is true as part of their evasion attempt bacteria constantly mutate, they cannot change their basic genetic form. This is why we believe we will always be able to recognize and destroy them."

"Would it be accurate to say—" Gadi hesitated a moment "—that you have invented the next generation of treatment?"

"We still have a long way to go, but we are definitely headed in the right direction. And it's interesting that you used the word 'treatment' instead of saying 'medicine.' I will elaborate more about the differences in a moment.

"One of the main problems yet to be resolved is the question of CRISPR's absolute precision. If we actually use CRISPR for editing the genome, the last thing we would want is for it to 'cut' the wrong gene. It is very easy to make mistakes in areas where the genome sequences are very similar. That's why the first algorithmic technology our company developed was the ability to confirm that the location where the CRISPR performs the cutting is precise and correct. Because we have raised and invested huge amounts of money in the company we have been able to attract the finest minds in Israel and America, both in the genetics research field and the field of mathematics. I have gathered around me a group of geniuses who constantly challenge themselves and each other. And Simon, the scientist who was attacked, is perhaps the most brilliant of them all."

Ronnie rose and began to walk about the room. "My scientists decided to challenge themselves with a more general question on their own free time. How could we build a mechanism that operates like the Waze navigation system, allowing us to direct our CRISPR to target any type of body tissue? Then, once it reaches the damaged tissue, lead itself to the specific location in the DNA of every cell building that particular tissue and replace damaged genes with healthy ones, yet leaving other healthy tissue untouched."

"Congratulations! You've just lost me completely." Gadi smiled when he saw Juanita shaking her head desperately as well.

"Let me help simplify things a little, Ronnie," Liah interrupted. "Since Ronnie has already explained it to me more than once, and I too wanted to tear my hair out in frustration the first couple of times, I believe I can offer you a layman's explanation. Think about a mail delivery. In order for the mail to reach its destination, we need to write down an address, which includes city, street, and street number. Think of the name of the city as the equivalent of defining the type of cell or tissue. The name of the street and the house number equal the specific place in the DNA we want to reach. And the content of the envelope is the healthy gene that needs to replace the damaged one, once it is cut off the DNA chain."

"Sounds simple." Gadi chuckled and then turned serious. "And who replaces the damaged gene with the good one?"

"The nucleus of the cell itself is the one conducting the exchange. When part of the genetic sequence is cut out of the cell, the nucleus panics and begins to seek out the missing part. We make sure it finds the one that arrived with the CRISPR and pastes it in place without realizing it isn't the gene that had been cut from it. Got it?"

"Just the major principle, but go on." Juanita seemed fascinated.

"You might be surprised to hear it, but the basic idea of using CRISPR to replace genes was around before Double N. But during the experimental stage, a frightening fact was discovered. CRISPR replaced not only the targeted genes, but sometimes, genes that were only similar. In other words, CRISPR is sometimes wrong. As Ronnie mentioned earlier, the first patent the company received was for the ability to make sure CRISPR arrives at the precise delivery address, not the one next to it, or a street with a similar name, then initiate the replacement process only at that exact address." Liah paused, then continued once she saw the principle had been understood.

"A much more difficult task is identifying a particular type of cell in the human body. The exact city address… How is this done? Well, it is extremely complex, both to explain and to perform. But at this stage, just assume Double N has found a way of guessing, based on a tissue's characteristics, what its address is. Furthermore,

Ronnie's mathematicians — and that was the biggest breakthrough — have found a way of describing this address in a simple mathematical way. Suddenly, it became feasible to effectively and accurately deliver a drug, gene, or DNA sequence anywhere in the body."

"Let's see if I got this straight." Gadi wrinkled his forehead in concentration. "Double N invented a mechanism that can carry genetic or medicinal cargoes anywhere in the body in a precise and error-free way. Am I right?"

Ronnie nodded. "Or to several locations in the body simultaneously," he added.

"So, you are actually the owner of a technology that could form the basis of all future curative methods, or, in other words, you are the CEO and major shareholder of a company whose real value is vastly higher than any current estimate?"

"Right again. But now, we need to hurry and meet the prosecutor from Bale's trial. We have to stop him before he reaches us. I know how Bale outsmarted the system, and that can help."

"So how exactly was he able to trick the system?" Gadi wanted to know.

Ronnie explained. By the time he finished, they were all open-mouthed.

CHAPTER 56

The phone wouldn't stop ringing. Martin Gibbons reached out and fumbled for the device that stubbornly insisted on waking him up. He cursed when he finally touched it and hurled it to the floor. The bothersome ringing continued. Martin bent and picked it up. "Hello," he answered in a drowsy voice.

"I expect this to be the last time you make me wait so long before answering," Bale's snakelike whisper scorched his ear.

All at once, the lawyer became fully alert and instinctively sat up. "I do apologize, Mr. Bale. How can I help you?"

"Do you have an answer from the police as to why they arrested me?"

"Of course." Gibbons relaxed. "I've had the answer since early last evening, but I didn't want to disturb your celebration."

"That's not for you to decide. Next time, let me be the one to decide whether I want to be disturbed or not. Now speak!"

An indulgent sigh was heard behind him. Gibbons turned his head. A naked girl was lying in his bed. Her loose hair covered her face. He tried to recall what she looked like but failed.

"You still there?" Bale's angry voice came through loud and clear.

"I apologize, I must have accidentally pressed the mute button," Martin answered quickly. "As stated, I contacted my informer in the police as soon as we arrived at the club. According to him, no incriminating evidence whatsoever had been received by the police. They immediately realized this was all part of a personal crusade conducted by the assistant district attorney, Julie Wilson, and aimed against you. Even though the police tried to dissuade her from her decision to immediately arrest you, she wouldn't back down and claimed your dislike of O'Shea had been apparent during the trial. She was convinced that the moment you were brought in, she would be able to goad you into admitting your crime. She was, at least according to my source, obsessed with arresting you that very night. The defeat she suffered during your trial has significantly hindered her chances of being promoted, and she is intent on having her revenge.

"When the duty officer refused to cooperate, she angrily left the station and returned an hour later with a court order for your immediate arrest. No one knows how she was able to get a warrant without possessing any proof of your involvement in any crime. I checked the identity of the judge who signed her warrant. I'm sure you won't be surprised to hear that it was the very same Judge Glenn Morrison who presided over your trial. I believe we have recourse to sue them for harassment."

"Thanks. Good job. We're not suing anyone." The call was disconnected.

The attorney turned around and looked at the girl lying in his bed. These little side benefits that came with working for Bale appealed to him as much as the generous pay that had been promised him the night before, while they were making their way to the nightclub.

CHAPTER 57

Bale stood by the bedroom door and watched Kate sleeping in his bed. A childlike tranquility bathed her angelic face. No one would have believed that behind those innocent features lurked a merciless killer. Her taste for blood and violence had unnecessarily complicated his interests more than once. Her violent attack on the scientist from whom she'd stolen the computer had been completely unnecessary. Bale had never believed her excuse of having deliberately resorted to violence in order to imitate the actions of the serial killer the police were after. He knew that Kate had relished every second of that evening's vicious attack. The precision of the blows and their intensity proved to him that she had purposely drawn out the attack as long as she could. After all, had it been him, he would have acted the exact same way.

Kate never ceased to surprise him in bed. He wanted to believe she was in love with him, but deep inside he knew that she was a sophisticated machine able to adjust herself to any situation and play any role, whether the highly skilled killer or the perfect lover. That was enough for him. After all, he wanted to believe that he too was an efficient, bloodthirsty machine. He was thrilled to the point of ecstasy by each of the murders he had committed with his own hands. Up until a few minutes ago, he had been convinced that Kate would be his next victim. He wasn't sure whether he should be pleased or disappointed by the news that no one had informed on him or had fabricated incriminating evidence.

Bale quietly drew closer to the bed, finding it nearly impossible to take his eyes from that little smile fluttering on her lips. He bent and stroked her swanlike neck. Before he could realize what was happening, Kate's hand sprang up to grip his wrist. She bent it back cruelly, while her legs rose quickly, wrapping themselves around his neck and twisting with the strength of a crocodile dragging its prey under the water. Bale fell on the bed, his arm stretched back painfully, and every bone in his body threatening to break or pop out of its socket. The pressure ceased as abruptly as it had begun, and he tumbled to the floor.

"I've warned you never to surprise me." Kate sat in bed with her legs spread, her breasts perked up proudly, and her lips curved in a defiant smile at the sight of Bale sprawled on the carpet, rubbing his shoulder with a pained grimace on his face.

Bale rose and took out a pistol from the night table drawer. He cocked it and aimed it at her head. The rage in his eyes seared her body. The smile never left her face.

"You want to kill me for having good instincts?" She rose from the bed, ignoring the weapon in Bale's hand, and walked naked to the bathroom. She stopped at the door and turned her head back. "Care to join me?"

Bale's hand trembled with a desire to pull the trigger. Finally, he turned and put the weapon back in its place. He went to the shower, where Kate was standing, and turned off the water.

"I just found out Julie Wilson wants nothing less than my head on a platter and has sworn to do everything in her power to frame me. Finish up and go follow her. I want to know what she's up to."

He pressed her violently to the wall, and with his free hand opened the stream of steaming water. Only when he felt the insufferable heat scalding the skin of his hand did he let go of her neck and leave the room.

CHAPTER 58

A sour taste rose up her throat. The cramps in her stomach had begun to ease, but the significance of the telephone call that had just ended hit her with a greater intensity and spread through every nerve ending. As soon as she saw Brandon Palmer, the district attorney's, name on the screen, Julie realized that what she'd feared most was actually about to happen. She had never, even during high-profile trials, gotten a call from him on a Sunday. He had a reputation for zealously keeping his leisure time for himself. Few in the district attorney's office dared call him during the weekend. Everyone knew that disturbing the boss outside his regular work hours was a career-ending move.

"Would you care to explain why I needed to get a phone call from the deputy mayor accusing the district attorney's office and the one heading it, me, namely, of harassing a citizen for no good reason?" Palmer's voice was strained with rage.

"Sir, I had reasonable grounds to assume—" she managed to say before his voice cut her off.

"Reasonable grounds? Since when do we pursue arrests on the basis of 'reasonable grounds'? Wasn't your monumental fiasco in Bale's trial enough? Now you feel the need to bring about an even bigger one? If you're trying to ruin your own career, that's fine by me, but don't do anything to drag me down with you."

"Sir—" Before she had a chance to say anything more, his next outburst poured like a stream of boiling lava into her ear.

"Next time something like this happens, I'll personally make sure you won't ever be able to find a job, even in the private sector. I haven't worked my ass off my whole career just for some hotheaded egomaniac like you to ruin it. Now, with your permission, I'd like to get back to my family. I'll see you tomorrow at 8:00 am in my office."

The bottom line of the conversation was as clear as a drop of blood on a bed of snow. And the blood was hers. What hurt her more than the lack of support from the man in charge was that everyone had warned her she was making a huge mistake. But her frustration over her defeat in the trial had made her act rashly. From the day she had finished law school and joined the district attorney's office, she had been warned of reactions motivated by anger and vindictiveness. Now, thirteen years later, she had fallen into the most obvious trap of the profession she so dearly loved. She had dedicated her entire adult life to her work. She had never had a steady relationship. Even her small apartment, furnished with furniture carefully selected from the finest design magazines and catalogues, lacked any personal touches. The alien and frigid air that dominated the apartment served as constant reminders of her misguided priorities.

Julie poured the last few drops of the recently opened bottle of wine into her glass and downed the contents in a single gulp. She stretched out on the couch with her hands behind her head and tried to prepare for the next morning's meeting. The more she thought about it, the more she realized the only way of getting out of the mess she'd made with any dignity at all was to hand in her resignation. A single tear that fell from her eye and crawled down her cheek broke the dam of restraint, and many more tears followed uncontrollably. Julie wiped her eyes with her sleeve and burst out laughing. The last time she had used her sleeve as a handkerchief must have been when she was twelve. Soon enough, the laughter turned hysterical, and Julie clutched her stomach, taking advantage of any momentary respite to get some air into her aching lungs.

The phone rang, startling her out of her thoughts.

"What now?" Concern quickly sobered her up and displaced the laughter. Julie hurried to the phone, which continued to ring. She did not recognize the number on the screen and so decided not to answer. The ringing stopped but immediately started up again.

"Who is it?" she answered aggressively.

"Hello. Am I talking to Julie Wilson?" It was a pleasant voice, laced with a hint of a foreign accent.

"Speaking. Who is this?"

"My name is Dr. Ronnie Saar, I am the CEO of Double N, a company specializing in genetic research. I believe I can explain to you how Arthur Bale was able to escape from punishment during his trial."

"You can do what?" Julie could hardly believe her ears.

"I'll be more than happy to meet with you to explain how Bale was able to hoodwink you and the rest of the judicial system. I understand you don't know who I am and probably wonder what my game is. I assure you, I have no agenda. If you Google my name, you'll see that I am a respected member of the scientific community. I am offering you my assistance as an expert. So, what do you say?"

"Can I get back to you in a few minutes?"

"Whenever you like. Goodbye," he answered calmly before ending the call.

Julie frantically typed Dr. Ronnie Saar's name into the search engine. The screen quickly filled with a list of links. Soon enough, she discovered that Dr. Saar, a Harvard graduate, was indeed a well-known figure in the field of medical entrepreneurship. In the past, he had sold a company for over four hundred million dollars. Later on, he had worked as a partner in a venture capital fund, and now he served, as he had said, as the CEO of Double N. The name of the company sounded familiar, and she typed it into the search box.

Serial killer strikes again! A Double N employee was brutally attacked in a Chelsea alley and was saved only thanks to the NYPD's quick response.

Julie leaned back. She was convinced the man she had just spoken to was serious. Unless he was an impostor, that is. She hurried to the Double N website, which was especially thin in content, with most of its web pages still under construction. To her relief, the website did include the management members' details and included Ronnie Saar's email address.

"*Call me. Julie.*" She wrote a brief email and sent it.

Two minutes later, the phone by her side rang. She snatched it and answered. "All right, let's meet. Where are you?"

"I'm in New Jersey, but I can meet anywhere convenient to you."

Julie looked at her watch. "I'd rather come to you. Everybody knows my face in New York. I could be in New Jersey in two hours. Does that work for you?"

"I'll meet you at Espresso Joe's in Keyport in two hours. Driving down here on a weekend shouldn't take more than seventy-five minutes."

"I'll see you in two hours, then." She disconnected the call and hurried to get dressed. She couldn't get over the feeling that the next few hours would determine her future.

CHAPTER 59

Espresso Joe's café had a long line out the door. Ronnie stood in the entry and looked around. The place was teeming with families craving a cooking-free weekend. Julie sat at a secluded table for two at the far end of the restaurant. Oversized sunglasses covered her eyes. Ronnie, recognizing her face from dozens of television appearances, waved at her and was answered by a slight nod. He made his way around the strollers and bags filling the aisles.

"Sorry, I had no idea this place would be so packed," he apologized as he took his seat. "Would you like to go somewhere else?"

"No. It's fine." She seemed intensely nervous, and he was sure her eyes were darting around, constantly examining her surroundings through the dark lenses of her glasses.

"I came alone." He tried to calm her while signaling a waitress that he'd love some coffee. "Are you hungry?"

"I already ordered a little something to eat," she said pleasantly, and then her voice turned businesslike. "I understand you have information regarding how Bale managed to outsmart the court. I suggest we forgo the small talk and get straight to the point."

"All right. In order for you to understand the explanation I am about to give, it's important that you have some sort of basic knowledge of genetics and an understanding of what we have developed at Double N. Therefore, I ask you to please be patient and let me start by providing you with the necessary background."

Julie Wilson removed her glasses and nodded to indicate she was ready. Her face was kind of gray, and eggplant-colored bags sagged under her eyes. This wasn't the same energetic woman who had arrested Bale only two days earlier in front of the television cameras. Her resounding failure, which was captured in headlines and on all the television channels, had taken its toll.

"The genome…" Ronnie began his explanation, and for the next thirty minutes went on to describe CRISPR's capabilities and the technologies invented by Double N, technologies he was convinced had been stolen from Simon's laptop. The coffee had gotten cold, but Julie couldn't care less. Occasionally, she nibbled at the cheesecake in front of her, but mostly she was too busy listening to pick up her fork. As Ronnie progressed with his explanations, it became apparent that she understood the scope of CRISPR's potential.

"Earlier today, my wife and a couple of friends helped me search the internet for information about Bale's trial. I was surprised to find material that made me suspect Bale had somehow tampered with his genetic tests." Ronnie finally addressed the subject that truly interested her.

Julie leaned forward, her hands clasped on the table.

"Allow me to repeat two facts introduced by McNeal, your expert witness in the trial. The first — our active genetic material forms only about fifteen percent of our DNA. We still do not fully understand the rest of the eighty-five percent. The second — that eighty-five percent contains patterns, which are actually a certain genetic structure repeating itself several times. Half of those repetitions come from the mother's DNA, while the other half comes from the father's. This is, by the way, how DNA paternity testing is performed. Since various repetitions reappear in twenty-two chromosomes, you can deduce with a very high certainty the odds of two samples belonging to the same person.

"In Bale's trial, two DNA-based tests were presented. The first relied on the fifteen percent of the genome, with which the suspect's face was reconstructed. The second relied on the remaining eighty-five percent, the only test currently admissible by the court. Lo and behold — the two results were contradictory."

Julie held her breath.

"In order to be acquitted, Bale had to discredit the forensic test results. He did not expect you to perform a facial reconstruction. Therefore, I believe that someone, and I admit that I can't hazard a guess as to his or her identity, concocted a CRISPR for Bale. This CRISPR was devised to cut out certain sequences in the tested twenty-two chromosomes and replace them with other sequences. In order to do that, he had to gamble that the test would involve taking a sample from one of two sources: the inner wall of his oral cavity, which is the standard way of retrieving DNA samples, or hair from his head, because hair was discovered at the crime scenes. He also had to gamble that you would not request a blood test. I can only assume that had you asked for a blood test, Bale's lawyer would have claimed your findings at the crime scenes involved hair and demanded an identical test. I must admit the way they altered the cheek cells was very clever. Neither you nor McNeal could have known that both samples would be manipulated."

Ronnie paused, trying to gauge Julie's understanding. Anger and frustration filled her tired eyes. He gave her what he hoped was an encouraging look and continued. "In order to do that, they needed the technology we developed at Double N, the kind that can differentiate between various types of tissue and act only on a specified kind. What made their work easier was that both types of tissue, that of the inner cheek and those of the roots of the hair, are externally accessible, a fact that increased the chances of a successful outcome for the genetic manipulation they had planned for these tissues. In all the video excerpts of the trial that I saw, I couldn't help but notice a water bottle regularly placed in front of Bale. I believe the water in the bottle contained a high concentration of CRISPRs that regularly changed the structure of Bale's inner cheek. What I still can't understand is whether this same bottle contained another CRISPR, which could somehow be absorbed by the body and reach the hair."

"That sneaky son of a bitch," whispered Julie. "Bale was extremely sick in the opening stages of the trial and wouldn't stop perspiring. He asked for and received authorization from the judge to shower four times a day and wash his hair with his own personal shampoo. I am willing to bet the shampoo contained the CRISPR necessary for the hair roots."

Ronnie smiled at her. "There you go."

"But how do I prove Bale actually did it? I'm sure they've destroyed all the water bottles and shampoo containers. Without any hard evidence, no court would agree to reopen the trial for obstruction of justice."

"Getting proof would be very easy. All it would take is a simple blood test. I'm convinced that his blood still contains the original DNA sequences."

"Are you saying he now has two types of DNA in his body?"

"Yes. The one that has been unnaturally changed as well as his original DNA. By the way, there is a natural biological phenomenon called chimerism, in which people carry two types of DNA in their bodies. I'm sure you could find a lot of material about it on the internet."

"Do you think Bale has to continue to use the CRISPRs programmed for him in order to maintain the change?"

"Good question. I don't think so. All the cells in our body are replaced once every eighteen months, more or less. When a cell reproduces itself before dying, it uses its own DNA. If the transgenic DNA is renewed, then the new cells would also carry that altered DNA. But, and this is a big but, because the technology is still in its infancy, if I were the scientist who developed this solution for Bale, I'd recommend that he continue to correct the sequences in his mouth and hair until I could examine him to make sure the reproduced cells had maintained their predecessors' qualities."

An agitated waitress came to their table. "Would you like something else?" she asked impatiently, eyeing their two half-full coffee cups and the nibbled cheesecake. A long line of anxious couples and families snaked around the waiting area near the restaurant door, and the waitress was probably hoping for new customers who would eat more and leave a bigger tip.

"Chicken salad, please." Julie smiled apologetically.

"I'll have a turkey sandwich with honey and mustard and a Coke, please." Ronnie followed the waitress with his eyes as she walked away tiredly.

"You do understand…" Julie paused, took a deep breath, and continued, "that should what you just told me become public knowledge, we would be flooded with retrial requests? If there is indeed a way of changing a DNA sequence, then all the evidence we used in previous trials to convict criminals would be called into question. Not because it's justified, but because the legal system would not know how to cope with this precedent. And in the future, criminals all over the world would turn themselves into what you just called chimeras. Every time a forensic test proved their guilt, they'd simply demonstrate that their bodies also carried other DNA sequences. They could claim that if they have them, perhaps other criminals were programmed with the same mechanism and therefore, carry the same sequences. This would be the end of genetic recognition-based convictions."

The waitress returned with their food, and Ronnie hungrily began to wolf it down. Julie picked at her salad with a pronounced lack of enthusiasm. The things she had just learned from Ronnie deeply disturbed her. It was only a few hours ago that she had seriously considered handing in her resignation and leaving the prosecutor's office. Now here she was, concerned about the future of the entire field of criminal prosecution.

"And what if people can use this technology you've invented to change their fingerprints? Even a slight change is significant. And a finger can easily be accessed." Julie kept running her hands through her hair nervously. She rose, then immediately sat down again. "You have to promise to keep this conversation and the information you revealed to me a secret until I figure out what to do next. Do you promise?"

"I promise. Unconditionally. Still, I'd be happy to get the authorities' help, should I need it, to catch whoever stole the information from me. I am concerned that the person behind the information theft might spread word of its criminal potential among members of the underworld. I am in a race against time to save my company, and you are in a race of your own to prevent this information from getting into the wrong hands. We are both after the same man or organization."

"Contact me when you have any new details. I promise to help where I can. Assuming, of course, the district attorney doesn't fire me tomorrow because of the mess I made during Bale's televised arrest." She smiled tiredly.

"Give him this piece of dynamite I just provided you with. If he has any sense at all, he won't allow anyone to fire you," Ronnie soothed her.

"Damn it, you're right." Her eyes blazed with sudden anger. She straightened up in her seat and raised a hand to flag the waitress for the check.

"That's all right. I'll pick up the tab. You can just leave if you're in a hurry."

Without a word, Julie rose and left the restaurant.

On the other end of the street, wearing an auburn wig, Kate was watching. Tailing Wilson from the moment she left her New York apartment had been easy. The prosecutor had not suspected for a moment that she was being followed and drove straight to the rendezvous point. Kate found it strange that although they both lived in Manhattan, they'd decided to meet someplace so far from their homes. There was only one possible conclusion: Dr. Saar had another apartment here, in Keyport.

She knew exactly what her next move would be.

CHAPTER 60

"Yes, Kate. Report." Bale sounded impatient.

"We have a problem. I followed Julie Wilson to a coffee shop in New Jersey, where she met with Dr. Saar, Double N CEO. They engaged in a lively conversation for over an hour."

"How the hell did they find each other?" Bale erupted with frustration.

"I don't see any way Wilson could have realized the connection between the information theft and the trial. On the other hand—"

"That CEO certainly could have," Bale completed her sentence, his voice seething with anger.

"Like I told you at our last meeting, that investigator he's brought in is impressive. Together, they make a dangerous pair. They definitely pose a threat to us." Her entire body was rigid with expectation, but she knew better than anyone that *he* had to give the order.

"You think you could get rid of them without leaving a trail leading back to me?"

Kate burst into relieved laughter. "Do I need to email you my resume?"

"When could you do it?"

"After Wilson left Saar, I followed him. I made the right choice, if I do say so myself."

"Get to the point!"

Kate ignored his agitation. "I followed him to a nearby apartment that isn't listed in Saar's name. His private investigator was there too. They met at the entrance to the building. It turns out he was waiting in the shadows to see if anyone was following his boss. If I hadn't worn a wig and kept my distance, I probably would have been caught. That man is really good. Killing him would be quite an intriguing experience." She chuckled with anticipation.

"Take your time, but be careful. If he's as good as you say, he won't go down that easily. Don't forget for a moment that he already had an encounter with two professional killers and walked away without a scratch."

"With all due respect to the professionals you sent to deal with him, and despite your denial that they were working for you, comparing me to them is a little insulting. But you're right, I promise to be careful."

The conversation ended, but the smile didn't fade from Kate's lips for a long time. She walked back to the coffee shop. Such a pleasurable task requires a tranquil mood and a full stomach.

CHAPTER 61

Julie Wilson had spent the night deliberating over the exact tactics she should employ during her meeting with Palmer, the district attorney. No closing argument she had ever given in court had carried such a decisive impact, certainly not for her personally. The man she would meet with in the morning was notoriously unpredictable. Still, she tried to anticipate the points he would address while reprimanding her and prepare satisfactory answers for each one. Toward morning, fatigue overwhelmed her and she collapsed, tired and desperate, on the living room couch. It all seemed pointless and hopeless. She suddenly understood how the witnesses she regularly prepared for trial felt once they were alone on the witness stand, being attacked by a hardhearted lawyer. Gloves off, no mercy. She had no doubt this would be the strategy of the person who was supposed to be in her corner. This would be a street fight, the realization struck her. And in such fights, he who strikes first gains the advantage. Talking and reasoning would only result in broken bones. All hers.

It was 7:50 am when Wilson entered the district attorney's office. His secretary's greeting did not bode well. It was clear she had started her day with a dose of misery. And the workday hadn't even officially begun.

"May I go in?"

"Yes, he's expecting you. But I'm not so sure you should," the secretary whispered.

"I don't think I have a choice," Julie answered with a forced smile and knocked on the door.

"Come in." Palmer's voice thundered.

Julie straightened an invisible wrinkle in her suit and stepped into the room.

"Sit." He pointed to the chair on the other side of his desk.

Julie sat down, careful to maintain eye contact, knowing she mustn't show any fear.

"I've never encountered such negligence as you demonstrated while working on the two Bale cases." His face was already flushed, he was so incensed.

Julie felt the anger she had struggled so hard to suppress begin to boil. The strategy she had considered seemed suddenly useless. "Bullshit," she replied calmly. "Would you like me to recite a list of all the stupid things you've done over the course of your career, mistakes you never paid for, just because you are a political animal and know whose ass you need to kiss at exactly the right moment?"

The district attorney was dumbstruck. No one had ever dared speak to him like that. "I'll make sure you'll live to regret those words," he whispered venomously.

"No, you won't. In the next few minutes, I expect you to pay close attention to what I have to say. I am about to present you with two options. One will ruin your career, the other could turn you into a king."

"Just who do you think you are to—" Fiery sparks flashed in his eyes.

"I'm the one about to save your career, although you hardly

deserve it. Now, I'm not going to tell you again." Julie took an envelope out of her briefcase and placed it on the table. "This envelope contains my resignation letter. You can accept it right now and end this conversation. Choose this option, and you'll find out what I wanted to tell you, but I assure you that it will hurt like hell. The other option is that you get back to being the manager I desperately need right now, one who actually supports his staff, so their successes will also be his own." She was unable to conceal the bitterness in her voice.

The prosecutor reached out and took the envelope. Julie rose and silently headed back to the door.

"Get back here at once."

Julie turned around. "Actually, I'm not sure I should. I'm tired of your power plays. Throughout my career, I've always treated you with all the respect due you. All I got in return were aggressive demonstrations of authority that served your insatiable ego. I came here today to expose a serious new threat to the entire judicial system. I'm still willing to do so. But, please" — she softened her voice — "stop these ridiculous mind games."

The district attorney examined her for a moment. Finally, he placed the envelope back on the table. "I apologize." He surprised her with his unexpected acquiescence. "Can we simply start over?"

Julie collapsed into her chair. "Sorry about my tone of voice, I haven't slept for two days."

The district attorney pressed the intercom button. "Two coffees, please."

He turned his head to Julie and smiled. "Oh, it wasn't just the tone, believe me. But I do like people who know how to stand up for themselves. You've just earned a lot of credit with me. I just wish

I seen this aspect of your character sooner. Now, let's hear what you have to say."

The door opened, and the secretary came in carrying a tray with two cups of coffee and a box of donuts. When her back was to her boss, she widened her eyes at Julie with a mute question. Julie smiled at her.

"When you two are done with the pantomime, I'd like to get back to the matter at hand."

The secretary, flushed with embarrassment, lowered her head and quickly left the room.

Julie looked back at the district attorney. "I hope you realize no one tampered with Bale's DNA tests. When the results came in, I was in complete shock. The only possible explanation was human error. But two things kept bothering me. The first —How did Bale's attorney know the DNA test would be erroneous? After all, if Bale had alibis for the murders, he would have presented them before trial. Trusting his client and gambling on a repeated test that could potentially bury his client, is the kind of rookie mistake a veteran like O'Shea would not have made. The second — Why did the two facial reconstruction tests we ran on the two DNA samples yield the same results?"

The district attorney looked at her intensely, hoping she'd get to the point soon.

"Yesterday, I received a call from a man I didn't know. It turns out he is the CEO of a company engaged in genetic research. Around the time of Bale's arrest, one of his employees was mugged and his company's intellectual property was stolen. The police did not think there was any connection between the robbery and the technology theft, but the CEO, afraid of losing his company, refused to give up and continued to investigate. The things that he told me made my blood run cold."

Time stood still. When Julie finished describing everything she had learned from Ronnie, she sat quietly, waiting for Brandon Palmer to speak.

"What do you think we should do? The way I see it, we can't afford to let the world find out what happened, so we are prevented from bringing Bale to trial again. On the other hand, he's a monster and we can't let him stay on the streets. If I know Bale, he'll put this technology on the market, and soon we'll be facing the same problem again." The district attorney's words were clipped, and it seemed as though he had aged several years over the course of the discussion.

"I have a plan. I think it's better that you don't know the details. If I get caught, you don't need to take the fall with me. Once you hear what's going on, you'll understand my plan is underway. That will be when I'll need all the support you can give me. If you agree, this conversation never happened."

"Take a donut for the road." Palmer smiled at her, tore up the envelope containing her resignation letter, and tossed it in the wastepaper basket.

CHAPTER 62

Gadi walked into the apartment and set the groceries on the kitchen table, then he took out a prepaid phone from his pocket and switched it on.

Ronnie looked at him with curiosity. "What's that for?"

"I was doing some shopping at the Stop & Shop. I saw they were selling disposable cell phones, and it gave me an idea. After I took out the two intruders in my hotel room, I checked their pockets. They each had a burner phone. I went through the call logs to see if I could figure out what this was all about. There wasn't much in there, in fact, each of them had only received two calls in the week before the attack. All the calls were from the same number. Other than that, the phones didn't have messages of any type. Apparently, those two weren't exactly social butterflies.

"I thought it might be a good idea to call that number and see who answers. The chances they'd answer are slim, but what have we got to lose? Anyway, I figured it was best to use an untraceable phone for my experiment. One we will destroy right after the call. What do you say?"

Juanita entered the kitchen and immediately joined the conversation. "About what?"

"About Ronnie doing all the grocery shopping from now on. There are just too many types of milk here in America. I wanted to slit my wrists by the time I was able to make a decision which of them to buy."

"Get out of here, both of you." She laughed as they raised their hands submissively and turned to go to the balcony.

Gadi searched through the notes he'd written in his cell phone, found the number, dialed, and switched the phone to speaker mode so Ronnie could listen as well. They could hear the phone ringing over and over. Gadi said, "Well, it was worth a—"

"You've reached Robert O'Shea. Please leave a message, and I'll get back to you as soon as I can."

Gadi looked at Ronnie, grinning. "Are you thinking what I'm thinking?"

"Robert O'Shea was Bale's lawyer during the trial. If we needed any more proof Bale was behind everything that's happened, we've got it."

The two went to the computer and watched, for the umpteenth time, the interview Bale had given to the independent journalist. They ran the interview nearly to the end and listened very carefully. "*How could I possibly know?*" they heard Bale's voice. "*If I knew who killed Robert O'Shea, my longtime friend, I promise you I'd turn him over to the authorities. Such a man deserves to be punished to the full extent of the law.*"

Worry spread across Ronnie's face. "It looks like Bale is covering his tracks by killing everyone who was part of his plan. I think that from this moment on, we must assume Bale knows about us. He tried to kill you once, and he'll try to do it again. If he finds out about my meeting with Julie Wilson, we'll all be in danger, including Liah and Juanita."

Gadi took the battery out of the disposable phone then smashed the device and tossed it into the wastebasket in Sam's study. "We need to stay clear of our wives until this is over. I don't want either of them hurt."

"I'll check with Sam to see if he has another vacation property far from here, somewhere we could send Liah and Juanita."

"Send who where?" asked Juanita, who was standing by the door, listening.

"Ronnie and I are convinced your lives are in danger, so we've decided to move you to a safe hiding place."

The ladle that hurtled through the air missed his head by less than an inch, landed with a clatter, and left a grease spot on the floor. "I'm not going anywhere!" She tossed a towel at Gadi. "Now clean that up!"

CHAPTER 63

"What's going on?" Liah was startled to see Juanita returning to the kitchen with an angry scowl.

"Our husbands are both paranoid. That's the only way to explain their behavior. Go talk to them before I kill them both." Juanita couldn't calm down.

"Now what?" Liah looked at Ronnie, who was sitting pensively at the desk, ignoring Gadi, who was busy wiping grease off the floor. Ronnie raised his head and looked into her eyes. The tranquility he saw in them surprised him. He cocked his head at her, and she sat on his lap and wrapped her arm around his shoulder while he told her what they had just discovered.

"Right now, we have two options. The first — hope they haven't tracked us to Keyport, leave you and Juanita here, while Gadi and I go back to New York. This would draw the fire away from here. The second — assume the worst has happened and we hide you somewhere far from us until the danger is over. Only if we know you two are safe will we be able to focus on the complicated task facing us. And before you say anything, yes, the police and other law enforcement authorities are already involved. I assume Julie Wilson has the wheels of the legal system moving, but I don't believe me, my family, or my company are at the top of her to-do list. Right now, all she cares about is seeing Bale behind bars.

And our two amazing and incredible pregnant women are not a priority."

"No problem." Liah surprised him with her continued calm. "Sam is supposed to come back home soon. We can talk to him about where we should go. I only hope he can find somewhere in the Caribbean for us, or at least Florida, if we have to compromise." She smiled in an attempt to ease the tension. "Leave Juanita to me, I'll explain to her that ignoring the problem or assigning blame won't solve anything."

Liah rose with difficulty and left the room.

The sound of a whispered exchange coming from the kitchen followed.

"Ronnie, if anything happens to Juanita or Liah, I'll never be able to forgive myself. We have to do something and do it fast. Waiting for Sam is not an option as far as I'm concerned. I want to take them to the airport right now. When Sam gets back, consult with him about where we should fly, and I'll buy the tickets on the spot. Since the banks are closed, I assume you don't have any way of withdrawing a few thousand dollars in cash. I'll just use Juanita's credit card. I'm not sure how much she has in her American bank account. Could you wire some money there?"

"Give me the bank account details, and I'll wire twenty thousand dollars right away. The girls should have no problem buying tickets anywhere in the U.S. or staying in the luxury hotel of their choosing."

Moments later Liah returned with Juanita. It looked like the drama was over for the time being.

Juanita went to her husband and kissed his cheek. "I'm sorry," she whispered, her eyes lowered.

"I love you," he replied and pressed her to him with a tight hug.

Ronnie updated the women on the plan.

"We'll have to pack," the two said in a single voice then burst into laughter together.

"There's no time." Gadi spoiled the minor celebration.

"Take it easy, Gadi. If they knew where we were staying, they'd be here already." Liah sounded less amused. "Another hour to pack won't change anything."

"An hour to pack? Show me what you want packed, and I'll do it for you in a minute," he said tensely.

"Packing is the easy part. Deciding what to bring is what takes up most of the hour," Liah teased him, desperately trying to maintain a playful atmosphere.

"Women…" Gadi sighed, relaxing a bit.

"Men…" Juanita sighed theatrically and flung up her hands.

"Shhh." Gadi's face turned serious. He rose quickly and motioned for the others to keep quiet. His sudden intensity did its job, and utter silence followed. None of them moved a muscle. Their eyes followed Gadi, who walked in silent, measured steps to the front door. The only sound in the apartment was the monotonous ticking of the grandfather clock in the other room.

Gadi placed his hand on the doorknob, which began to turn.

CHAPTER 64

Sam squeezed out of the taxi. He gripped his suitcase with one hand and gave the driver a few bills for the ride from the airport with the other. He didn't even hear the driver saying thanks. Since leaving California, his mind had been preoccupied with his business. The decline everyone had predicted for shopping mall sales thanks to the ever-increasing stream of customers who preferred to do their shopping online, had begun to take its toll on the ability of his clients to uphold their contractual obligations. Too often during this last business trip, he'd had to use various threats to force them to make good on their commitments. His representatives who ran his businesses day to day had long warned him about the deterioration in payment ethics. "Ethics" was a word he had never applied to the business world. As far as he was concerned, the principles were clear and simple: Contracts had to be honored to the letter.

Sam stepped into the building lobby and nodded to the guard at the station like he always did. The guard said something about his lady guest, but Sam ignored him. If Juanita or Liah had done something out of line, the guard could just take it up with them himself. The elevator was waiting, and he dragged his suitcase inside, slipping through the closing door at the last moment. In his heart of hearts, he hoped his guests weren't in the apartment. More than anything he needed a warm bath and some rest. *Age has finally caught up with me*, he tiredly thought.

The elevator door slid open, and Sam stepped out into the hallway and headed for his apartment. While he was fumbling in his pocket for the key, he felt the cold blade of a knife pressed against his throat.

The voice of the woman standing behind him was even colder. "Thanks for your help. Now take out the keys and open the door slowly. Don't do anything stupid, I'm sure you know a quick slitting of the throat has a brutal impact on the vocal chords as well."

"You're making a mistake," he hoped his voice sounded steady.

"Shh… not another word. I have no interest in you, otherwise you'd be dead already. But if you force me, I'll be more than happy to kill you along with everybody inside. Right now, your survival depends on my good mood, so I strongly suggest you keep me happy by cooperating." She pressed the knife harder, and he felt a drizzle of warm blood trickling down his neck.

"Settle down, I'm taking out the key." Sam bent a little to reach in his pocket. As he did, the pressure of the knife against his neck eased off dramatically. Without hesitation, he snapped his head back. A sickening crunch was heard as his skull crashed against the attacker's nasal bones. She uttered no sound, but her grip weakened slightly. He quickly turned around in the hope of escaping, but he stumbled over the suitcase. The sudden pain in his back was excruciating. The keys slipped from his fingers and he fell to his knees with his hands twitching. The last thing he felt before his face met the floor was a sharp stinging as the knife was drawn out of his back.

Kate bent, wiped the knife on Sam's shirt, returned it to its sheath, then took the keys from the floor. She fiddled with the key ring, searching for the right one. She'd already drawn her pistol, and it was hanging casually by her thigh, silencer at her knee. She would kill the CEO and whomever else she found in the apartment with a precise shot to the forehead. She decided she'd have a little fun with the arrogant detective though, perhaps even a lot of fun, as long as he didn't make too much noise. She found the apartment key and gently inserted it into the lock, when the door in front of her quickly opened.

Gadi stood in front of her, his eyes wide at the sight of the gun barrel directed straight at his chest. Out of the corner of his eye, he saw a man lying flat on the floor in the hall, blood seeping from his back.

A twisted smile rose to Kate's blood-smeared face. "Gadi, right? I'd heard Israelis were renowned for their hospitality, but I never, not in my wildest dreams, expected you to open the door and invite me in to rid the world of you and your annoying—"

Gadi reached out and violently torqued the forearm above her gun hand. Sharp crackling followed, as the bones in her wrist shattered from the brutal twisting. The gun fell to the floor. Gadi quickly struck at Kate's sternum, but she managed to evade him and kicked his groin. His entire body turned into a bundle of pulsating pain. As Gadi doubled over, taking sharp breaths, Kate turned on her heel with the grace of a ballerina and hurled the side of her leg toward his temple. He quickly ducked even lower and dealt a powerful kick to her ankles. The force of the blow made her fall on her injured hand. They both crouched on the floor, breathing hard. The pistol that had fallen from Kate's hand glinted to their left. Sam looked at them with hollow eyes. The blood continued to ooze from his back.

If blood is flowing, it means his heart is still beating, thought Gadi. *I have to end this quickly.*

Kate demonstrated no outward sign of the terrible pain she must have been suffering. "You're better than I thought. It would be exquisitely entertaining to kill you and then slowly torture the woman standing behind you."

Gadi started to turn his head, when Kate launched her attack. Juanita's scream made him step aside, and the kick Kate had aimed at him from an impossible angle merely glanced off his temple. Gadi scrambled to his feet. Kate's right side, he knew, was more vulnerable. Her broken hand wouldn't allow her to defend herself properly. He flanked her from the right, blocking her path to the pistol. Kate moved with surprising speed. Instead of trying to grab the gun, she rolled to the other side and drew her knife. Still rolling on the ground, she flicked it at Gadi.

Gadi, on his way to pick up the gun, was unable to change direction, and the knife lodged in his thigh. He collapsed to the floor and with sheer force of will, grabbed the pistol and fired a volley of shots at Kate. Astonishment spread over her face when the first bullet hit her chest. She died before the next three hit home.

Through the mists of pain, Gadi felt Juanita's hands stroking his head and heard Liah giving orders, the instincts of the physician she was, overcoming her fear and shock.

"Ronnie, call for two ambulances while I start with the necessary first aid."

"Keep the baby safe," muttered Gadi before losing consciousness.

CHAPTER 65

Ronnie Saar closed his eyes. The adrenaline had long since drained from his body. He needed every last ounce of will power he could gather to keep focused on the tasks at hand and force himself not to follow Gadi and Sam to the hospital. The sight of Juanita sitting on the living room floor in shock and Liah spattered with Sam's blood, her eyes wild, made him understand what was important right now. He had to move them to a safe place before they were exposed to another attack. He was no longer fighting merely for the future of his company. This had become a battle for his life and the life of his loved ones. It was clear Bale wouldn't stop until they were all dead. The single telephone call he'd managed to make before the apartment was flooded with police officers and paramedics was to Julie Wilson.

"Which one of you is Dr. Saar?" he heard a voice calling. A man of about forty-five stood a short distance away. He was about six feet tall, with a slim figure and hair that grayed at the temples. A major's insignia glinted on his uniform.

Ronnie raised his hand, and the major approached him. He gave Ronnie a penetrating look, examining him with interest. "My name is Major Hardy, from the New Jersey State Police, and I'm in charge of this investigation. You must be a very important man to have the New York State Attorney General ask his counterpart here in New

Jersey to provide you with anything you need, no questions asked. He made it clear that he personally vouches for you."

Ronnie decided to forgo the niceties. "Do you have a hiding place, somewhere where you keep government witnesses safe?"

The major looked at him with surprise. "You've been watching too many movies. We call such places maximum security prisons here. Why are you asking?"

"I need to keep my wife and the wife of my injured friend away from any potential risk. They're both pregnant." He wasn't sure why he added that last bit of information.

Hardy hesitated for a moment, then rummaged around in his pockets. He finally took out a heavy key ring that reminded Ronnie of a school janitor's. He detached two keys, scribbled something on the back of a business card, and handed them to Ronnie. "On the back of the card you'll find the address of a summer house belonging to my wife's parents. They're long past the age where they enjoy going out there, so they handed it over to us. The kind of hours I'm working, we haven't gotten the chance to drive up there even once." A rueful smile crossed his face. "I think they'd be happy to hear the house was being put to good use. Don't worry, I'll tell them only after the fact," he added when he saw the worried creases on Ronnie's forehead.

"Thank you." Ronnie shook the major's hand. "I hope I'll be able to repay you one day."

"You do know attempting to bribe a state official is illegal." Hardy gave him a serious look.

"No, I just…" Ronnie started to answer but stopped when he saw a smile curving the corners of the policeman's mouth. Ronnie smiled with embarrassment. "Excuse me. I seem to have lost my sense of humor. I guess having a family member fighting for his life and a best friend in the hospital with stab wounds will do that to a man."

Hardy gave him a reassuring pat on the shoulder. "I'll send a patrol car to the underground parking lot. Get the women down there, and the patrol car will take you out of the building so you won't need to face the journalists lurking outside or, possibly, one of the attacker's allies who might have stayed behind." He paused for a moment, hesitating. "On second thought, I'll ask the officer to take you all the way to the summer house."

"I really don't know how to thank you enough."

"Well, for starters, coming back and telling me what the hell happened here and who's behind all this would be a great help."

"I promise to do everything in my power to help," answered Ronnie, recalling Wilson's warning not to even hint to anyone about Bale's involvement in the incident. He knew that he needed time to think of some story that would make sense, yet still remain fair to the lawman who was going out of his way to help him.

The drive went by quickly, and once the girls were settled in the luxurious cabin, the police officer volunteered to drive Ronnie to the hospital.

Hanging around the hospital waiting room was nerve racking, but fatigue soon got the upper hand and Ronnie fell asleep on an uncomfortable sofa.

"Mr. Saar?" he heard a voice above him.

He opened his eyes and quickly got to his feet, looking anxiously at the weary doctor.

"I'm glad to tell you Mr. Storm is out of danger. He's been trans-ferred to the intensive care unit, but I assume we'll discharge him to the regular post-op ward, where you'll be able to visit him, in about twelve hours. He was very lucky, if I may add. I understand he was involved in a fight or an assault. I'm not a forensic physician, but judging from the angle in which the knife was stuck in his back, I'm willing to bet he tripped just as the knife entered his body. If the blade had continued straight down from the penetration point, it would have torn his heart in half. Whoever stabbed him possessed a thorough knowledge of anatomy or was extremely adept in hand-to-hand armed combat."

"Thank you, doctor, both for the good news and for saving his life."

"I don't know who took care of him immediately following the injury, but whoever did was truly the one who saved his life."

"It was my wife. She's a doctor," Ronnie said with a hint of pride in his voice.

"Well then, if she's looking for a job, please promise you'll send her to me first." The doctor smiled pleasantly and went on his way.

Ronnie took the elevator down and walked to the emergency room. Gadi was lying in bed, his thigh adorned with an oversized bandage.

"Twenty stitches," he told Ronnie as soon as he saw him getting close. "If I hadn't broken her wrist in the beginning of the fight, she'd have taken me without breaking a sweat. There's no dirty trick in the book that girl didn't know." There was real admiration in his voice.

"Yes, but she's dead, and you're going to be a father sometime this year." Ronnie smiled tiredly.

"Where are they? You know the danger hasn't passed yet." Gadi tried to sit but instantly fell flat on his back, his face twisting with pain.

Ronnie told him about Major Hardy and the help he'd offered.

"Wow. That would never have happened back home." He chuckled. "We don't have any cops with golden hearts. Plus, no civil servant can afford a summer house. Or any other house, for that matter."

"The girls are safe. You are going to stay in the hospital for another day, and Sam will be in the intensive care unit at least until tomorrow. If I don't catch some sleep soon, I'll probably end up in intensive care too. I'm going to check into some random hotel, but tomorrow morning I have to get to work. I have a few important meetings that can't be postponed. Considering Double N's delicate situation, I can't demonstrate any signs of distress. Once I finish with my meetings, I'll come to discharge you from the hospital, so together we can decide on our next steps." He gave Ronnie's bandaged leg an amused look. "In light of your current situation, perhaps that wasn't the best of phrases to use. See you tomorrow." He patted Gadi's leg gently and headed out.

"We still need to find out who stole that information from your company," Gadi called after him. His loud voice annoyed a passing nurse, and her angry glare made him shut his mouth. *I think I know who's involved in the theft*, thought Gadi, *and you're not going to like it, not one little bit.* He followed his friend's broad back as Ronnie disappeared through the sliding doors.

CHAPTER 66

Monday morning's schedule was full of meetings with investors. Derek Taylor, the sole original investor remaining, had managed to get some friends from other VC funds excited, and a positive atmosphere prevailed throughout the discussions.

At the end of each meeting, Ronnie tried to get hold of Michelle, his secretary, but to no avail. Her disappearance had started to nag at him. Since she had begun working at Double N, she hadn't come to work late even once. It was Michelle who'd updated him about today's last-minute changes in his schedule and made sure he had all the background material provided by Derek. She had even called him the day before and reassured him she intended to arrive at the office early. Now it was already noontime and there was still no sign of Michelle. The employee he'd sent to her apartment returned and told him he'd buzzed her door for a long time but got no answer. Even though he could think of no possible connection between the attack on his loved ones and Michelle's disappearance, Ronnie could not get over the idea something bad had happened to her.

Thinking about last night reminded him he hadn't called Wilson to thank her for her help yet. He dialed her number.

"Yes, Ronnie. Is it important? I'm crazy busy." An urgent conversation was heard in the background.

"I just wanted to thank you for all your help yesterday and assure you that I haven't shared my suspicions with the police."

"Excellent, and you don't need to thank me, you earned it. I'll talk to you later. There's been a very interesting development regarding the subject we're both interested in. I may need your help. Bye for now." She disconnected the call without waiting for his reply.

"What did you think about today's meetings?" Derek stepped into his office with a pleased smile.

"They went even better than anticipated. It looks like you did a great job preparing your colleagues. It seemed like all of them, except for one perhaps, were instantly willing to invest in the company."

"You're right, I did prepare them well," Derek said lightly then he turned serious. "But, and correct me if I'm wrong, all through the discussions I got the feeling you were stalling and that perhaps you're not really interested in my colleagues' investments. Unfortunately, that was also how they felt. If that's the case, I think it would have been decent of you to inform me of this change of attitude before I pulled all those strings and called in all those favors. I came into today's meetings with the understanding we needed to raise at least fifteen million dollars and came out of feeling utterly confused. Perhaps you'd care to explain?"

Ronnie gave Derek a dispassionate look. "I'm sorry if that's how you feel, Derek. I'm still interested in raising the amount we agreed upon, perhaps even more. But it is exactly because they're your friends that I feel guilty about withholding some important information. Both from them and from you. You're right that I should do the decent thing."

Derek nervously crossed his arms on his chest. "What do you

mean you're withholding some important information from me?"

"What I'm about to tell you must remain in this room." Ronnie watched for agreement in Derek's eyes.

"All right." Derek's voice rose on the last word, making it almost a question and signaled at Ronnie to continue.

"Last night, there was an attempt on my life. The assailant also tried to murder Sam, whom you know, and Gadi, my friend. My wife and Gadi's wife were also present at the time of the attack. Sam was severely injured and is currently in intensive care. It was only Gadi's courage and skills that saved us. Gadi himself was injured in the struggle and needed quite a few stitches in his thigh. He too, is still hospitalized. Until we understand who is behind these attacks and until we are able to neutralize them, I feel that I would be betraying a trust by taking any money from investors."

Derek looked at him open-mouthed.

"I meant to tell you about it before the meetings, but I simply didn't find the opportunity. I'm sorry if I've caused you any discomfort."

"A murder attempt?" Derek came to his senses. "What is going on with this company?"

"I believe this has something to do with the information theft and the attack on Simon. Gadi and I have no intention of giving up our investigation. I guess we stepped on the right toes, and the people behind the robbery decided to strike back. I already have my suspicions regarding their reasons for stealing our information, but I've no idea who actually stole it. I'm in contact with the DA's office in New York and am currently cooperating with them, but they forbade me from giving any additional information."

Neither of them spoke for the next few minutes. It was apparent that Derek found the information extremely difficult to digest. "Are you saying that my life is in danger as well? If Sam, another investor, was attacked and severely injured should I assume I am to next on their list?"

"I don't believe you are in any danger. Sam just happened to be there. We were all guests in his apartment for the weekend while he was away on a business trip. He was unfortunate enough to return from the trip just as the murderess decided to strike. It was completely unrelated to him being an investor in the company."

"Did you just say 'murderess'?"

"It's a long story. As I said, I can't provide any more details right now."

Derek cleared his throat several times but was unable to speak. Finally, he rose and stood on trembling feet. "I'm sorry, Ronnie. I'm just not sure this is what I signed up for when I decided to continue to support Double N. I need some time to rethink all this mess. I promise to share my decision with you soon."

He left the room, while Ronnie remained seated with his eyes on the floor. The world around him had crumbled more than once, but this was the first time he had no idea how to cope with the situation. The phone on his desk seemed to scream and startled him out of his chair.

"Ronnie Saar," he answered.

The caller's statement was short and sharp. When he was finished and the call ended, Ronnie remained seated in his chair, his face deathly pale. Suddenly, his situation just a minute before seemed like heaven when compared to the new world he found himself in.

CHAPTER 67

When he arrived at the hospital to pick up Gadi, Ronnie was told Sam was still in the intensive care unit. Respiratory complications, the nurse told him. "Not uncommon in such injuries. There's nothing for you to do here. We have your phone number, and we'll let you know once he's transferred to the other ward."

Gadi's discharge was quick and efficient. The medical staff said Gadi must be in a wheelchair until they left the hospital grounds. Ronnie helped Gadi climb into the leased SUV and carefully placed his injured leg inside the cabin. He closed the door, and with Gadi's eyes following him with concern, walked around the car and climbed into the driver's seat.

"All right, you're way too quiet, Ronnie, talk to me." Gadi's face contorted with pain as he shifted in his seat to observe his friend more closely.

"Michelle was found dead in a hotel room. I wasn't given any other details. I don't know if she was alone, if it was a natural death or a murder. Nothing. I tried to get hold of Wilson, but she doesn't answer my calls. My heart goes out to that poor girl. If it turns out her death has anything to do with something we or the company did, I'll never be able to forgive myself."

"Got it. And your solution is to wallow in depression and self-pity. Fantastic. Wake me up once you snap out of it." Gadi leaned his head back and shut his eyes.

"Because being insensitive and sarcastic is better?" Ronnie struck the wheel with both hands.

Gadi opened his eyes. "All I'm saying is that we don't have the luxury of sinking into depression. You can't know for sure that her death had anything to do with her job. On the other hand, these people have tried to eliminate us several times already. So right now, I suggest we both get a little 'insensitive' and start doing some serious investigating. Unfortunately, my leg is killing me, so I'll need your help. If you can't help me, hire someone who can.

"Juanita, Liah, and both our unborn children need us. So, with all due respect — while I'm not about to start whining — for the first time in my life, I am afraid. Not for myself, but for the people I care about most in the world. So, what's it going to be? Are you going to help me in trying to help you, or am I on my own in this fucking investigation?"

A smile lit up Ronnie's face. "Gadi, I love you. Thanks, I needed that wake-up call. Ok, what's next?"

"I suggest we start at the office. I'll go through Michelle's desk and see if I can find anything. I don't have much hope of actually finding anything, but it's time for a consistent, step-by-step, thorough investigation. After all, someone must have told Simon's attackers when he left the office. There's a good chance it was Michelle."

"Are you kidding?"

"That's one of the options. We'll check it out first and move on if that's not correct."

"I see that you already have it figured out. Who do you think the other options are?"

"Let's start with Michelle and take it from there." Gadi refused to elaborate.

A brand-new wheelchair waited for them at the entrance of the Double N building. Gadi reached out with his hand to make it easier on his friend, who helped him to the chair. Moments later, he found himself behind Michelle's desk.

"Looks like the woman had no secrets, at least none that she kept in the office. All the drawers are open, nothing's locked. Everything looks innocent. Leave me here, and I'll call you when I'm finished." Gadi did not wait for Ronnie to leave before he began to systematically go through the stuff in Michelle's drawers.

An hour passed and Ronnie, overcome with impatience, returned to Michelle's workstation. "Have you found anything?"

Gadi spread out a series of pictures of Michelle with another young woman about her age. Most of the pictures had a golden beach as their background, while the rest had been taken in various locations, most of them unfamiliar to Ronnie and Gadi. "Do you have any idea who the other girl is?"

"Yes. I went by her cubicle once and she happened to be looking at one of those pictures. For some strange reason, she became apologetic and embarrassed, as though I had caught her doing something wrong. She said the woman was her best friend, who'd moved to Denver after her husband got a tempting job offer and left Michelle in New York all alone and lonely. She told me she had often considered leaving everything behind and moving to Denver but knew her friend's husband wouldn't take it well. She had tears in her eyes when she told me the story. I believe the story was true and painful for her."

"Hmm…" Gadi suddenly looked preoccupied. "Perhaps this

explains who took their pictures."

Ronnie took another look. "I don't see anything odd about these photos. This is the Michelle we had all grown fond of. She was always cheerful and loved to be the center of attention."

"Can I keep these pictures?"

"I'm afraid the police will probably want them."

"We'll split them, then," said Gadi indifferently, examining a few of the pictures and pocketing them. The rest, he placed back in the desk's top drawer.

Ronnie looked at him, barely able to restrain his laughter. "You'll never change, will you?"

"Who knows, maybe once I'm a father. Right now, there's no immediate change on the horizon. Now I'd like to search the drawers and phones of the rest of the staff. I'm sure you think this violates their basic right to privacy, and this is where you come in. As the workplace belongs to the company, I can do it of course on your authority, but I'd like to see their reaction when you ask for their permission."

After a split second of hesitation, Ronnie turned away with an exasperated expression. "You wait here and do nothing before I come back."

A few minutes later, Ronnie returned to the lobby, followed by every one of Double N's employees. They exchanged baffled looks at the sight of Gadi in his wheelchair with his leg in a brace and wrapped in blood-spotted bandages then looked back at their boss as he began to speak.

"I'll try to be brief. I'm about to ask you something that you'll all think I have no right to be asking. But first, let me give you some background. Yesterday, there was an attempt on my life, and possibly, the lives of my family. Had it not been for my friend Gadi here, who, as you can see, was injured during the struggle, I wouldn't be standing here talking to you."

Time seemed to have slowed. No one in the lobby moved or said a word.

"And if that were not enough, a few hours ago, Michelle was found dead in a hotel room." Ronnie paused and looked from one employee to another as hands pressed to mouths gaping with shock and eyes widened with fear. "This has to stop. Therefore, I ask that you allow Gadi, who is a licensed PI, to search the contents of your desk drawers and check your phones. If any of you has a locked drawer or cabinet, I'd appreciate your cooperation in opening it. Same applies for your phone's security code. I truly don't believe any of you are involved, but in order to move on, we must clear you of suspicion. After giving it much thought, I reached the conclusion that at this stage I do not want to involve the authorities and asked Gadi for his help. Now I'm asking for your help as well. Please let me know if I have your consent for making this drastic, yet necessary move."

A commotion filled the reception area as all the employees simultaneously voiced their opinions. Ronnie raised his hand for silence.

"I have absolutely no problem with that," Simon shouted into the sudden quiet.

One by one, they all gave their permission for the search and placed their personal cell phones on Michelle's desk.

"I really appreciate your willingness to cooperate. I give you my word, nothing that is found will be made known to me, unless Gadi believes it to be directly connected to the terrible events I've just described.

"For those of you who are not familiar with him, allow me to formally introduce Gadi Abutbul, my best friend, a former military police detective, and the owner of a private detective agency. I assure you, if anyone can solve this mystery, it's Gadi. We can use this unexpected free time to convene in the conference room. I think it's high time I updated you on fundraising and several other administrative subjects I've wanted to share with you for a while."

"Simon" — Gadi turned to the first employee who had agreed to the search— "I have very limited mobility right now. Would you mind accompanying me and helping me move around? I will see to it that Ronnie briefs you later on."

Simon nodded and began to push the wheelchair.

Balance sheets, graphs, and charts were displayed on the screen. Presentations came and went. Hours passed, and people had begun to shift restlessly in their chairs when Gadi finally showed up, pushed by Simon.

"Thank you. I'm sure you'll be happy to learn that I haven't found anything suspicious. I'd like to thank you all again and offer Simon a special thank you for his kind help. By the way, Simon, could you please stay with Ronnie and me for another minute?"

The others left the room and the door closed behind them.

Gadi did not wait a second. "Simon, forgive me for being blunt, but is it possible your attacker was a woman?"

The scientist's face reddened in embarrassment. "A woman? Didn't you see what I looked like after the attack?"

"I'm skilled in several martial arts, and this is the way I look after being attacked by a skillful female assassin. So, put the macho attitude aside for a moment and try to remember. You described your attacker as being skinny, perhaps emaciated, tall. Perhaps it was a taller than average woman? Try to remember the way your assailant moved, walked, or anything else that might help us identify him or her."

Simon glanced at Ronnie briefly, then pursed his lips, straining to recall the events of that terrible evening. "Now that you bring up the possibility, I'm starting to think the attacker did have ballerina-like movements. The blows covered me like a swarm of bees. And…" He paused for a moment and scratched his receding hairline.

Ronnie and Gadi both waited patiently.

"And he, or she, had this hoarse, fiendish laugh I'll never forget." A tear trickled from his eye. "Now I know that she took sadistic pleasure in beating me."

"She's dead. She can't hurt you anymore." Ronnie patted his shoulder and wheeled Gadi out of the room.

Simon remained by himself, staring at the white wall in front of him.

CHAPTER 68

Julie Wilson and Brandon Palmer sat quietly in Palmer's office, their uncomfortable expressions indicating just how problematic it would be to approve the plan she had just outlined.

"And why do you think Homeland Security would be interested in this subject?"

"I have no idea. Perhaps they've come across a similar death in one of their own investigations. Perhaps they believe a terrorist organization is involved. But we shouldn't be wasting time on speculation." Julie sat up a little taller in her seat and peeked through the transparent glass panel running across the milky glass door. Two men wearing black suits, white shirts, and polished black shoes were standing in the lobby next to the DA's office. *Amazing how much they look like their stereotypical movie portrayals*, she thought.

There was a light tapping on the door, followed by the soft creaking of the door hinges, as the DA's secretary ushered the two guests into his office.

"Something to drink?" She examined them with curiosity.

"Coffee, black, two sugars."

The other agent raised two fingers to indicate he wanted the same.

The four shook hands, exchanged business cards, and took their seats at a round table in the corner of the room.

"Two days ago, the body of a young woman was found in a Manhattan hotel room." Julie decided to take the initiative. "The postmortem yielded two facts. The first, before her death, the woman had sexual intercourse without a condom. We took a DNA sample of the sperm and identified the owner with one hundred percent certainty. The second, the cause of death was arterial aneurysm in a large number of blood vessels, a kind of orchestrated, simultaneous collapse. Our medical examiner recalled a memo from DHS asking to be notified of any cases like that. He followed through, and I assume that is what brought you two here. We would love to hear why you are interested in this particular cause of death."

The two agents engaged in a silent, eye-to-eye conversation. "Who was the victim? Was she a member of any law enforcement agency?" The agent, completely ignoring Wilson's question, responded with one of his own.

"Michelle Herrington. She had no connection to any law enforcement agency."

"I'd like to ask that a pathologist working for us be allowed to review your findings."

"Gladly."

"Thank you." The two rose and turned to the door.

"Sit back down," the district attorney's voice thundered. "I'm not impressed by your games. Mess with me, and the next thing you know, the New York State Attorney General will be on the phone to the Director of National Intelligence. I think he would be disappointed to hear the different security agencies under his command are unable to cooperate, won't he—" he glanced at their business cards "—Agents Ferguson and Tucker." The two hesitated for the blink of an eye then returned and sat down.

"Getting back to my question." Wilson smiled at them, trying to lighten the mood, "What's your interest in this?"

"Several months ago, our retinal scanning detection system denied an employee entry to the building where he had worked for several years. Since a retinal eye print cannot be altered, we conducted a thorough DNA examination of the man in question. The examination yielded more strange results. Before we were able to question him, he collapsed and died. The cause of death was similar to your victim's."

Julie was unable to contain her enthusiasm. "What do you mean by 'strange results'? Did the DNA test results contradict the ones in your database, or—" she paused for a moment, afraid to ask the next question "—or did you discover a phenomenon called chimerism? Did the man have two different sets of DNA in his body?"

The agents shifted nervously in their chair their eyes widening with surprise. Even their extensive training could not have prepared them for Julie's question. It was one of their agency's best-kept secrets. "How did you know that?" Tucker erupted.

"How did I know what?" Wilson feigned innocence, taking a prosecutor's professional pleasure in watching her tactics make professionals lose their composure.

"That the man had two sets of DNA."

"I guessed. And my next guess is that the hair and inner cheek cell samples yielded different results than the blood tests."

"Since you have no way of knowing that, I assume you have come across a similar case," Ferguson said, his voice an impressive baritone.

"Indeed. Allow me to bring you up to speed and share with you the problem we are faced with." Julie's smile was gone. No more fun and games.

An hour later, after she had gone through, point by point, the explanation she had gotten from Ronnie Saar, Julie summed up, "In order to make the problem go away permanently, we need your assistance."

The two agents nodded their agreement. "We'll do anything we can to help."

CHAPTER 69

It was 9:00 am when a knock on the door made Ronnie and Gadi tense up.

"Just don't tell me it's another assassin." Gadi made a face. "Haven't they learned their lesson yet?"

Ronnie looked through the peephole. A police officer was standing outside holding a handwritten sign, which he raised for Ronnie to see. It said: *By the DA's order, I'm responsible for your safety.*

Ronnie unlocked the door and opened it. "Thank you. Would you like to come inside?"

"No, but if you could spare a chair, that would be great."

Ronnie handed him a chair and the officer left.

"I need to talk to you about something important." Gadi had turned serious.

"Talk." Ronnie lay on the couch and covered his face with his arm. "My eyes are burning from exhaustion. I hope you don't mind if I shut them for a couple of minutes. You can be sure I'll be listening to your every word."

"As I've already told you, I was unable to find any clear proof that any of your employees acted against the company. Honestly, I didn't expect to find anything. We've known for a long time that we are faced with a highly sophisticated organization. As a professional investigator, it would have been insulting, nice, but insulting, if I'd found a printed confession. I guess such miracles happen only in cheap thrillers. What I did find were internal Double N communications, correspondence between employees, and an endless number of pictures people keep on their phones, especially ones taken at various hangouts and tourist attractions here in America and around the world."

"Interesting information, but why are you telling me this?"

"For some reason, Americans like to take pictures of themselves with their car in the background. As I had nothing better to do, I copied the license plates from the pictures." Gadi took a handwritten list from his pocket. It contained three columns — employee name, license plate number, and vehicle owner. "I sent the list to your friend, Julie Wilson, and asked her to find the names of the vehicle owners for me. A short while ago, I got the information back from one of her assistants. I didn't really expect to find much, but I did learn one very intriguing bit of information."

Ronnie sat up, the fatigue instantly disappearing from his face.

"Most of the vehicles in the pictures," Gadi continued, "belonged to various leasing companies or to the employees themselves. What attracted my attention was a vehicle appearing frequently in the pictures of one employee but registered to someone who does not work for Double N, a man named Sean Young."

Ronnie looked flabbergasted. "Dr. Sean Young? From G-Pharma?"

"You know the guy?"

"Who doesn't? He's one of the most brilliant geneticists in the world. He is admired by everyone even remotely related to the field. He founded G-Pharma a few years ago, and soon the company became a worldwide industry leader. I believe that even Wyatt

Robinson's fund invested in them. In fact, when Wyatt had offered to invest in Double N, I questioned whether such an investment would not pose a conflict of interest for them. Only after they had committed to a complete compartmentalization of information, did I allow them to invest in my company."

"That didn't end too well, now did it?" Gadi smiled sadly.

"Right, but it's no use crying over spilled milk. At the time, they claimed most of G-Pharma's activities were related to drug research and development, while we at Double N are developing a technology allowing targeted drug delivery. In other words, they manufacture the explosives, while we create the missile's guidance system, so there is no conflict of interest between the two companies."

"But, should they get their hands on your technology, they would take over the market and become the industry's undisputed leader." Gadi was suddenly overcome with excitement.

"Hold on, Gadi" — Ronnie grabbed his arm — "whose pictures showed Young's car?"

Gadi ignored the question and turned his telephone screen to Ronnie. A slightly blurry image appeared on the screen. "Do you recognize this face?"

"It's Sean Young. Where did you get that?"

"It was reflected in the photographed person's glasses."

Ronnie looked like every last bit of strength had suddenly drained from his body. "Gadi," he pleaded, "what photographed person? In whose pictures did you find the reflection and the pictures of Young's car?"

Gadi lowered his eyes. "In the pictures Michelle left in her drawer. I believe that when you caught her staring at those pictures, she was actually focused on the reflection of her lover, who had taken them, and not on the girlfriend she claimed to miss so much."

Ronnie's eyes desperately sought any indication that Gadi was mistaken.

Gadi remained silent for a while. "Ronnie," he eventually said softly, "I know this is hard for you to swallow, but I need another favor from you, and please don't argue with me. I only ask you to trust my instincts and follow my instructions down to the last detail."

Ten minutes later, Ronnie left the apartment. He wasn't at all sure he would be able to keep his promise to Gadi.

CHAPTER 70

Ronnie hurried to the hospital elevators. Sam had been transferred to the fifth floor. Last night had been long and arduous, following Gadi's revelations earlier in the day. It would never have occurred to him that Michelle, that lively, seemingly trustworthy girl, could be involved in this. That she would be able to tell Young, her lover, about Simon — enabling his attack — was disturbing enough. But that she could then go and visit him in the hospital, demonstrating concern and sadness that seemed utterly genuine, was truly hard to accept.

The elevator doors opened, and Ronnie looked around for the right ward. The smiling nurse behind the reception desk referred him to room number eight and added, "Visiting hours end at nine, then the doctors' rounds begin."

Ronnie raised a hand in affirmation and hurried to Sam's room. His cousin was lying in a large bed attached to many tubes and wires. In this condition he looked nothing like the man Ronnie had come to love and appreciate.

"How are you feeling?" He held Sam's hand with concern.

A faint smile flashed on Sam's lips. "Amazing," he whispered. "Things can't get any better than this."

"The doctors say you are going to come out of this without any permanent damage. They say you were extremely lucky to have tripped just as the knife went in."

"Yes. Would you believe I owe my life to a suitcase?" A tremor laced his voice as he spoke.

Ronnie squeezed Sam's hand in an attempt to cheer him up. "It's all over now. It turns out Bale was indeed behind the information theft. He is going to be arrested sometime today. I don't know the exact details, but the prosecutor is convinced he can't possibly get out of this one. Additionally, Gadi discovered the identity of the person behind all the developments used to keep Bale from being convicted in his trial. And also—"

"Who is it?" Sam's whisper interrupted Ronnie's report. "Does he work for a competitor?"

"Yes. Someone from G-Pharma, a company whose activities overlap with ours. But it seems the man's actions were independent of the company itself. I believe that if we present the G-Pharma CEO with the facts, we will be able to get a written guarantee preventing them from using any of our information that might have leaked to other employees. Perhaps there is a silver lining to this sad business after all. This could turn into a fruitful future cooperation between the two companies. I'm very optimistic. Your investment in my company might yet yield you a lot of money."

"But how could they have known when Simon would be going out with all the information on his laptop?" Sam began to cough, and his entire body convulsed with pain.

Ronnie, worried, looked over at the monitors, which had begun to beep loudly. A nurse came running into the room. She examined Sam and reattached a sensor that had come loose. She gave Ronnie a scolding look. "He needs to rest. I suggest you say goodbye now."

"It's all right," Sam whispered. The nurse left the room, shaking her head reproachfully.

"Perhaps I should leave?" Ronnie stood to go.

Sam reached out a hand weakly. "Answer me one question first. You've always suspected an employee was involved. I very much hope you were proven wrong."

It was obvious Ronnie was having trouble bringing himself to speak, but his body language said it all. "I'm afraid I wasn't wrong. It was Michelle. We're still uncovering the exact details, and I still find it hard to believe Michelle betrayed us, but that is what it looks like right now."

Sam remained silent.

"All right, cousin, I'll leave you in peace now. Try to rest as much as possible."

"Hold on. I'm still processing what you just told me. Michelle is such a sociable, nice young woman. I find it hard to believe she is tangled up in this. What did she say when you confronted her?"

"Unfortunately, she was found dead last night in a hotel room. I guess we'll never know why."

"Dead? How?"

"From what I understand, she suffered a circulatory collapse of all major blood vessels in her body. She would have had no chance even if it had occurred in the hospital."

The monitors erupted into a fresh chorus of chirping.

Ronnie rose from his seat. "I'll come back later today. Do you need me to get you anything?"

Sam was pale and exhausted. "In the cabinet over there, you will find the clothes I wore when I was hospitalized. I believe my cell phone is in one of the pockets. Please take it out and put it under my pillow. Injured or not, I must continue to attend to my business affairs. And please don't argue, cousin," he continued in a feeble voice, seeing Ronnie was about to protest.

Ronnie placed the phone under the pillow as he had been asked to. "I'll bring you a charger when I come back. Looks like your battery is running out."

"Thank you for coming." Sam closed his eyes with exhaustion.

CHAPTER 71

The morning had started badly. Extremely so. His wife squirmed with pain. The trickle of blood running from her nostril did not bode well. Not a sound came from her mouth, but the searing, accusing looks she kept giving him said it all. He tried to get through to her, but she turned her head and refused to listen. His heart was breaking. Could it be that the deal he had signed with the devil would end without him being able to save his wife? He refused to give up. If only he could have a little more time, he was convinced he'd be able to save her. The past few weeks had seen impressive progress in his research team's accomplishments. He himself had served as a human guinea pig for some of the treatments. But his wife continued to fade away before his eyes. The CTC, CBC, and protein blood tests had shown significantly better results, but her body, weakened by the illness from which she had suffered for so long, was unable to recover.

He felt his phone vibrate. It was an unidentified number. He hung up and returned the device to his pocket. The phone vibrated once more. He rejected the call, only to have it vibrate again immediately.

"Who is this?" he shouted enraged and saw his wife cringe at the sound of his voice. He left the room to avoid upsetting her further.

The chilling voice at the other end of the line sounded familiar.

"This is Mr. Brown. My sources in the police tell me they intend to come to your house to arrest you in a few hours. They've discovered you are behind the murder of a woman named Cheryl or Michelle — something like that. They even connected her death to the death of that homeland security employee. You will be facing double homicide charges, and the DA will do his best to make sure you never see daylight again. The way I see it, you have two options. One is to somehow vanish from the face of the earth, and the other—"

"How did they figure it out?" Young's voice trembled with fear.

"The one who caught onto you and told the police is an Israeli investigator hired by Double N's CEO. Based on what I was told, they have solid evidence of your guilt. Even if they don't, Homeland Security would never let you go unpunished. They are merciless when it comes to their own people."

"And why are you telling me this? Are you afraid I'll inform on you? Do you think I'd—"

Cold laughter cut his words short. "You've never met me, and you don't know who I am. The woman who brought you the stolen laptop is dead. As hard as it may be to believe, this is merely a courtesy call. You've provided me with excellent service, and I thought I'd do you a favor in return. Before making any rash decisions, I suggest you think of your wife as well."

The phone went silent, but Brown's barely concealed threat reverberated in the room. Brown knew about Michelle. There was no way they could know about her. He had not left any traces, besides sperm cells. But he was confident that when those sperm cells were tested, they would match the DNA of Arthur Bale, the man who had been released thanks to the mechanism developed by the team at G-Pharma. The same mechanism that had caused the contradiction in the recurring DNA tests.

Young hated Bale with a vengeance. Bale was responsible for his moral decline. Michelle's murder, so he'd hoped, was not to have been in vain. Her death was supposed to send to prison the man who had ruined his life. Now, by some ironic whim of fate, his destiny was tied to that of the man he despised. Or perhaps it wasn't. According to Mr. Brown, whoever he was, perhaps even Bale himself, he was faced with two options. In actuality, he had only one option. A sense of defeat began to spread through his body. The realization that he had only one route of escape from the humiliation awaiting him dawned on him with ugly intensity.

Young returned to his wife's room and looked at her lovingly. She seemed a tiny spot on the white sheet covering the wide bed. The full-bodied, gorgeous woman he had fallen in love with had turned into a doleful pile of skin and bones. Tears poured from his eyes. The selfishness of his actions had suddenly become terribly clear. He had never truly thought of her welfare. His behavior was the result of ulterior motives that had become grievously obvious to him and burdened his conscience. It was time to put things right.

He sat gently on the bed, shivering upon seeing how she instinctively recoiled from him. "My love, I'm sorry for the suffering I've caused you. I am going to put an end to it this very instant. I won't try to keep you alive against your will anymore. I promise."

Slowly, the woman turned her emaciated face toward him. The tangles of hair stuck to her cheek made her look like a hunted animal. "Really?" she whispered hopefully.

He reached out and stroked her face. Tears continued to trickle down his cheeks, but he did not notice them. "Really," he whispered into her ear.

"You will help me die?" she found the strength to ask him.

He hugged her fragile shoulders. "If that is what you want." His voice trembled.

A smile curved her dry lips, and her sunken eyes lit up briefly. He suddenly saw the face of his beloved breaking through the sickness and pain. He knew with certainly that this was the image he wanted to remember during the last moments of his life. He took from his pocket the syringe and ampule he had been carrying for months and without a word, injected the contents into the IV tube dangling from her forearm.

"Thank you," she whispered, and in a moment her eyelids fluttered briefly then went still.

Young bent over her, closed her eyes, and kissed her forehead. Next, he disconnected the tubes from her shriveled body and covered her with a clean sheet from the closet. He returned to the medicine cabinet and took out an unmarked vial. He drew up its contents into the syringe and lay beside his beloved. Without hesitation, he plunged the syringe into a protruding vein on his arm and pushed the liquid into his body. The burning sensation quickly spread.

He turned on his side and hugged his wife's body. "I'm coming to you, my love." And then he was gone.

CHAPTER 72

Ronnie burst through the door of the G-Pharma offices and hurried to the reception desk.

"I'd like to speak to Dr. Schmidt, your CEO."

The receptionist looked at her computer screen. "Your name? Do you have an appointment?"

"My name is Dr. Saar. I am the CEO of Double N. I don't have an appointment, but I'm sure Dr. Schmidt would be very interested in listening to what I have to say."

"I'm sorry, Dr. Saar, but Dr. Schmidt is extremely busy today. I suggest you leave your name and number with me. I'm sure his secretary will contact you soon."

The phone on the reception desk began to ring.

"Go ahead, answer it. I'll wait." Ronnie knew what was going to happen next. The conversation he'd had with Julie Wilson before he'd entered the G-Pharma offices was brief. After he'd updated her on Gadi's discoveries, she had immediately agreed to his request.

"Thank you." The receptionist smiled at him and picked up the phone. "G-Pharma, how may I help you?" Her smile instantly vanished. "Yes. I'll call you right back." The receptionist quickly typed on her keyboard, her eyes following the information on the screen with concern. She picked up the receiver and dialed, completely ignoring Ronnie, who watched her, amused.

"May I please speak with Ms. Julie Wilson?" There was a brief pause. "Yes, ma'am. Certainly, ma'am," she stammered uncomfortably before hanging up. "Excuse me, I'll be right back," she murmured to Ronnie, and before he could respond, she got up and broke into a run toward the elevators, abandoning the reception desk.

A few short moments later, the elevator door opened and an impressive man in his fifties emerged. The receptionist walked behind him with her eyes lowered to the floor.

"Dr. Saar? I understand you're looking for me and have friends who know how to push the right buttons." Schmidt sounded curious.

"I most certainly am, and I definitely do." Ronnie extended his hand with a broad smile.

It was a brief handshake.

"Come with me, please." Schmidt led him to a small conference room adjacent to the reception area.

Ronnie sat, while Schmidt remained standing. "I'm very pressed for time. I'd appreciate it if you could get straight to the point."

"Gladly. A few months ago, one of my employees was violently attacked and had his laptop stolen. It was only by some miracle that he wasn't killed. I am in possession of conclusive evidence, which I have shared with the New York District Attorney's office, that the man behind the attack and the information theft works for G-Pharma."

Schmidt slowly sank into the chair next to Ronnie's. "What are you talking about?"

"The person who stole the technology from us is Dr. Sean Young. I find it difficult to believe you were not aware of his illegal activities." Ronnie gave him a hard look.

"Sean Young? Are you sure? What proof do you have?"

"I assume that you know what your development manager is working on these days?"

Schmidt nodded, and panic began to spread on his face. All the suspicions he had harbored for the past few months, suspicions he had preferred to ignore, now came back to haunt him.

"I'm going to guess that he is working on perfecting an efficient mechanism for targeted drug delivery. I also believe you won't find it surprising to learn that this is the technology that was stolen from us. Both I and the prosecutor in charge of investigating this matter, are convinced that applying a little pressure on your development staff would bring the truth of this matter to light." Ronnie's voice had grown husky with anger.

"Needless to say, I am shocked by your accusations. Let me prove my integrity by confirming that this is indeed the subject Young and his people have been working tirelessly on for the past few months. Unfortunately, Dr. Young did not come to work today, otherwise I would confront him immediately. If it turns out that he is behind this, I give you my word that I will personally help in bringing him to justice.

"I am aware that I am not in a position to be asking for favors, but I believe that if you allow me a certain level of discretion in handling this situation, without involving the police and the DA's office right away, all parties involved will benefit."

Ronnie closed his eyes and rubbed his forehead with his fingers. He felt instinctively that Schmidt was telling the truth, or that at least he had not been actively involved in the plot. He opened his eyes and examined the CEO, who looked back at him anxiously.

It seemed the man fully understood the gravity of the allegations leveled against the company under his leadership.

"You have until tomorrow morning. After that, I'll make sure the DA's office is brought in on this. For your sake, I hope you don't make the mistake of abusing my trust by trying to destroy evidence. That would make you an accomplice.

"Good day." Ronnie lingered a moment, waiting for a reply that did not come, then he left.

CHAPTER 73

The alarm clock wouldn't stop ringing. Julie waved her hand frantically in the hope of silencing it, but to no avail. A sigh of relief escaped from her mouth when the annoying ring stopped and silence returned to the dark room. She cracked open one eye and peeked at the clock. It was 6:30 am. She had gotten into bed only two hours earlier. The alarm clock came to life again. She smacked the off button, lowered her feet to the floor, and dragged herself to the shower.

With eyes still droopy with sleep and without waiting for the water to heat up, she took a deep breath and walked under the stream. She uttered a scream then leaned her forehead on the white tiles and tried to restrain the shiver passing through her. The shock of cold water did its job, and Julie began to feel energized. Soon the water began to warm up, making the tremors go away. She had a long and busy day ahead of her. The day before, she'd had a lengthy telephone conversation with Gadi and Ronnie. The information they'd given her regarding the identity of the scientist behind the DNA tampering was important, but at this stage, they possessed no concrete proof of Young's involvement. Their theory, so she had explained to them, still had quite a few holes in it. She promised to look into and take care of that matter at a later time, but right now, the mission facing her was very clear: putting Bale behind bars for the rest of his life.

It was just short of 9:00 am when Julie Wilson walked through the doors of the Department of Homeland Security building. She was heading for the reception desk, when she heard Martin Gibbons calling her name. She stopped and waited for him to catch up.

"I demand to be present at Mr. Bale's interrogation. Legal representation is the constitutional right of every citizen in America."

"You mean to tell me that they didn't allow you inside?" Wilson feigned confusion.

"Indeed." Hope ignited in Gibbons' eyes.

"I wonder why. The only reason I can think of is that Bale is charged with serious felonies involving national security. If I'm not mistaken, such circumstances allow the authorities to appoint a lawyer who is acquainted with the National Security Court laws. Or perhaps it was merely because you don't have the appropriate security clearance." Julie gave him an empathetic smile. "I promise to look into this. Who knows, if they allow me, I might even provide you with an explanation. Now please excuse me, I'm late for an important meeting."

"With my client?"

Julie Wilson shrugged while presenting her ID to the security guard.

Brief moments later, she stepped into a spacious interrogation room. Ferguson and Tucker, the two agents from the day before, were already there. Across from them sat Bale, a smug grin plastered on his face. At the end of the table sat a scrawny man wearing a suit that looked two sizes too big. His thinning hair belied his youth. His darting eyes gave him the appearance of a child lost in a crowded store. He seemed somewhat terrified.

"Hello, Ms. Wilson. I should have guessed you were behind

this nonsense. It's sad to see you haven't learned your lesson and continue your futile efforts to frame me. I must say you are starting to seem pathetic. I really pity you."

"I recommend you don't waste any pity just yet. You're going to need it for yourself soon enough."

Contemptuous laughter filled the room.

"I suggest we get started," Ferguson interrupted Bale's laughter.

"I'm not saying a word without my lawyer," Bale replied stubbornly.

"The attorney appointed to represent you by the National Security Court before which you will stand trial over the course of the next few days is present." Ferguson nodded toward the young man, who responded by giving him a panicked look through the thick lenses of his glasses.

"We don't expect you to answer any questions. In fact, we'd much prefer it if you'd shut your mouth and listen; we're tired of your theatrics. You are charged with the planning and execution of the murder of Sunil Gupta, a Homeland Security agent. In addition, you are charged with the murder of Michelle Herrington. If you're lucky, you'll end up getting two consecutive life sentences without the possibility of parole. If you're a little less lucky, which is much more likely, the court will set up an appointment for you with a potassium chloride injection. If it were up to me, and happily, it actually is, you will never again take a breath as a free man. The trial will be conducted behind closed doors, presided over by a National Security Court judge. I'm sure your new attorney is going to do his best to defend you, but in light of the evidence in our possession, he hasn't got a chance."

"Guard!" the agent shouted out.

The door opened, and two burly security officers entered the room. "Take the prisoner to a secure cell."

Bale looked about him in astonishment. "What are you talking about? This is the first time I've heard either of those names."

The agents stood up. Wilson did as well. The young lawyer remained seated. He seemed unable to decide what he should do next. The security officers stood on both sides of Bale, gripped him under the arms, and raised him effortlessly from the chair.

"There's been some sort of mistake. You know this won't hold water in court. Give me some more information about the allegations against me, and I'll prove this is another plot devised by the esteemed prosecutor, Ms. Wilson."

Julie turned on her heel. "I'm sorry, Mr. Bale, but I'm not actually the one behind these charges. I'm merely here as an observer."

The guards began to drag Bale out of the room. His desperate attempts to free himself from their clutches were of no use. "I demand to speak with my lawyer," he shouted furiously, straining to turn his head back. The security officers kept moving.

"Bring him back inside and let him to speak with his attorney," Tucker instructed. "Let us know when they're finished."

CHAPTER 74

The lawyer waited until Bale was back in his chair and his hands were cuffed to the metal ring embedded in the center of the table. His slender fingers held a white handkerchief and were occupied with cleaning the lenses of his nondescript glasses. Occasionally, he raised the glasses, inspected them under the light of the caged bulb in the ceiling, then returned to obsessively wiping them. His eyes did not look panicked any longer, merely nearsighted.

"Allow me to introduce myself. My name is Rafael Ortez, and I serve as defense counsel in cases involving matters of national security. I may look young, but I am thirty-three and have eight years of experience."

"And how many cases have you actually won?" An involuntary mocking tone colored Bale's words.

Ortez ignored the contempt in Bale's voice. "I'd say over fifty percent, but this is not about me. The sooner you deal with that, the better. I'm all you've got, and you'd better get used to it. And before you ask, I can't think of a single case in which a national security judge allowed a defendant to switch attorneys. You could try to defend yourself, but I highly recommend against it. Homeland security law is different from anything you've previously encountered."

"I'm accused of the murder of two people whose names I've

never heard up till thirty minutes ago. So, as I see it, you shouldn't have any problem improving your winning percentage."

"I certainly hope so." Ortez opened a folder and began to quickly flip through the dozens of pages it contained. "I suggest we start from the very beginning. With your permission, I'll forgo reading the details and provide you with a summary of the main points of the allegations against you."

Bale eyed him with curiosity. The young man had changed before his eyes and suddenly projected supreme professional confidence.

"Sunil Gupta was a DHS employee. The man underwent manipulations that changed the characteristics of his genetic identity. Before researchers were able to find out who he had been in contact with in the period prior to the change, he died of a general circulatory collapse. To be more graphic, every blood vessel in his body simply melted. A cruel death, I'd say." The lawyer examined Bale for a moment, then continued. "At the time of his death, there was no similar recorded case in the history of forensic science. Two days ago, the body of Michelle Herrington, a secretary employed by Double N, was found. When—"

"Double N, you say?"

"Yes. You know them?"

"I've heard of them, but I have never been in contact with them."

"Good. It turns out Michelle Herrington died in the same way as Sunil Gupta. An arterial aneurysm in a large number of blood vessels. Before dying, she'd had sexual intercourse. A DNA test of the sperm cells found in her body indicated without a doubt that you were the last person who was with her, or more precisely, the person who had intercourse with her."

"What?" Bale roared.

"The hotel room also contained a bottle of wine with traces of genetic materials — CRISPR, they call it. I haven't had the chance to study the subject yet, but the Homeland Security people seem certain this is what caused the genetic manipulations that caused the circulatory collapse of both victims. In light of these findings, it was decided to define the material found in the wine bottle as a biological weapon, a weapon of mass destruction."

"But I have nothing to do with any of that. I have no idea how my sperm..." Bale stopped mid-sentence, and his face paled, sick understanding sweeping across it. His new DNA had been planted in the body of the woman with whose murder he was now being charged. Only two people could have possibly done that.

"The agents investigating this case," Ortez went on, completely ignoring his client's sudden mood swing, "are aware of how you put one over on the court by changing the DNA profile of your hair, cheek, and possibly other places. They also realize you needed to perform a preliminary experiment before gambling your life on this tactic. The best place to conduct the experiment, or so you thought at the time, was the Department of Homeland Security. It was clear that should you be able to outsmart the world's most advanced forensic lab, you'd also be able to outfox the civil judicial system. And you were right.

"All these facts tie you to both murder cases. Therefore, in my opinion, and based on my experience, your case is about to ruin my success rate rather than improve it. Furthermore, the moment you are found guilty, the three previous murder charges, which were illegally dropped, will be reinstated. The way I see it, you are faced with five consecutive life sentences. Or maybe what is a better option for you — the death penalty."

"But I honestly don't know this Michelle person. You have to find out who did it, find the real culprit."

"I have to tell you that based on the information I have, it is pretty obvious you were the one who committed the crime, and therefore, the system is convinced of your guilt."

A knock came from the door. One of the security officers entered and handed the lawyer a folded piece of paper. Rafael Ortez carefully read the message it contained and turned to Bale. "Dr. Young, the man who apparently prepared all your genetic potions, has just signed a state witness agreement. He will testify that you threatened his life and the life of his ailing wife. He will admit under oath that he concocted the materials for you and handed you the bottle of wine that caused Ms. Herrington's death."

"I'm obviously being framed," Bale squealed with a hollow voice.

"I'm afraid that a simple genetic test will prove the theory I just outlined. I don't know how to say it in any more basic terms: This is the most clear-cut case ever brought before a military court."

"So what? You're giving up on me?"

"Of course not. Based on my experience, I'm certain no security agency would be interested in news of a new weapon of mass destruction, developed by a private person, being leaked to the media. In order to prevent this, it is obvious they would need to place you in solitary confinement for life. This would involve vast amounts of money, even for a system such as ours. Similarly, I am convinced that the criminal justice system wouldn't be interested in exposing the fact that DNA tests can be manipulated. The massive number of retrial requests would bring the judicial system to the point of collapse. Therefore, and only after threatening that we would demand a trial, I managed to get a settlement agreement for you.

"You will be charged with white-collar felonies and serve a sentence of fifteen years. You will surrender to the state two hundred and fifty million dollars hidden in your Jersey Island bank accounts. If you have any additional funds, you will be permitted to keep them for the days following your release." He grinned like an accomplice. "You will agree to prevent any information of your exploits from ever being revealed. Neither now, nor after your release. If there is ever the slightest suspicion that you have broken this promise, I assure you that nothing will stop them from making you pay. You might simply disappear. And trust me – it's happened before.

"If you agree, I will call in Ms. Wilson and your attorney, and in their presence, you will sign the paperwork. It has already been approved by Judge Glenn Morrison."

Bale's face was an ugly green. He could barely keep himself from vomiting. "All right. Bring them in, and I'll sign it," he whispered miserably.

In a far-off room, at the end of the corridor, a joyous cry broke out.

"I told you Rafe would do a fine job. He may not be a lawyer, but he's certainly the best undercover agent we've ever had. As you've just seen, the man can transform into any character in the most convincing way."

"I'm so jealous. I wish we could get away with those kinds of tricks." Julie laughed and went out to meet Martin Gibbons.

CHAPTER 75

"I'm still not sure that showing our cards to Schmidt was such a good idea," Derek Taylor said with visible discomfort.

Ronnie shrugged noncommittally. "I guess we'll know soon enough. The G-Pharma representatives are supposed to be here in—" he glanced at his watch "— five minutes. I hope you're wrong and they have come up with a solution for the problem they caused. They wouldn't have called me after midnight and asked for an appointment first thing in the morning unless they had something urgent and serious to say."

"And that is exactly what's bothering me. I don't think our problem has a solution that would be acceptable to both parties," Derek answered right before the temporary secretary popped her head into the room.

"Your guests are here."

Ronnie and Derek got to their feet and asked her to show them in. They all shook hands and introduced themselves.

"Schmidt, G-Pharma CEO, and I believe you two know Roland King." He nodded politely at Derek.

"Harold Hoffman, G-Pharma's legal advisor."

"Welcome," Derek began, his stern expression standing in stark contrast to their guests' amiable deportment. "If we had known lawyers would be present at the meeting, I don't believe we would have agreed to it."

"Please allow me to explain, Derek," Roland King intervened. "We brought our legal advisor to add an official dimension to the offer we would like to propose to you. I believe you will be pleased by the end of this meeting."

Derek leaned back, but his arms remained crossed on his chest, and his eyes were narrowed suspiciously.

"Yesterday, after Dr. Saar left the G-Pharma offices," Roland took charge of the conversation, "Dr. Schmidt telephoned Dr. Young but was unable to get hold of him. At the same time, he asked me to come to the office to assist him in further investigating this matter. Together, we summoned the team that worked with Young on the new developments and determined, with a high level of certainty, that G-Pharma is in up to its ears in a criminal act perpetrated by one of its senior employees."

"You mean to tell me that our proprietary information has been shared with more of your company employees and is now possibly available to the public?" There was no doubt that Ronnie was panicking.

"I have even worse news, but I ask that you please let me finish," Roland remained calm. "I don't know if you are aware of this, but a few months ago, Dr. Young's wife became terminally ill with lung cancer with metastases that had spread throughout her body. We believe Young stole your technology in an attempt to save her. When we were unable to contact him — and by that point, I had already been brought in on the matter — we assumed he had taken his wife to the hospital and had turned off his phone. It was only that night, after having repeatedly failed to reach him that Dr.

Schmidt decided to go to Young's house in New Jersey." Roland looked over to Schmidt, who took a deep breath and continued the narrative.

"There was no answer when I knocked on Sean's door, but all the lights in the house were on. I tried the door and was surprised to find it unlocked. I went inside and called out his name. When he didn't answer, I began to search the house. I found Sean and his wife lying dead in each other's arms in their bedroom. From the looks of it, I assume they took their own lives together."

"I'm sorry to hear that," Derek said evenly. "But that does not diminish your responsibility as a company for what happened. As for you, Roland, I have to admit that you and Wyatt being partners in the same fund has often made me wonder about the possibility that information had leaked between the companies, reached Young, and made him aware of what we are developing here."

"Derek, please, I can assure you I didn't hear anything from Wyatt, and I certainly didn't pass any information to Young, but today, I know for sure that Wyatt could have prevented this mess from snowballing if he had only acted professionally at the right moment."

Ronnie and Derek instinctively leaned forward.

"Sometime after your technology was stolen, there was a board of directors meeting at G-Pharma. Your technology was introduced by Dr. Young as a new breakthrough, and investors were asked to invest additional funds in the company, allowing G-Pharma to become the leader of the targeted-drug industry. Because of a crisis in one of my companies, I was unable to attend the meeting, and I asked Wyatt to stand in for me. When Dr. Schmidt told me about the questions Wyatt asked during the meeting, it became clear to us that even back then he realized the technology being discussed had been stolen from Double N."

"Son of a bitch." Ronnie slammed his fist on the table. "That's why he offered to buy our company for a pittance. He wanted to whitewash this crime. I won't—"

"Please settle down, Dr. Saar. Very early this morning, I confronted him with the facts and threatened him with a civil lawsuit. As of ninety minutes ago, Wyatt was dismissed from all his duties in the fund and also surrendered all his holdings. It is for you to decide whether or not to file suit against him, personally. Once word of his misconduct is known, he'll carry the burden of this disgrace for the rest of his life. He will never work in the industry again. I believe that would be punishment enough. And besides, if it went to trial, there's no guarantee you'd win."

"I, too," Schmidt spoke up, "have resigned my position today. From the very start, I suspected the speed with which the technology suddenly emerged in our company was unreasonable, but out of convenience, and quite possibly greed, I chose to ignore it."

As Ronnie and Derek absorbed that information, Roland began talking again. "Despite this unfortunate incident, I can't let it go unsaid that G-Pharma is a wonderful company with fantastic products and loyal employees. The company has already had close to a hundred million dollars invested in it. I'd hate to see it go to ruin." Roland continued, "That is why I'd like to put the following offer on the table. Let's agree to merge G-Pharma and Double N. Ronnie would be appointed CEO of the joint company and we, the G-Pharma investors, would give him a free hand to construct the joint company according to his personal vision. That way, it would no longer be a problem that much of Double N's technology has leaked to a few of our employees. And before you ask the obvious question — I thought of a merger of equals. I'm sure you'll agree that this is an adequate arrangement."

"Very much so," answered Derek. "Which is why I don't understand why you are proposing it."

"Because together, we would be worth so much money that all parties involved would only gain by it. On the other hand, if we start squabbling in the courtroom, none of us would make any money. Ever."

"And the rest of your investors would agree to this?"

"That's why I'm here." The legal advisor pushed a document bound in a transparent plastic folder across the table. "Inside, you will find the principles of the merger and the signatures of all the G-Pharma investors, as well as all the members of its board of directors. I'm sure that once you delve into the details of the document, you'll be convinced that no legal games are being played here. I understand you'll want some time to read the documents, but if you accept that this is indeed our offer, we would be pleased to hear your reply immediately."

Derek rose and extended his hand to Roland. "Gentlemen, I believe you've just found yourselves new partners."

EPILOGUE

A wide smile spread on Sam's face when he saw Ronnie and Gadi step into his room. He was lying in bed with his chest bare. The color had returned to his cheeks, and if it weren't for the steady beeping of the cardiac monitor in the background, one wouldn't have guessed he had been fighting for his life a mere week before.

"So, we're both getting better real fast, eh, Gadi?" He laughed out loud. Sam's laughter died quickly under their glares. "What happened, cousin? Did someone die?"

Gadi sat in the armchair next to Sam's bed, and Ronnie remained standing, leaning against the wall.

Ronnie's voice trembled with repressed rage. "Why did you betray me, Sam?"

Sam looked at him, startled.

"Allow me, Sam, to ask you several questions that have been bothering me for quite some time," Gadi jumped into the conversation. "How do you explain why that woman did not kill you the moment you arrived at the apartment? What reason could she have had to try and neutralize you with a knife when there was a loaded pistol equipped with a silencer in her pocket?"

Sam shrugged. He looked at Ronnie then returned his gaze to Gadi. "How can I guess the processes of a cold-blooded killer? Perhaps she was a sadist? Perhaps she wanted to use me as a human shield once the door opened? I don't understand. What's going on here?"

"And why didn't you scream? Why didn't you to try and warn us?"

"I was too shocked to utter a word."

"I don't think so. When I heard the elevator, I hurried to the door. The only noise I heard outside was a suitcase being dragged. A moment before I opened the door for you, it got very quiet, and then I heard you say, 'You're making a mistake.' This is not something a man surprised by an assailant would say. It smacks of familiarity…"

"Ronnie?" Sam looked at his cousin, pleading.

"I repeat my question," said Gadi. "Why didn't you scream and warn us?"

"I'd just gotten back from a business trip; how could I have even known you were in the apartment?" He tried to rise to a sitting position, but Gadi's hand forced him back down.

"You knew that Liah and Juanita were pregnant. Juanita told you even before telling me. You knew they were living in your apartment. You also knew when we arrived. After all, you left a broken washing machine in the parking spot. Still, it never occurred to you to scream and warn any of us?"

"I was so frightened that it didn't even cross my mind."

"Or perhaps you believed your business relationship with Kate would save your life." Gadi's voice dripped with contempt.

"What is this, some sort of prank?"

"I'm afraid not. Do you know what helped me put it all together? When Kate came inside the coffee shop in New York, where the three of us were sitting, I could see in her eyes that she recognized one of us. It was only later on that I realized she did not even know what Ronnie or I looked like. It was *you* that she identified."

"She couldn't have recognized me, because she didn't know me."

Gadi waved his hand dismissively. "When Simon let everyone know he was about to take the material for the design review and go home, you were in the office too. Ronnie suggested that you wait half an hour and have dinner with him, but you refused, claiming some unexpected matter required your attention. The real reason for your urgent departure was that you had to update Kate or Bale that an opportunity to steal the computer from Simon had presented itself."

"If I remember correctly, I simply needed to get back to New Jersey for a business meeting and with the traffic at that time of the day, I was afraid I was going to miss it." Sam's face had settled into a benign expression.

"Isn't it strange that you remember the incident so clearly? Sounds like an alibi you knew you might need one day. But I agree, so far, all the evidence is circumstantial. What really bothered me from the moment of Simon's attack was the basic question of how the attackers could have even known about the technology developed at Double N and the breakthrough that had taken place a mere few days before. What—"

"Ronnie, come on!" Sam sounded frustrated. "You yourself told me Michelle was Young's lover, and she must have been the one who handed him the information."

Ronnie's entire body seemed to shrivel. "Until this very moment, I prayed with all my heart that Gadi was wrong. But, per his request, I never mentioned Young's name in your presence. When Gadi first asked me to keep his name a secret from you, I was furious. I couldn't believe, nor did I want to believe, that you, my own flesh and blood, were the one who betrayed me. We both know that even if I'd placed all the information on Michelle's desk, she wouldn't have the necessary understanding or knowledge to separate the wheat from the chaff. In her job interview, she mentioned that she had worked at G-Pharma and had always been fascinated by working in the company of brilliant people dealing with things she would never be able to comprehend. It wasn't Michelle who relayed the information that Simon was leaving the Double N offices with the material. It was you."

"You are both out of your minds. Why would a rich man like me do such a thing? I have more money than I could ever spend in a single lifetime."

A mocking smile crossed Gadi's lips. "Perhaps now you do. Blood money you've received from Bale. You've gotten used to making easy money, and it didn't matter if it resulted from the pain and misery of others. I ran some checks and discovered all the shopping malls you built in the beginning of your career turned into monumental financial disasters. The company that took them off your hands at bargain prices, but allowed you to keep managing them, was an unknown entity registered in the Cayman Islands. I'm sure you won't be surprised to hear we've discovered this company happens to be a client of Mr. Bale's. To be more precise, Bale also owns the company."

Sam's eyes glazed over into an expressionless stare.

"Are you ashamed to admit that you are Mr. Brown, and you were nothing but a failed businessman turned into Bale's puppet?"

Sam violently pushed away Gadi's restraining hand and sat erect in his bed. "Get the hell out of my room, both of you. You'll hear from my attorneys yet. Especially you, Ronnie, you ingrate. By the time I'm done with you, cousin," he venomously spat out each of his last words, "you'll be left with nothing. Nothing! You haven't a single shred of proof for any of the nonsense you've accused me of. Not a single one."

The door opened, and Julie Wilson stepped into the room accompanied by a uniformed police officer.

"I assume, Mr. Storm, that you haven't heard the latest news. Yesterday, Bale signed a plea bargain with the state. As part of the deal, he will serve a fifteen-year sentence and hand over two hundred and fifty million laundered dollars to the state. This morning, Ronnie contacted me and shared Mr. Abutbul's suspicions. He begged me to help him prove you were innocent. The only way of doing that, in his opinion, was to convince Bale to tell us who was behind this whole idea of tampering with the DNA tests. All that Bale agreed to tell us was that a certain Mr. Brown was behind the idea. He claimed he had no further information about that mystery man."

"So, I'm innocent, as you yourself can see." His face reflected his relief.

"With the agreement of the New York District Attorney," Julie ignored him and continued, "and with the understanding that we could not allow a man who might simply join forces with another crime syndicate and continue to wreak havoc on the judicial system to remain free, I offered Mr. Bale an opportunity to improve his agreement with the state. He was very appreciative of the opportunity to retain an additional fifty million dollars. You wouldn't believe how he went out of his way to thank us. He was so happy that he eagerly identified your picture out of hundreds we placed in front of him."

Without another word, Ronnie turned and left the room.

ACKNOWLEDGMENTS

This book could not have been written without the aid and support of numerous good people.

First and foremost, Benni Kopelovitz, a childhood friend who came up with the idea of writing a novel revolving around CRISPR and did not rest for a single moment, constantly providing ideas, assisting with logistics, and lending his uncompromising and painstaking approach. I have never had a tougher critic.

To Ruthie Weiner, the amazing genetic scientist, thank you for letting me in on the secrets of the world of genetics and for simplifying such complex and complicated subjects, so I could do the same for my readers.

To Ron Hibel from the Israel Police forensic laboratories, who found the time to come to my house during late night hours and assist me with all the forensic identification technology-related matter.

To Eilam Oren Domoshevizki, my beloved son-in-law, for his constructive remarks.

To Yaron Regev for his meticulous translation work.

To Julie MacKenzie, the amazing editor with whom I've had the pleasure and honor of working on all my books.

And, of course, to my supportive family, for allowing me to vanish from their lives while I worked on this book.

Thank you all.

Made in United States
North Haven, CT
16 June 2022